THE CRYING GAME

John Braine was born in 1922 and was
educated by St. Bede's Grammar and
on leaving school had a variety of jobs.

In 1940 he became an assistant at Bingley
Public Library where he worked, except for a spell
in the Royal Navy between 1942 and 1943, until
1951 when he became a freelance writer in
London. In 1954 he returned to librarianship for
three years and then became a full-time writer. In
1966 he left Yorkshire and moved to the south of
England and he now lives in Woking with his
wife, son and three daughters.

John Braine's first book, *Room at the Top*, was
published in 1957 and filmed in the following
year. The second novel, *The Vodi*, was published in
1959 and three years later, *Life at the Top*, which
was subsequently filmed. His more recent novels
are *Stay With Me Till Morning*, 1970; *The Queen of
a Distant Country*, 1972; *The Pious Agent*, 1975;
Waiting for Sheila, 1976; and *Finger of Fire*, 1977.

As well as writing books, John Braine has been
a TV reviewer for *The Spectator*, film critic for the
Daily Express and book reviewer for *The People*. He
also writes TV scripts.

John Braine

The Crying Game

MAGNUM BOOKS
Methuen Paperbacks Ltd

A Magnum Book

THE CRYING GAME
ISBN 0 417 04940 4

First published in Great Britain 1968
by Eyre & Spottiswoode Ltd
Reprinted by Eyre Methuen Ltd 1978
Magnum edition published 1980

Copyright © 1968 by John Braine

Magnum Books are published
by Methuen Paperbacks Ltd
11 New Fetter Lane, London EC4P 4EE

Made and printed in Great Britain
by Richard Clay (The Chaucer Press) Ltd
Bungay, Suffolk

I know all there is to know about the crying game
I've had my share of the crying game
First there are kisses
Then there are sighs
And then before you know where you are you're saying goodbye.

from the song 'The Crying Game' by Geoff Stephens

reproduced by courtesy of
Southern Music Publishing Company Ltd

for Pat again

The time of this novel is shortly in the future

one

My new life began when my cousin Adam Keelby came into the Salisbury one muggy September evening. It was seven o'clock exactly, and for over an hour I had been huddling in the corner of an alcove – as if taking shelter from a storm – staring alternately at the *Evening Standard* and the brass-topped table. I didn't even want to look around me; I'd been interviewing a television personality and felt as though there was nothing left of me.

The television personality, Harry Morgate, lived on admiration materially and spiritually, if spiritually is the right word. It wasn't enough to nod or to shake one's head or to use noncommittal phrases; continually he set little traps to ascertain whether one was really listening.

'Refresh my memory,' he would say. 'When exactly did I become a prisoner of the Japs? God, it's ridiculous, I want to forget . . .' And the rather protuberant eyes under the thick black eyebrows would seem about to moisten with tears; he would be actually frightened that one wasn't listening. On the box his raw egotism gave the impression – at least to some critics – of exuberant vitality, but in three dimensions it was like being forced to look at a deep wound.

There would be no difficulty in producing my usual sort

of piece, bright and chatty but fundamentally deep and thoughtful – *Gadfly or earth-mover? Sage or titillator? What lies behind that telegenic mask?* What lay behind it, actually, was a huge store of quotations, a first-rate sense of timing, and a phrase, sentence, and even paragraph to describe every human situation. There was also the quiet happiness conferred by £25,000 a year and a block of television shares bought in those early days when sound and sensible City men were turning up their noses at any venture so speculative.

This wouldn't, of course, appear in the article. In fact, after an hour's slow absorption of draught Guinness, I had succeeded in putting Harry Morgate out of my mind.

And then something worse took over. I was lonely. I wasn't lonely because I was shy; I couldn't have held my job down for a single day if I hadn't been able to chat up perfect strangers at a moment's notice. In fact, I was noted in the office for my instant charm. There were times when, wheedling an interview out of someone who only wanted to crawl away and hide, I was rather disgusted with myself.

I wasn't lonely because I was ugly or deformed: I was an inch below six feet with good teeth and a clear skin, and not very far from being handsome. My nose had rather over-shadowed the rest of my features as a child – I think it had grown to maturity before the rest. Now it might fairly be described as commanding; it was one of my private conceits that I looked like a soldier. My hair was the usual English mousy brown, but it was thick and springy and I kept it brutally short. I always dressed well – I couldn't afford Savile Row but I never went below Austin Reed standards. And I always had a bath every day; not that this is very important. Women are less fastidious than they're supposed to be, and men don't notice until one actually begins to stink. But it did mean that I always felt, as it were, ready for action, fit to go anywhere.

I wasn't lonely because of any physical deficiency; and I wasn't lonely because I was poor. At twenty-seven I earned just above £3,500 a year and fiddled another £1,000 on expenses. And I had a tiny flat in Chelsea, which I always described as being off the King's Road. It was actually nearer the World's End than Sloane Square, but, undeniably, it was off the King's Road.

I had what I'd dreamed of since I was sixteen: a place of my own in London, a place where I could take girls, a place where I was absolutely free, where no-one knew or cared what I did as long as I didn't inconvenience them in the slightest way.

In Charbury – even more than Bradford, the archetypal West Riding city – I had never for one moment been free of surveillance. The atmosphere was that of a mill village. No matter how discreetly you behaved, whatever you did or said was common property within twenty-four hours – in fact I sometimes had a notion that it was considerably less – that one performed, as it were, on a brightly-lit stage for the amusement of the whole city. I remember taking a Jamaican girl, who was studying medicine at Leeds University, to the Alhambra in Bradford once. It was once and once only, because we decided that we weren't each other's cup of tea or, for that matter, Blue Mountain coffee. But for years afterwards I had to put up with clumsy jokes about khaki babies at home and requests to join anti-apartheid demonstrations at the University. And yet I couldn't remember having encountered even one person whom I knew at the theatre.

In Charbury you were never alone. You were never lonely either. And as I sat there in my cosy alcove at the Salisbury, finally tired of staring at the evening paper and the table, I was suddenly and thoroughly homesick. I tried to cast myself in the part of the dispassionate observer, making mental notes of the conversation of the customers who were mostly theatricals or trying desperately hard to look and sound like theatricals. But I would cheerfully have exchanged the Salisbury for any Charbury pub, even the most relentlessly modernized one, all chrome and plastic, even the dingiest and roughest one in Bradford Road where, they used to say, the gutters literally ran with blood every Saturday night.

I liked the Salisbury because somehow or other, despite all the celebrities who liked it too and who had said as much in a thousand interviews, despite it being genuinely in the heart of London's theatreland, which made one feel part of a brewer's advertisement, it was nevertheless one of the few remaining Victorian pubs, solid and comfortable and respectable, in which above all the noise there was a positive drowsy quietness. But I wasn't likely to find any company there.

And that was all I wanted. I didn't want sex either. It wasn't, for instance, that I would exactly have turned my nose up at the red-haired girl in green slacks, so tightly stretched that I would see the outline of her knickers, who stood in front of my table arguing about David Mercer ('Essentially, dear heart, he's as artificial, as mannered, as *decadent* as Oscar Wilde or Pinero') with a young man with a full beard but no moustache. The effect was that of a pie-frill and I was in the mood to tell him so. As she leaned forward to take a cigarette from him her white sweater moved up to show an inch of white flesh.

I began then, despite myself, to work out an approach, but I knew that it would come to nothing. Precisely because it was a theatrical pub, one of the few in London which a woman who wasn't a whore or a Lesbian could visit unaccompanied, one couldn't pick up women in the Salisbury. The girl turned her head towards the door momentarily and I was able to see her face – green eyes, a snub nose, not quite enough chin, but in full face her make-up would conceal the fact. I looked away from her and took the Larranga which Harry Morgate had given me out of its aluminium tube: I had been saving it for later to show off with after a tête-à-tête with the girl I was sure to meet before the evening was out, but there wasn't going to be any such occasion. I needed to introduce the pleasure principle into my life here and now.

What I really wanted was to have a drink in male company, simply to relax. And, come to think of it, that was easy enough. There was company in the Press Club, at El Vino's, at Poppins, at indeed almost any pub in Fleet Street. There was company at the newspaper office, even female company; journalists don't all clock off at half past five, and they always have time for a drink. But that wasn't what I wanted. For once, after Harry Morgate, I was disillusioned with my job, I had no desire to talk shop, printer's ink had ceased to be a delightful perfume.

The choice was looming up. Either stay at the Salisbury and get quietly soaked – I was nearing the point of no return, the third pint – or go to the cinema by myself. Or phone Theresa which, inevitably, matters being as complicated as they were between us, would lead to trouble.

I scraped the end from the cigar with my thumb-nail and took out my lighter. A hand pushed the lighter away.

'Blasphemy, my dear fellow, blasphemy.' A book of matches was flung on the table.

'You haven't changed, Adam,' I said. I lit the cigar. The book of matches was, I noticed, from L'Ecu de France.

'You're wrong, mate,' he said. He pulled off his short grey raincoat and sat beside me, flinging it on the seat. Somehow or other the red silk lining and Mr Fish label continued to be displayed to the full advantage. He took out a packet of Russian cigarettes. 'You're quite *bestially* wrong. I'm richer and more successful, corrupt in every way.'

He had, since I'd last seen him over five years ago,

acquired or been acquired by a Chelsea accent, drawling, curiously toneless, slightly Cockney, always apparently on the verge of parodying itself.

'It's nice to see you,' I said.

'And it's nice to see you too. I always regarded you as one of the few human beings in that bloody awful dump in which we had the misfortune to spend our youth. I don't go back there, not since Mama died.'

He blew out a mouthful of cigarette smoke. The smell asserted itself even above the cigar, more acrid than Turkish, more aromatic than Virginian. It put me in mind more of incense than tobacco, it seemed part of his general décor, if that's a word one can apply to human beings.

'I go back quite often,' I said.

'You have a family, Frank. A father, a mother, three sisters. But what do you mean go back often? I thought you were still with the *Gazette*.'

'I've been here six months,' I said. 'I'm with the *Argus* now.'

'Why the hell didn't you look me up?' There seemed to be genuine indignation in his voice.

'I didn't know where you lived,' I said. 'We seemed to have lost touch. Or rather you never bothered. We all wondered what we'd done to offend you. I don't mind for myself, but my mother — '

He ran his hand through his hair which now, I noticed, was so short as to be almost crew-cut.

'I know, I know. But for a long time I couldn't even bear to think of Charbury . . . Besides, I ran into a certain amount of trouble there. But you'd know about that, of course. Everyone else in Charbury did.'

'Edna's married now,' I said.

'God help her husband then. It wasn't even her that was the trouble. It was those frightful boozy brothers of hers, behaving like characters from a Victorian melodrama. Do

14

you know what that creep Raymond actually said to me? In the eighteenth century, he said, I would have *called you out*. I didn't know what the hell he was talking about for a moment . . .'

'Do you remember when that boulder dropped on his toenail?'

'God, do I not. I pushed him home in that handcart I had. He howled all the way from Goodwin Woods. I can still see that big dirty bleeding toe. . . .'

We had picked up the threads again as if they had never been dropped. As he spoke, the Chelsea accent seemed to lose its cutting edge, the outline of the thin face to become less brusque and authoritative. In fact, the bright young executive clothes – pink shirt, floral tie, fawn mohair suit with no turnups or breast pocket, brown and white correspondent shoes – seemed to be, as they would be in Charbury, clothes for a masquerade.

'Raymond's married now too. Very big wedding. Top hats and morning suits and every last one of them pissed as newts. Raymond's not far off seventeen stone now.'

'He always was a greedy pig. It doesn't seem quite real now. The whole damned city doesn't seem real. I can't believe now that there was all that trouble just because Raymond came home early and caught me screwing Edna.'

'You certainly left under a cloud.'

He smiled. 'Yes, indeed. Charbury's a moral city. Never mind, I'd have left anyway.' His pale blue eyes – cold and wary in contradiction to the long black eyelashes and the small but full mouth – were restlessly scanning the room. 'Have a drink, Frank.'

'Have one with me,' I said automatically.

'No, I still have an expense account. The firm pays more tax, that's all. Unless you're from overseas. So I'll put you down as Frank Batcombe of New York. Bastards!'

I knew it was the Government to whom he was referring. 'I'm with you there,' I said. That, when he had lived in Charbury, had been a great bond also.

'I don't read your paper regularly – the Telegraph's good enough for me – but I come across it from time to time. It's pretty sound. Sounder than the Telegraph about some things.'

'Are you still in advertising?'

The girl with red hair who had left the room a moment since, now reappeared and changed the playwright under discussion to Ionesco. Adam saw the direction in which I was looking and half-smiled. Then – it seemed unimportant at the time – his neat but piratical features distorted in a grimace of pain. The half-smile returned and became a real smile, showing a mouthful of teeth so white and regular that they obviously must have been capped.

'Public Relations,' he said. 'Same thing essentially.' He nodded at the girl. 'She's a silly bitch. Always yapping about the Theatre of the Absurd, or Committed Theatre. It just used to be the Theatre once. . . .'

'It wasn't her mind I was interested in.'

'She'll not see thirty again. And she's divorced one husband and she's well on the way to getting shot of another. . . .' He had lowered his voice. 'Want to meet her?'

Later I was to learn that he offered to introduce one to any woman one looked at with any semblance of interest, even if he didn't know the woman. There was no offence in it – it was as if he'd offered one something trivial and amusing from a shop window or a plate of cockles and mussels from a street stall.

I shook my head, not because I cared whether the girl was married or not but because though he meant it kindly enough, there was something a little too lordly, a little too suggestive of coins being thrown to the cheering multitude, about the offer. But already the girl had noticed him and had come over to us, leaving the young man with the pie-frill beard in the middle of a sentence.

'Dear heart!' she cried and kissed him. 'Why did you just *sneak* in? Don't you love me any more?'

'This is Wendy Halmstead,' Adam said. 'My cousin. Frank Batcombe. A journalist. Big man in show business. Makes and breaks the stars.'

'You're a bloody liar,' she said. 'I mean, he's no doubt a journalist but he's not showbiz because I know them all.'

'He might be showbiz one day,' Adam said. 'You be nice to him and he'll be nice to you.'

She sat down beside me. Suddenly there was a sense of tension.

'Cousin Frank doesn't have much to say for himself, does he?' She had an atmosphere about her of tiredness and the wrong sort of meal, of pork pie and beer for lunch and spaghetti and Algerian wine for dinner. She seemed clean enough, but I felt that she'd bathed hastily in a tiny and chilly bathroom like the one in my flat off the King's Road. She didn't look positively ill; but if I'd been told she was suffering from a fatal disease I wouldn't have been in the least surprised. And for all that, she was powerfully, rankly attractive.

'I'll interview you if you like, Wendy,' I said. 'I've done Harry Morgate this afternoon.'

The celebrity name, like some religious incantation, commanded her interest. Adam broke in.

'Sooner you than me. Christ, I well remember doing a job for this children's charity which he's said a thousand times over is good and noble and heart-warming, bla bla bla. And our managing director believes all this and we're doing the job for nothing, that's the cream of the joke. And what did old Santa Claus Morgate ask for and get, just for opening a bazaar? Three hundred guineas, that's what. It isn't the money, he had the nerve to say, it's the principle of the thing.'

The dark face was contorted with hatred. 'It's time he was dead,' he said. 'If you want to destroy the sod, Frank, I'll give you absolutely all the dirt. Wendy was very thick with him once, weren't you, dearest?'

'I'd nearly forgotten,' she said. 'Give me a cigarette, Adam.' He pushed over the box of Russian cigarettes. 'Oh Jesus, no, they're weird. Like bad drains and cheap eau-de-cologne.' She looked at me.

'I smoke cigars,' I said.

'I'll have a cigar then.' I brought out my tin of Mannikin cheroots, the biggest I could afford at that period.

'Better still.' She lightly stroked my hand as I lit the cheroot for her. 'You have a steady hand. Nice skin too.'

I felt like a bull at an auction mart. Her hand continued its stroking. Long-fingered with nails a little grubby, it seemed to have a life of its own like some small animal.

'I try to keep fit,' I said. It was difficult to speak.

'Don't we all?' Adam said. He knew what was going on under the table, even knew that it was for his benefit rather than mine; but he seemed merely slightly amused.

'What school did you go to?' Wendy asked me.

'The same one as Adam. St Theo's. It's a Papist grammar school, actually.'

Her eyes widened. The hand continued lightly to caress my thigh. I was now almost in physical pain.

'I always thought it was pure fiction. The Charbury grammar school bit, I mean. It wouldn't have surprised me if he hadn't been to bloody Eton or Harrow and was just pretending to be prole.'

'I never tell lies unless it's absolutely essential,' Adam said. 'You look such a fool if you're found out.' He was looking towards the door.

Wendy laughed. 'In PR and never tells a lie unless it's absolutely essential? They'll put you in Madame Tussaud's, I shouldn't wonder.'

Adam rose abruptly and went over to the bar. He came back with a pint of Guinness for me and a half of bitter for Wendy. I noticed that he didn't bring one for himself.

'Going anywhere special, Frank?' he asked.

I shrugged my shoulders. 'Just repairing the tissues after Harry Morgate.'

'How well I know the feeling. When I was first in PR I used to crawl into the most sordid little pubs I could find and just sit for hours in a state of deep shock. Well, let's go and have a nosh-up somewhere . . . Wendy?'

'Some other time,' she said. Her fingers gently tapped my thigh, moved up towards my groin, then moved away again. She was smiling broadly now.

'What's your phone number?' I asked her.

'I'm in the directory, dear old Frank.'

'Drink up,' Adam said. 'It seems quite evident now that the dilapidated old Thespian whom I came here to see is not, in fact, turning up.'

He was taking charge, as he always had done. But, as always happened when he was about, a period of time which had seemed scarcely to be breathing had regained its colour and jumped out of its sickbed.

'I must go,' Wendy said. 'I'm expecting a friend.' She glanced at her enormous wrist watch with the Union Jack face. 'In fact, here he comes now, weighed down with sorrow, as usual, the poor sod.'

Adam pulled a face as she stood up and waved at the young negro who had just entered.

'Fascist beast,' she said. The negro was small and moved with the lightness of a boxer or a dancer; his tight lavender-shade slacks and loose-fitting purple Angora sweater somehow gave his flat impassive face an air of menace. I felt a purely atavistic pang of jealousy and hatred, an urge to take Wendy away from him.

'Come on,' Adam said, and almost pushed me out of the pub.

'You don't like to see it, do you, rotten racialist swine that you are?'

'Speak for yourself,' I said.

He smiled. 'Ah, I *am* a rotten racialist swine generally. But that's a *good* nigger, even if he does go in for folksong. Comes from Rhodesia; his father's loaded. You know, the rick blacks are O.K., just like you and me. It's the poor ones are the trouble. . . . Didn't know he was having it off with Wendy, though.'

'It's rather old-fashioned,' I said.

'That's it exactly, Frank. She's only doing it to shock people, but she's twenty years behind the times. No-one cares now. I don't know what exactly you have to do to shock people these days. In fact, that's one of my problems. . . . Look, let's just dash into the Old Mitre.'

We dashed into the Old Mitre for the duration of a Guinness for me and a glass of sherry for him. Like the Salisbury, the Old Mitre with its dark panelling and stained-glass windows always had a soothing effect upon me; but when I proposed another drink Adam shook his head.

'We must move on,' he said. 'One last attempt to track bloody Dick Sancreed down, and then we're finished.'

'I thought Dick Sancreed was dead.'

'That's the point. That's why I want to run across him, casual-like. So I haven't even asked anyone behind the bar if they've seen him. Not that I would, anyway.' He imitated a whining Cockney voice. 'Hey, Nelly, 'ave you seen old Jack tonight? The bloody barmaid never has seen old Jack either, and the chap who's asking doesn't care if he never sees old Jack again. It's just a way peasants have of demonstrating that they've got friends . . .'

There was a hardness in his manner I hadn't noticed before, and the attempt to impress me never seemed to cease. I didn't in the least mind what he said about peasants; but as we went into the Arts Theatre Club and up the stairs into the members' lounge, I wondered if, the next day, he might not be recounting examples of my own incredibly gauche behaviour to someone like Wendy or, for that matter, her black friend.

But in the lounge at a window seat he seemed to relax.

'Sometimes I'd like a nice uncomplicated job like yours,' he said.

'Who told you it was uncomplicated?'

'You've got a paper to bring out every day, that's something clear-cut. You're not dealing with imponderables, you're not trying to measure what can't be measured. Damn it, even in advertising you've got a yardstick. You sell the product or you don't. That's all . . .'

It was growing darker now, the lights were coming on, the evening was beginning, the time at which one either had an engagement to dinner or a party or filled in the hours at the cinema or a strip club, and ended with a snack at a Wimpy Bar or a Golden Egg or a Lyons. There had been too many evenings like that for me recently, but Adam's insolently self-sufficient expression, the way he wore his expensive clothes and ordered a drink, were the evidence that he never needed to kill time, that he was never short of company.

'You don't seem to have done badly out of the imponderables,' I said, taking his lapel between my finger and thumb. 'You didn't buy this under sixty guineas.'

'Ay, lad,' he said, assuming a Yorkshire accent. 'A bit of good stuff this. And the tie is Pierre Cardin, not that one can wear the label outside, more's the pity. That's the main thing in PR, actually. Packaging oneself. Unless one's related to the Managing Director, of course . . .'

'Your Oxford degree might have helped,' I said.

'It got me a copywriting job at J. Walter Thompson's a long time ago, but that's all . . . Where are you living now, by the way?'

'Off the King's Road. The wrong end. I've been going to move for some time, but you know how it is. One's overcome by sloth most of the time. I only use the place to sleep in anyway.'

'What sort of place have you exactly?'

'What they call a flatlet. A glorified bedsitter with a shower compartment and a recess for a Baby Belling, in fact.'

'Haven't you thought of sharing a bigger place?'

'You have to be careful. Or else you find yourself living with a queer or a loony or a crook.'

'Too bloody true. I live in Hampstead now. Sometimes it's rather a fag getting there but it's worth it. Too many artists and politicians and swine of that kind about the streets, but at least they're prosperous swine. And the air's marvellous. Look, why not have a trip there with me? You haven't anything else on, have you?'

I agreed, doing my best to put on some show of indifference. He hadn't bothered all these years to discover whether I or my parents were alive or dead; he wasn't now going to be permitted to assume his former position of leader, even of master.

In the taxi – Adam never used public transport because, he said, of the smell – he told me of starving in a bed-sitter in Bayswater on his first coming to London, how he'd landed the job at Thompsons, moved on to LPE, then on to another firm, and now into public relations. 'It's the ultimate,' he said. 'At least, for the time being. It isn't a big firm, so I'm polishing apples like mad, working day and night and all that jazz. As long as you continue to talk fluently and occasionally funnily and even more occasionally colourfully, and even more occasionally still display enormous integrity, you have it made. Where else would I get £5,000 plus expenses at my age?'

'There must be more to it than that,' I said as the taxi went up Haverstock Hill and the special atmosphere of Hampstead – sexy, untrammelled, yet prosperous and secure – struck me softly like a pretty girl's playful blow.

'Naturally. If anything we promote turns sour we'll be in a right old mess. Our overheads are fantastic, and they've damned well got to be. But mount a successful campaign and the customer's positively dazzled. Because all of a sudden he's no longer anonymous or lumbered with the wrong image. Everyone knows he's there. How should they not, since we've informed everyone in his particular line that he does in fact exist?'

We turned off Church Street and turned again, keeping in the direction of the Heath. What I couldn't believe was that any of the houses contained real people. They were too newly painted, too clean and shiny, there was far more than the usual proportion of Rolls and Mercedes and Lancias outside, the flowers in the window-boxes were too fresh; around the next corner the film cameras must surely be waiting. Hampstead had once been a mixture of middle-class and Bohemian; now it was all just plain rich. There wasn't anywhere left to be scruffy, poor, or wild; each house gave the impression of being under inspection always, like a soldier in a crack regiment.

But now we were travelling down a road of larger detached houses, one of which at least was boarded up and deserted. This was a road of mansions which would now be blocks of flats and institutions; and it would always be quiet and slightly melancholy, as it was now, since it was a road of people who lived alone.

But northwards there was open space, the grass and trees and bogs of the Heath. It never was my favourite street;

there were too many buildings there which, like the commercial college and the sub-sub-department of the Ministry of Defence, were closed and dead out of term time or office hours. And there were, naturally, no children living there. It wasn't that I wanted to pat them on the head or to watch them at their play, or indeed that I very much desired their presence. But a street without children is like a wax fruit under a bell jar; there will be, so to speak, no possibility of smell or mess, but there will also be no change and no growth.

'This is it,' Adam said to the driver. The name, Shalott House, on the tall stone gateposts, had recently been repainted white.

The fallen leaves rustled under the wheels of the taxi; the drive, bordered by laurels, broadened out by the house itself. There were two old-fashioned gas standard lamps at the bottom of the steps and a small stained-glass lamp over the porch. All three were lit; two of the first floor windows and all the dormer windows had lights in them. Unless Shalott was the builder's or original owner's name, it wasn't at all what one was expecting, but solid red brick Dutch style with a rather beetle-browed front porch, built to last some time in the early 1900s. There was no evidence anywhere of romantic dilapidation; this was a property that had always been well maintained.

Adam brushed aside my offer to share the taxi fare. 'You're from New York, remember.'

He stood at the door for a moment sniffing appreciatively. 'No smoke here, Frank. This brickwork's as good as new. Just weathered nicely now.'

The hall was lit by a cluster of wall lights, one on each wall. The brass stems – dolphins and seahorses and mermaids – hadn't been cleaned for a long time. But the tesselated floor was spotless. The staircase was broad and painted white and there was a narrow strip of plain ochre carpet, not very far from being threadbare. There was a pile of letters on a marble-topped table by the window. Adam flipped through it. 'Bills, bills, bills,' he said, and stuffed them in his pocket without opening them.

'There really should be a butler to open the door,' I said.

Adam smiled. 'Just what I've always felt,' he said. 'They did have a butler here in the golden days. He slept up in the attic, and spent his days in the basement. Basil – that's one of the chaps I share the flat with – sleeps in what used to be his pantry.'

He opened a door to the right of the stairway and led me into an entrance hall or, to be more accurate, cubicle. There was a walnut table and a spindly gilt chair in the cubicle. On the walnut table was a silver tray with a litter of visiting cards on it. I noticed that those bearing titles had somehow contrived to find their way to the top of the pile. Adam grinned at me. 'The great thing,' he said, 'is not to show the whole name. Just the Duke of, the Hon., the Right Hon., His Excellency the, and so on . . . I used to put them on the mantelpiece, but all the best people say that this is frightfully vulgar. The loo's through the door on the left if you need it.' He flung his coat over the chair and took mine from me. 'The coat rack's fallen off the cloakroom wall. I'm going to put it back eventually, but I'm not terribly good at that sort of thing. If only my old man were alive now, he'd really have fixed this place up.'

'What happened to all his books?' I asked as we went through the door immediately in front of us.

'I've got some of them here. The rest are in storage.'

I drew in my breath sharply as I looked around me. What I saw was not what I'd been expecting. Somehow the notion was firmly implanted in my head that bachelors, even in Adam's salary bracket, either lived in minute flatlets or, if they had room to move, in a state of dusty bohemianism at the very best, surrounded by empty bottles, unwashed crockery, and yellowing newspapers. And the rooms of their flats were arrangements of partitions, oddly proportioned; but this room, looking out to the front of the house, was the original drawing room; the run of the cornice and picture-rails was unbroken except at the section by the door.

Adam, from over his shoulder as he was drawing the plum-coloured velvet curtains, said, 'For God's sake, sit down, Frank, and stop pricing everything. You're not in bloody Yorkshire now.'

'And I'm not the Country Mouse,' I said sharply, taking an armchair by the big stone fireplace where now stood an electric fire. The fire was brand new, as was the radiogram and tape recorder and twenty-three inch television set and, indeed, everything mechanical and portable in the room; but the furniture and carpets and even the curtains were heavy and old-fashioned and hauntingly familiar.

Adam switched the fire on. 'Sorry,' he said, 'We nerve-ridden Town Mice tend to be rather hectoring.'

He went over to a huge Chinese lacquer work cabinet with gilt dragons on a red background. 'Do you want Guinness, Frank? Or there's some beer in the fridge. Or you can have vodka or gin or whisky or brandy – but what you'd rather have is some wine, surely? I don't really drink anything else myself. Not rare old vintages; just fermented grape juice.'

'You haven't left me with much choice,' I said, as he brought out a bottle of Spanish burgundy. I leaned back in my armchair; I'd almost forgotten how pleasant it was to sit in comfort in a more than decently-sized room without feeling any pressing necessity, as it were, to sing for my supper.

He poured me a glass of wine and lit himself another Russian cigarette. I took out my packet of Mannikins.

'No, no,' he said, rummaging in the cabinet. 'Don't

smoke your own.' He threw me a packet of White Owl cigars. 'Chap in the office gave me these the other day. They're not Havana, but they're smokeable. Do you remember when we had our first smoke? Woodbines, going home from St Theo's?'

'That was after we had that stupid clot from the Ministry of Health.'

'I know. It struck me that there must be something good about tobacco if he was against it ... Well, what's your considered opinion of my squalid little pad?'

'It's too good for you,' I said. 'It must cost you a packet.'

'Not quite. I share it with two other chaps. Basil Staverton – he's a solicitor – and Gordon Shilmoor, who's what is termed as a rising young executive. Of course, I had a hell of a lot to put down in cash when I took over the place, but it's well worth it.' His face momentarily softened, at the same time became savagely greedy. 'I'd give up the hell of a lot to hang on to this place. You still don't know what it's like living away from home, Frank. Christ, when I think of the wretched places I've been in, the horrible diggings, the horrible people there ... and the bed-sitters, which are just as bad in a different way ...'

'You'll get married,' I said.

'I know all about that. You begin with a flat, your wife keeps on working, you put away her salary and then when the bambinos arrive you get a little box in the suburbs with a bloody big mortgage and the solicitor congratulates you on saving so much income-tax. And then you get a bigger box, and then a still bigger box, and your mortgage is so enormous that really the Inland Revenue should be owing you money, but you still have to pay it out —' He drained his glass quickly and poured himself another.

I was rather surprised by his vehemence; I hadn't myself at this time thought very seriously about marriage, but neither did I have any strong feelings against it. I now have an £11,500 box in Chertsey – four bedrooms, oil-fired central heating, a ninety per cent mortgage – and if my family grows may even acquire a bigger box, all as Adam foretold. But I've never seen it as otherwise than inevitable. That was the difference between us. I mumbled something noncommittal about there being plenty of time yet, and then my attention was taken by a large framed photograph on the wall opposite the drink cabinet.

I went over to look at it more closely. The girl in the photograph was, quite unmistakably, Wendy Halmstead, standing naked against an oak tree. There was a rug and a hamper on the grass. Her arms were behind her head to lift up her breasts; they were smaller than I had imagined they would be, but she was much younger; the faint lines that her face was etched with now must have taken five or six years to acquire, and the way in which she held herself was easier, less studied, almost coltish. It was a very good photograph, dramatically black and white, startlingly clear; so good, in fact, that it aroused in me not sexual desire but a strange sadness: the body that I was looking at was already being changed, bit by bit losing its spring, imperceptibly being coarsened, worked over as if by a malevolent masseur.

'Déjeuner sur l'herbe,' Adam said. 'That was when we were engaged. Four years ago. No, five, I'd just gone to work for Thompsons.'

'You never told me.'

'It was just after my mother died. It didn't last very long.'

'What happened?'

He seemed embarrassed for a moment. 'Another woman. Mind you, I'm not sorry. I suppose I was feeling all alone in the world, a poor little orphan boy, and she was there, and she's a bit older than me. But it wouldn't have done, it wouldn't have done at all. She's been married and divorced since then, and she's having trouble with her present husband, who seems an all-round twat, but who am I to throw the first stone?'

'Does she know the photo's there?'

'Know?' Adam laughed. 'She'd play the devil if ever I took it down. She's very proud of it.'

I continued to stare at the photograph. There was a reproduction of a Byzantine Madonna next to it; I fancied that the half-smile on Wendy's face and on the Madonna's face were uncannily alike.

'You're still on good terms with her?'

'Why not? As long as I don't have to marry her. Not that I could now: that's one of the advantages of being a Papist. If I were you I wouldn't look at that picture any longer, though. She's a wild one, is old Wendy. Poor bitch, she lives in a perpetual state of confusion. . . .'

'Don't we all?'

He filled up my glass again. 'No, Frank, we do not. We wouldn't be here if we did.' He walked over to the far side of the room and bent down to inspect the wall. There was a yellow stain there, glaringly obvious against the pale blue wallpaper with its formalised pattern of white flowers. Adam tried to rub the mark off with his handkerchief but without success. 'I wonder who the hell did that,' he grumbled.

'Put something in front of it,' I said impatiently.

He moved an armchair. 'Gordon, probably, staggering about in his cups. Not that I should grumble, he won't be here much longer. He's going to Bradford, poor devil. And now I've got to hunt about for someone to take his place . . .' He straightened a Toulouse-Lautrec reproduction of a brothel scene: a fat naked man lolling back on a rumpled bed, his face suffused with satisfaction, his penis flaccid, and a bored-looking woman pulling her stockings on.

'No *post coitus triste* there,' I said.

He grinned. 'Is there ever? Even when you know it's the wrong person and the wrong time and the wrong place?'

He straightened the framed First Communion certificate that hung next to the Toulouse-Lautrec and went back to the drink cabinet.

'I've put a lot of work and money into this place,' he said. 'I can't have just anyone living here. There's always some sodding woman wanting to move in, but that only leads to sorrow. And if you advertise, not only do you get a shoal of letters to go through but, as you rightly say, half are queer and half are crooks. And I don't like agencies.'

He still had the tendency to worry a subject to death, even to force his listener to share his interest in it.

'I'm hungry,' I said. 'I can't sit about swilling wine on an empty stomach much more. If I do, I'll be sick all over your pretty blue Axminster carpet.'

'You once were,' he said. 'It's from the drawing-room at home. God, what a time I had scrubbing it and soaking it with TCP! The sofa's from our house too, and the armchairs. I had loose covers put on them all. And those nesting coffee tables and the dining table and the sideboard and the grandfather clock —'

He continued the inventory, but it was superfluous. The heavy furniture, mostly Victorian, belonged to this room more than it ever had belonged to any room in Adam's home in Charbury; it needed space to come into its own. The mahogany table, for instance, which stood in one corner of this room now looked almost light and graceful; in Charbury it had taken up nearly half of the dining-room even when not completely extended. To see it here was, after the first shock had passed, warmly, almost voluptuously comforting, like the stock pulp story situation of the man meeting the Plain Jane from next door in the Big City and discovering her anew as a grown-up, an exciting mature woman. The wine was by now beginning to affect me. I belched loudly.

'We may as well have a bite here if you're going to make those nauseating sounds,' Adam said.

I followed him into the passage beside the drawing-room. Here the walls were distempered plain white, but the mosaic patterned tiles continued. There were two other doors on my right, and overhead there was a naked 40-watt bulb. 'My room there,' Adam said. 'Bathroom and W.C. next to it. I'm going to put down some carpet here one of these days.'

The kitchen was a large room with a new gas cooker, a huge black refrigerator, a scrubbed deal table and six Windsor chairs. There was a pile of dirty plates and cups and saucers on the draining board. On the white-painted open shelves were a great many jars of spice and herbs; from the dust on them it didn't seem as if they were ever used. The walls were distempered in the identical bleak white of the passage.

I shivered. 'Christ, this certainly lacks the woman's touch,' I said.

Adam was taking plates and glasses out of the cupboard by the door. 'There's a heater over the door,' he said. 'I'm not really a kitchen man, to tell you the truth . . . Fetch in a bottle of vino, will you, Frank?'

When I returned the table was already set and he was cracking eggs, frying bacon, and cutting bread almost simultaneously.

'This is the limit of my cooking,' he said. 'The time for a bachelor to beware is when he becomes too dab a hand with the old paella and fondue and all the rest of it. The next stage is those pretty whimsical teacloths on the wall and swopping recipes with your chums.'

He ate quickly, in fact almost wolfishly. I had only half-finished when he pushed his empty plate away and lit a cigarette.

It was then, and very briefly, that I received the warning signals. He was impatient for me to finish my meal, he wanted me to eat at the same rate as he did. I was, to judge by his expression, being tried and found wanting. But it was the kitchen – so tidy, so bare, so institutional – that triggered off the warning signals. For there hung over it the sense of a great loneliness – not a sad loneliness, but a self-satisfied loneliness, a sterile loneliness.

And then I had finished and the plates and cutlery were whisked off the table and we were back in what he had told me must always be called the living-room, and the warning signals grew fainter and, disregarded, stopped. I was drinking wine with my cousin Adam, I wasn't anything like drunk, but I was mellow; and something of the old hero-worship was returning. Only Adam, I thought, comparing the way he lived with the way that I – and indeed all the bachelors of my acquaintance – lived, could manage it. It wasn't simply that he lived in greater comfort than the rest of us; the flat was an extension of his personality.

'I wish I lived in a place like this,' I said. 'God, it must cost you a packet.'

'Less than you think. Eighteen guineas a week. Of course, there's all sorts of conditions – so bloody many, in fact, that it's difficult to see exactly what the poor tenant *can* do. The landlord's a rather nice old boy, name of Cohen – he has a flat on the first floor, but he's not here very much. Mostly tours the Continent trying to earn a few coppers to save himself from destitution, or so he says. And on the top floor is Simon Cothill, of whom you may have heard.'

I shook my head.

'Um. Well, that's one of his problems right now, like poor old Dickie Sancreed. He's a photographer and a bachelor, and likely to remain so. He comes to our parties too.'

'I have heard of him,' I said. 'He was always in the head-lines once.'

'He survives, don't worry about that. The good old Homintern never lets its members down. But somehow or

other life has passed him by. It's probably the male meno-
pause. He has an assistant whom he calls Carlos. Carlos is
really the absolute end and —' his face was distorted by
genuine hatred – 'one of these days I'm going to fix bloody
Carlos good and proper.'

'You do go on a bit about fixing people,' I said. 'But you
always were a good hater. Remember our Enemy list?'

He smiled. 'We used to tick them off as misfortune over-
took them. Are they all still alive, do you know?'

'I'm afraid they are. All except old Atlas' – this was the
P.T. master at St Theo's – 'and he got cancer.'

He made the sign of the Cross. 'Poor old sod. I wouldn't
have wished that on him. But that's the way the cookie
crumbles. You put a curse on a chap and you never know
how it's going to end.'

'I wish it'd work with the Government,' I said.

He made a noise imitative of retching. 'Don't talk about
it. I have it all day at work. If it isn't South Africa, it's
Rhodesia, and if it isn't Rhodesia it's Vietnam. I just make
vague and sapient noises when anyone talks about politics.
My politics is *me*. When they have an election I vote for the
chaps who'll tax me the least, and that's the most I hope
for.'

He went over to the window and pulled back the blind.
'Look here,' he said, beckoning me over. 'In the morning
you see trees and grass and you open the window and it's
fresh and clean. And down below, and that's what's best of
all about it, they're all breathing in carbon monoxide and
sulphur and river sewage.'

'How many rooms have you?' I asked him. It was as if I
were going to buy the place; suddenly, whether from professional curiosity, or from alcohol or a combination of
both, I was consumed by a desire to know all that was to be
known about the flat.

'Five, counting this and the kitchen. And not counting that

33

weird little entrance hall and the bathroom and shower stall and two cloakrooms.' There was a note of proud tenderness in Adam's voice, and he was looking round the room as he spoke, and not at me.

'It's funny seeing all this stuff again,' I said.

Inside the china cabinet I recognised the Dresden shepherdesses and blue Wedgwood pieces and the two elaborate Swiss musical boxes – a farmyard and a scene from *Les Sylphides* – and the rose-tinted glassware that had been accumulated by Adam's mother. The rosewood grandfather clock, some hundred and fifty years old with a hand-painted sylvan scene on the face, ticked away reassuringly. And I could even remember the occasion of some of the pieces being added to the collection – my own mother had brought her back the farmyard musical box from Lausanne and I myself had given her the little blue Wedgwood jar for her birthday.

'I had a job hanging on to it,' Adam said. 'You see those two Fred Lawson water colours there? When my mother died, my bloody Uncle Jesse was so kind as to offer to take them off my hands. And this Chinese cabinet, which Mother was given by my Auntie Harriet. And the Dresden. And that big German jug.' He mimicked a quavering Yorkshire voice. *'Ee, lad, tha'll noan be wanting all this old junk, not a young bachelor like you.* They were all hovering around like vultures. So were the dealers. I must have broken their hearts. They really thought I didn't want the stuff. You could see them rubbing their hands, because they know the value of everything, the sanctimonious greedy bastards . . . So I put it all into storage and then this place came along unfurnished. It wasn't advertised, I heard of it through a mate of mine at LPE.'

I was looking at the pictures. 'There's a Graham Sutherland here. And an Eric Gill.'

'My father bought them, not me. Uncle Jesse said that

the Gill drawing was indecent – he meant the pubic hair – but it'd do for his study. And there's a Jacob Kramer over in the corner there, next to the Sacred Heart. He was a friend of Epstein's, a coming man and all that, and then he did a Rimbaud and went to live in Leeds.'

The Kramer was a pleasant little nude in oils, perhaps a little too slick. Next to it was a big heavy wooden crucifix, at least three feet long. The figure was painted in glaring primary colours, the face contorted with agony. There was no doubt of the Son of Man dying in agony and despair.

'One of my own purchases,' Adam said. 'A fun thing really, like the posters' – there were posters of a farm auction in Skipton in 1885 and an execution by shooting in Johannesburg in 1899 – 'and the handcuffs.' He lifted up the heavy rusty handcuffs next to the Johannesburg poster. 'They're a ton weight. Supposed to date from the Crimean war, but I doubt it.'

'You're a decadent old sod,' I said affectionately.

'I'm my own shop window. This place is part of it. Mark you' – he pointed a long finger at me – 'I like things like old handcuffs and I like crosses that make me think of death. That cross shakes a lot of the lousy pagan buggers who come here. You wouldn't believe to what lengths they go to assure themselves they're going to live for ever – I mean physically for ever.'

I couldn't be quite certain from the expression on his face whether he was serious or not.

'I'm glad your simple faith remains untouched,' I said.

'There was a period when it didn't. The Wendy period. But then I came to with a jerk and looked at all the stupid pricks around me, not knowing whether they were coming or going, always agonized over Apartheid or Hiroshima or starving Indian peasants . . . So I grew up.'

The doorbell rang, or rather chimed. It was so strident that involuntarily I jumped, spilling a little wine.

'Sorry I didn't warn you,' Adam said. 'I think Cohen bought that bell from a fire station. Excuse me.'

I heard a man's voice, more aggressively Cockney-cadenced than Adam's and yet more emphatically King's Road.

'Adam love, have you any coffee or even tea? I've run right out.'

'I'll look. Don't stand in the doorway like a vacuum cleaner salesman. Come in and have a drink.'

A man who at first sight appeared no more than thirty appeared at the doorway, his hand on Adam's shoulder. The main overhead chandelier was not switched on; as he came closer I saw that he was certainly much older than thirty, the short blond hair tinted, the face heavy with talcum.

'I'm sorry, Adam. I didn't know you had company.'

'Oh, Christ, Simon, don't say it in that revoltingly coy way. This is my cousin, Frank Batcombe, whom I ran across in the Salisbury. Frank, Simon Cothill, the photographer. A quid for five artistic poses in black and white, two quid for colour.'

Simon wriggled like a small girl who wants to go to the W.C. but can't bring herself to ask.

'He's beastly, you know, Frank. Actually, I'm mostly in fashion.' He held out his hand; it was cold, with stubby fingers.

'What do you do for your daily bread, Frank?'

'I'm a journalist.' I named the paper and his eyebrows – which were very much darker than his hair – shot up.

'Oh, that's very good. I mean, it's still solvent. I work for them from time to time.'

Adam looked at him sardonically. 'I'll get you some coffee,' he said. 'Have some vino, Simon.'

'I shouldn't really,' Simon said. 'I'm a vodka man, really. The purest spirit there is.' He poured himself a glass and

36

took a sip. 'Vino indeed. Obviously you're not doing business with dear old Adam, or else he wouldn't give you this muck. Honestly, love, you ought to see him when he's with someone he thinks he'll get something out of. Oh, it's all "I'd appreciate your opinion of this hock I've just got in" or "let's be devils and have some of this very unpretentious champagne" . . .' He raised his voice. 'Do you hear me, Adam?'

Somehow or other he had come very close to me; he smelt very strongly of a faintly lemony cologne. 'Eau Sauvage,' he said. 'And I can see what you're thinking, my dear Frank.'

'I wasn't thinking at all,' I said.

'Oh yes, you are, Frank. I'm a great student of human nature, you know. I can tell you a lot of things about yourself immediately. You're about twenty-seven. You're a bachelor. Unfortunately you're hetero. And you're an observer. You're a nice boy but you're an observer.'

'That's not hard to guess,' I said.

He sipped the wine, giving the impression of actually putting his tongue into it like a cat. His suit was a lavender coloured tweed with a matching waistcoat cut like a pullover. His red bow tie was the colour of his silk breastpocket handkerchief. The shirt was the exact colour of his suede shoes. He seemed to preen himself as I looked at him.

Adam came in with a packet of coffee.

'You know I like the Continental blend,' Simon said.

'I'm not running a bloody shop,' Adam said.

'It'll have to do. Thank you, my dear Adam. I'll repay you a hundred fold.' He offered us a packet of Gauloise. Adam took one; I shook my head.

'Wise man, Frank. I puff puff puff all the time. Mind you, I don't inhale. I can't really smoke when I'm in the darkroom you see, so I make up for it outside.'

'I thought you were smoking something else these days,'

Adam said. 'There was a damned peculiar smell in the hall the other day.'

Simon reddened. 'I don't really know what you mean.'

'Yes, you do. Pot. Hemp.'

'Oh, I'm sorry about that, Adam dear. Really I am. I didn't know you felt so strongly about these things —'

'You know bloody well what I feel. The hall smelt like a nigger brothel.'

'Truly, I'm sorry. But I do assure you with my hand on my heart, it wasn't me. Pot isn't my sort of vice, knowing as I know that the ensuing publicity just isn't good for someone in my business. My bread-and-butter is the British middle-class —'

'So is mine,' Adam cut in. 'You tell that little whore Carlos to smoke his stinking reefers somewhere else. Or I'll tell him with my boot-end.'

'You needn't be quite so *crude*,' Simon said. 'Couldn't it have waited, meaning no offence to dear discreet Frank here?'

'No,' Adam said. 'Because the next thing we know, Carlos will bring his mates here and he'll have himself a real ball. And the fuzz will arrive, and there'll be real trouble. And everyone at Shalott House will be tarred with the same brush. And Cohen, and I shan't blame him, will be forced to throw us all out. Look at your lease if you don't believe me.'

'I'll have a word with Carlos. I promise you faithfully that I won't let him touch the stuff again. It isn't addictive, you know. It's only a phase —'

Adam made a rude noise. 'If you believe that, you'll believe anything. Anyway, I don't give a damn whether it's addictive or not. I won't have it stinking up my home, and if you want to know, I'm not so keen on Carlos living here, either.'

Simon giggled. 'I like to live dangerously, my dear. To

feast with panthers. You mustn't begrudge me my pleasures.'

Adam shrugged his shoulders. 'Please yourself. By the way, you're coming to my party on Friday, aren't you?'

'Depends who's there.' Simon put his glass of wine aside. 'Give me some vodka, you mean thing.'

Adam gave him a glass of vodka and a bottle of Schweppes Bitter Lemon. 'Some customers for you. And perhaps a few for me. Try to bring at least one new bird, will you? Mislingford may be there.'

'Yes, yes.' Simon looked as if he were about to weep. 'Dear God, what a life it is, never a moment to call one's own. I can see it's all new to you, my dear Frank, your face is so fresh and unlined. You remind me of a boy I once knew. He was only twenty-one. Just twenty-one. And he'd been in remand homes. Christ, *homes!* – all his life. His mother was a whore and his father was a thief, and he never had a chance until he met me. And then what did I do for him? I bought him that sodding motor-bike. The one he'd got wasn't fast enough . . .'

He glanced at his watch, a gold bracelet Piguet. 'My God, it's eleven o'clock, and Denise is phoning!' He drained the vodka in one gulp, not bothering with the Bitter Lemon, and flashed me a brilliant smile. 'I'll see you again, I hope, dear sympathetic Frank.'

When he had gone, leaving the smell of Eau Sauvage behind him, Adam took out a bottle of brandy.

'Simon is rather horrible, isn't he? Mind, he's damned useful. And I'm useful to him. He has contacts and I have contacts and, above all, he has an unlimited supply of birds. He's the best unpaid pimp in the business.'

The brandy was smooth in my mouth; it seemed both to dispel the metallic aftertaste of the red wine and to transform it into something richer.

'I'll have to be moving,' I said.

'Hell, it's early yet. Stay and meet Basil. He's out with some chick or other. But he's always in before midnight, like Cinderella. Afraid he'll turn into a dock brief or something.'

I went to look at the photograph of Wendy again. The cleft between the legs seemed to be more deeply indented than ever I'd seen on any woman. 'Christ, I really could do something for her.'

'No doubt, Frank. And no doubt she'd be glad of it. But she'd eat you up, I warn you. And she's drinking like a fish these days. Funny you should have noticed her, though. Funny I should have come into the Salisbury for that matter. It isn't my usual stamping-ground.'

'I'm glad you did.' The brandy was loosening my tongue. 'There are times when I feel like taking the next train back to Charbury. I mean, it's hard work getting to know people in London.'

'That's been my job for a long time. Getting to know people. You know what they call the chap who stands at the entrance of the Methodist chapel before the service? The smiler-in. That's what I am, Frank, the smiler-in. Mostly the people I meet want something from me or I want something from them. Mostly be damned . . . All the bloody time. As for the women, they want sex or marriage. Yes, even old Wendy wouldn't mind trying her luck again . . .' He held out the brandy bottle. I shook my head. 'You know, Frank, when first I came to London I hardly knew anyone. I had eighteen quid a week and a lousy bedsitter in Earl's Court – a divan bed and a gas ring and a wash basin. But, believe me, to all outward appearances I was earning ten thousand a year. You see, it doesn't cost any more to go to Mass at Brompton Oratory or Farm Street than it does to go to your own parish. And unless you're a real old lush, you can make a gin and tonic or a lager last for hours at the Ritz or the Dorchester or the Savoy. The great secret is never to mix with the peasants, never to wear anything that looks cheap, never to wear a dirty shirt or a frayed tie. Hell, it's all old stuff now, there's at least a million books written about it, but I discovered it for myself. Remember, Frank, that ordinary people smell. Mix with them, start treating them like human beings, and the smell rubs off on to you.'

'I hadn't thought about it before,' I said.

'That's your great charm, Frank. You never have done.' He looked at me appraisingly. 'Tell me, do you really like journalism?'

I can see now that he was already beginning to plan how to rearrange my life; he couldn't understand how any young man with my qualifications could want to be anywhere except in public relations.

'It's better than a lot of jobs I could mention.'

'That's very negative, Batcombe,' he said, using the favourite expression of our Latin master at St Theo's. 'You must burst through the eggshell of negation, my boy.'

'Negative be damned,' I said. 'I like the job. I even like the paper.'

'So do I. It's very sound, particularly on capital punishment.'

'I agree with you entirely.' At this stage I wasn't quite sure what I was agreeing with him about; as soon as I said something, aphasia descended upon me.

'Good. Good. To tell you the truth, I was a bit bothered about that. I mean, you went to Charbury University and Charbury is full of foul perverted Communists and, indeed, Progs of every kind. Progressives, I mean.'

'At Charbury they were always asking you to join things and to protest. But I didn't. I don't care to protest about anything except personal matters.'

He nodded slowly. 'My sentiments exactly. I refuse to stand up and be counted. To hell with my suffering black brothers in South Africa and Rhodesia too. To hell with the homosexuals, to hell with the unmarried mothers, to hell with the homeless —'

'And down with Oxfam!' a voice cut in. A small, stocky man had bounced into the room. He was about Adam's age with bristlingly black hair and gold-rimmed spectacles; there was about him an air of almost lunatic cheerfulness.

'Down with Oxfam!' Adam repeated in a ritual tone. 'Frank Batcombe, Basil Staverton, a crooked lawyer, the mouthpiece for all the big gangs. Frank's a cousin once or twice removed, Basil. Mick on his mother's side like me. He's now a journalist.'

Basil shook my hand briskly. 'Which paper? Or rather which journal? For the word journal, as few people know, means daily.' He poured himself a large brandy as I told him.

'An admirable paper,' he said. 'Not far enough to the right, but then what paper is?'

He sat down opposite me, his hands clasping his ankle. 'I've wasted a great deal of time and money tonight, all in a vain attempt to persuade a young lady to divest herself of her clothes. Hell, she didn't have all that many on, it wouldn't have been any great effort to her.'

'Lucy?'

Basil nodded.

'She's a roaring Lesbian, you idiot. She wouldn't have gone out with you at all, except that Trixie's modelling in New York.'

'I wondered,' Basil said. 'I wondered when she asked for a pint of bitter. But, unlike you, I'm not an expert in such matters.'

I seemed momentarily to see claws rake out and Adam to wince; but he quickly recovered himself.

'All I can say is,' he said, 'that you're a glutton for

punishment. You'll end up paying a pound a lash, you really will.'

'No doubt I shall,' Basil said. 'But they can't all be kinky or virginal. It's just that my luck hasn't been in lately.'

His cuff-links were, I noticed, massively golden, and his dark grey suit was cut to minimise his extreme broadnesss Even when still – and he wasn't, unlike Adam, given to fidgeting – he radiated energy. I felt that now he was inspecting me, filing away a complete report.

'Basil,' Adam said, 'Frank here is going to take up residence with us.'

'Wait a moment,' I said. 'You haven't asked me properly yet.'

Adam scowled. 'I should think you'd jump at the chance, you silly sod.'

'It needs thinking over.' It had actually been in my mind ever since I had entered Shalott House; but I didn't like the way in which Adam, within so short a time, was already taking decisions on my behalf.

'Nonsense. You're the ideal candidate. You're clean in your habits, you're not queer, and you don't appear to be a Communist. Not that it matters these days. Some of my best friends are Communists.'

'Jolly decent of you not to mind,' I said. 'Actually, I'd come like a shot, but I still have a bit of trouble with the old leprosy. I keep losing a finger here, a finger there —'

'As long as it's nothing worse,' Adam said. 'We very often have delicate little birds folding their wings, so as to speak, in our nest.'

'I do in my own little nest in the King's Road,' I said.

'Ah, but do you have room enough for orgies? And if you did, wouldn't your neighbour object at the first scream?'

'Adam,' Basil said gently, 'don't try to persuade Frank –

43

or rather bend him to your will – quite so assiduously. There's plenty of time before Gordon leaves.'

'I'm sorry,' Adam said. 'I know very well I'm a power-maniac. Anyway, come to the party on Friday and we'll have a talk about it then.'

Basil took a gold half-hunter from his waistcoat pocket. 'I must go to bed soon. Alone, as I hoped I would not be. It rather appears, however, as if Gordon has been more fortunate than I, if indeed I is the pronoun for which I am searching.' He sipped the brandy. 'He keeps this under lock and key, Frank. I advise you to drink as much of it as possible; a considerable period will elapse before you taste it again. It isn't a rare old liqueur as drunk by Napoleon, either. It's just that he's excessively parsimonious. In short, bloody mean.'

'What on earth do you want to go to bed for? It's not midnight yet.' Adam's tone was petulant, almost whining.

'Because I am overwhelmed by fatigue,' Basil said. 'And because tomorrow I must be in Court, and it's imperative that I look my shining and resplendent and keen-eyed best.'

'Simon's been in to borrow some coffee,' Adam said.

'He's rather a menace, isn't he? Has he promised to bring some breasts along to the party, though?'

Breasts, as I was to learn later, was part of the private language of Shalott House; it was only applied to bedworthy girls as guests.

'As usual.'

'But not also as usual, I hope, that turd Carlos?'

'Not if I can help it.'

'He is one of the few human beings I detest. Once one could have looked forward with pleasure to seeing him hanged. Or at least jailed for the sin of Sodom. Now they can't even be punished for that.'

'Don't worry,' Adam said. 'He'll end up in jail one way

or the other. But not, if my plans work out, whilst he's under this roof —'

The phone rang. When he answered it, his face seemed immediately to break up, to grow older. 'No, for God's sake, no!' His voice was shrill. 'Why me, then? Am I the only bloody man you know? No, you mustn't even think of it. No. Absolutely not. You'll kill yourself. Christ, how did you get home anyway? Well, don't blame me. It's late in the day for that —' His knuckles were white with the pressure of his grip on the phone. 'Twenty minutes,' he said finally. 'Yes, of course I know where it is. Goodbye.'

Basil poured himself some more brandy. 'Wendy again,' he said. 'You should tell her to get on with it. In my experience, which is more exhaustive than you would suppose, those who threaten suicide rarely commit it.'

'Shut your effing trap,' Adam said savagely. 'You don't know Wendy. I do. And give me your car keys, mine's at the garage.' He stood for a moment frowning after Basil had handed him the keys. 'If I hadn't run across her tonight . . . Something's put her on the bottle again, if it isn't something worse than the bottle. . . .'

The effects of a bottle and a half of wine and two large glasses of brandy seemed suddenly to be not apparent.

'I'll get a cab,' I said.

'No, I'll take you, you're in her vicinity, actually. Jesus, why does it have to be me? What about her bloody husbands? What about that walking heap of dandruff she was drinking with? What about Little Black Sambo with whom presumably she's spent the evening? But it has to be me, it has to be old Muggins, and she'll keep me up until five in the bloody morning raving on about her unhappy life and how no-one loves her. . . .'

'You'd better get on with it, then,' Basil said. He seemed to be enjoying the situation.

Adam turned abruptly and strode out of the room; I could hear him starting the car before I had picked up my coat and got out into the hall.

Basil's car was a Renault R4 shooting brake, crammed with books, coats, rugs, boxes, and several large objects which in the dark I couldn't identify. Adam drove fast and hard, swearing under his breath all the time; as we turned into Haverstock Hill on the amber I distinctly felt the two offside wheels leave the ground and heard all the car's contents shift.

'Sorry about that,' Adam said, jamming the brakes on as a taxi shot out of a side turning. 'I mean, dragging you out like that.'

I heard the taxi-driver shout something; Adam grinned and started again with a jerk; I leaned back and half-closed my eyes, wishing that I'd had the moral courage to refuse the lift.

'Does she often do that?' I asked him, more to take my mind off the speed at which we were travelling than from any genuine interest.

'About twice a year. That's about how often I see her. London's a small place, Frank. One only has chums of one's own kind, and sooner or later one runs across those chums.' His tone changed. 'That's what I love about the place. It's my village now, you see.'

I opened my eyes to find that we were turning into Queensway. In the middle of the road two men were fighting, surrounded by girls. Adam narrowly avoided them, the tyres of the Renault screaming; I looked back to see them continue the fight in the gutter.

'I had a room in this district once,' Adam said. 'Not for very long; I found one of the other tenants peeing in the bath. But that's another good thing about London. There's quarters which are low and rotten and nasty and dirty. I always go this way to cheer myself up.'

I found myself roaring with laughter. 'So you can be reminded how well off you are?'

'Just so. It's quite near here. A West Indian family in the basement, a brothel on the ground floor, a loony old bachelor on the first floor and an equally loony old spinster with three cats on the second floor. God, the smell! Cats and dry rot and fried fish and vomit. Then I moved.'

'You've suffered, Adam,' I said. 'I'm surprised you're not embittered.'

'I knew it was only temporary,' he said as he drove out into the Bayswater Road. 'I only wish that this business with Wendy were temporary. But she's never going to get off my back. I can see this sort of thing happening the rest of my life ... The worst of it is, I wouldn't touch her with a bargepole. I never liked her very much, even when we were engaged. . . .'

He continued to grumble about her until we arrived at the King's Road, still full of people at midnight, but unmistakably on the verge of quietening down. Soon they would all discover that it was merely a long street full of closed shops and closed pubs and that all the excitement it had seemed to offer at the beginning of the evening was merely the invention of hacks like myself; only in the expensive houses and flats off it by Cadogan Square and Glebe Place and Radnor Walk was the evening just beginning to swing. I had discovered this for myself on my arrival in London, exploring the length and breadth of Chelsea on foot only to discover what I could equally well have discovered in Charbury, that the rich live in a world of their own.

'Isn't your flat somewhere near here?' Adam asked.

'Turn right by the World's End.'

The street was deserted here; this was the wrong end of the King's Road, with every other house boarded up and, it almost seemed, every other street demolished. There was a glaringly new shopping arcade on the left; it might have been anywhere. This was where the pretence petered out, this was the D and E Income Group King's Road, this was where the Fairy Snowman and Mazzawattee Maharajahs and Miss Camays called, where a buckshee five or ten or twenty pounds or even only one pound was worth having.

'I'll see you on Friday then,' Adam said as he stopped the car. He glanced up at the peeling exterior of the house. 'Christ, are you living here as a penance?'

He had something there, I thought, as I briefly inspected the pile of letters on the bamboo table in the hall, found nothing, and went up the stairs to my room on the top floor, feeling suddenly tired and older than my years. The house was clean enough; it smelt, in fact, rather over-poweringly of carbolic acid and strong soap. And Mrs Jessup, who cleaned my flat once a week was if anything, fanatically clean. I had come here because it was cheap, because it was clean, because there was never likely to be in the lifetime of the landlady, a Mrs Kennedy from Mount Rath, either a West Indian family in the basement or a brothel on the first floor.

But the whole house was dingy, with no prospect of a face-lift; it was due for demolition and in the meantime was simply a profit-making machine. Somehow the heart had gone out of it; there would be no parties there, no festivities, no births, perhaps even no deaths. The paint on the doors would not be renewed, the faded curtains and faded wallpaper and paper-thin carpets would not be replaced.

Until I'd visited Shalott House, I hadn't thought of the place where a bachelor lived as being of any importance. It was merely a base of operations, a place to sleep in and to keep my clothes and books. Now, opening the door of my flat, I looked forward to what faced me with something like horror.

The breakfast dishes would still be in the sink in the tiny kitchen, the divan bed would still be unmade. There would still be the big patch of damp on the wall by the dormer window, the green stains on the wash basin; and the W.C. still wouldn't flush properly until the fourth pull on the chain. But it wasn't these things which really mattered. It was that in the whole place there wasn't one piece of furniture that could ever have had any associations for anybody, that hadn't, to judge from the look of it, been bought secondhand in the first instance. Black floor, a dark red carpet, dark red lino of almost the same shade, fawn wallpaper, brown paint – it was all drab, all intended not to show the dirt, the only patches of colour being the white sheepskin rug by the gas-fire and the TV, which were both mine. And they because of their newness only served to make their surroundings still more drab.

And, by some peculiar alchemy, the flat absorbed my attempts to give it individuality. The Picasso Blue Period *Mother and Child*, the four Toulouse Lautrec posters, and the Douanier Rousseau *Sleeping Musician* might as well have been part of the pattern of the wallpaper for all the effect they had. And if they had been the originals it wouldn't have been any different: that room belonged only to itself. It wasn't haunted, there was not even any sense of anyone else having lived there; it was merely quietly, sullenly paranoid, desiring only to be empty.

I put a shilling into the meter and lit the gas fire. For a moment the room was more cheerful, almost, in fact, easy. But after I'd undressed and put on my pyjamas and, shivering, brushed my teeth, I lay awake for a long time with the light on, frightened for the first time since childhood, of the dark. And as finally alcohol and fatigue pulled down my eyelids I realized what it was that frightened me, who might open the locked door – not a ghost, and not any kind of demon, but simply myself, myself in the cosy green-and-white striped Viyella pyjamas I was wearing now, smelling of Guinness and wine and brandy as I was now, and lonely and lost and two hundred miles away from home as I was now.

two

When I awoke the next morning I didn't exactly have a hangover, but my mouth was dry and my head was throbbing. The room was both cold and stuffy; I lay there for ten minutes hating it. I hated the cheap plastic handles on the built-in wardrobes in the alcoves by the fireplace, I hated the gate-legged table in the centre of the room, I hated the mean little suite – of the kind described as *cottage* – of a two-seater sofa and two fireside chairs, I hated the dwarfish yet heavy sideboard with disproportionately large metal drawer and cupboard handles and short immensely thick legs. I hated the blotchy mirror over the fireplace with the peeling gilt frame. I hated the blue screen which hid the wash basin in the corner, I hated the three dining chairs with their worn rexine seats, and I hated most of all the dressing-table. The dressing-table was solid Victorian mahogany, and in itself without offence; but its presence reminded me that this wasn't a real flat, but a bed-sitter with a bathroom – or rather shower compartment – and kitchen attached.

I took a cold shower, dried myself briskly on one of the huge towels my mother had given me for Christmas, and completed the first stage of recovery. By the time I had brushed my teeth, washed out my mouth with Listerine, shaved, and drunk a glass of Alka-Seltzer, recovery was nearly complete. There were only left the stages of strong tea, toast, the morning paper, the first cheroot of the day and, finally, dressing.

It was whilst I was dressing that I became aware that I hadn't fully recovered from the night before and wasn't likely to. Living alone, one builds up rituals, one cares intensely – more than one should – about personal possessions, about not only what one does at certain hours of the day, but about what one thinks at these times. What had never before failed to give me comfort in the morning was the inspection and enumeration of my clothes. One light grey worsted suit faint blue overcheck, one dark grey worsted, faint red and green stripe, one plain navy blue lightweight mohair suit, one plain fawn lightweight mohair suit, one lovat green thornproof tweed suit, one dark blue Harris tweed jacket with leather-edged cuffs and elbow-patches, two pairs of dark grey slacks, one dinner jacket, two evening shirts, two dozen pairs of socks, two pairs of black calf shoes, two pairs of brown calf shoes, two pairs of brown suede shoes, one pair of sandals, thirty ties – I remember all these articles of clothing and the pleasure, small but reliable, which I would take in deciding what I would wear each day. I was not under the illusion that I should be promoted for my spruce appearance; it was simply part of my general picture of myself these days as something of a dandy.

But as I dressed this morning I remembered Adam's clothes, I remembered Simon Cothill's clothes, I remembered even Basil Staverton's. Whatever combination I chose – and any combination which doesn't actually involve indecent exposure is acceptable in a newspaper office – I shouldn't look as arrestingly well-dressed as they; I should merely be adequately covered. Neat but not gaudy – that awful phrase of awful old Polonius just about summed it up. Any boring old cliché, I felt, as I finally settled for the dark grey worsted suit, plain blue shirt and plain maroon tie, would sum up any aspect of my character. I had arrived in Fleet Street, at least I hadn't stuck in Charbury, but I wasn't in the main stream. At my age, there wasn't much time left, I was perilously near the stage where I'd cease to be Young Batcombe, pushing, bright and eager. Young Batcombe had the world at his feet, Young Batcombe was always coming up with something provocatively, shockingly new, Young Batcombe was a card, a likely lad, whose sins would be forgiven him. But Good Old Batcombe would be part of the office furniture, reliable, steady, always delivering his copy on time, always checking the facts; not to be sacked precisely because of his reliability, and not to be promoted precisely for the same reason.

The fact was that Adam had, as usual, gone one better. I didn't feel envy, only astonishment that he should have got, or should be well on the way to getting, all that he wanted so quickly.

He always had, I thought. We had gone to the same parochial school, we had gone to the same grammar school. It was I who had the highest marks at both schools, it was I who had the better Matric. But it was Adam who had gone to Oxford and I to Charbury University. And it was Adam who was being paid £5,000 a year, nearly half again as much as I was.

I rinsed my cup and saucer and plate and knife and put them into the blue plastic rack on the sink. When I came home that evening they would be dry. When I came home. . . . I didn't want to come home that evening, because it wasn't home. I could look around for something better; but what I really wanted would cost all of £20, nearly one quarter my salary.

The gas fire spluttered out. I rummaged through my

pockets for another shilling and failed to find one. So I had been cheated of my morning browse through the paper. I lit another cheroot and put on my raincoat; it was unfashionably long as, I realized gloomily, all my top coats were.

It was cold that morning, with rain in the wind; the rush hour was already beginning and I took my customary pleasure in walking slowly down the King's Road looking at the shop windows. The pleasure wasn't derived from being on the King's Road, which at that time of day is as sleazy and unwelcoming as any other street in London, nor was it derived from what was in the shop windows; the men's clothes on display seemed to me fit only for homosexual prostitutes and the furniture and bric-à-brac junk of the kind that in Charbury they'd have had to pay people to take away. The pleasure of that morning saunter was that I didn't have to rush, that ten o'clock was soon enough for me to start work. So most days I walked to the office, varying my route each time, building up a taxi-driver's knowledge of that part of London. To walk there gave me the feeling that I was making the city my own, beginning, as it were, to take off some of her outer layers of clothing. I even had then the idea of writing a book about London, but it came to nothing, there had been too many others there before me.

That morning I went into Kensington through Warwick Gardens where G. K. Chesterton had once lived – I was still naïve enough to experience a small but authentic thrill as I passed his house – and walked to the West End through Kensington Gardens and Hyde Park. I stopped for a moment by the Albert Memorial; the rain was still holding off and the sun had come out. I stared up at the huge mass of stone with delight and love and bitter regret: here, whatever Victoria's intentions, was a monument not to her dead husband but her country's power. A young man like myself, looking at it when it was newly built, might have dreamed of carving himself a juicy slice of that power and wealth, of having a hand in the affairs not merely of a country but a continent, he would have had the chance of being something not very far from a god.

I came to with a start and looked at my watch. I had been standing there for a quarter of an hour. I walked off briskly in the direction of Hyde Park Gate, my feet scuffing the fallen leaves. It was time for something new to happen, it was time for a change. Somewhere within the city was to be found everything that I wanted – or at least everything that one man could get in England in this decade of the twentieth century. It was all there for the asking, if I only knew where to ask.

I enumerated my assets. Five feet eleven, all my own hair and teeth, square but not fat, in good physical shape, an Honours degree in English, a hard worker, reliable, conscientious, and with something else – a burning conviction at certain moments that the world was a wonderful place, and the ability to communicate this conviction. And I had the ability to make people like me, was even able without being too obvious about it to switch on the old quiet unaffected boyish charm.

But I hadn't got what Adam had got. I would pass muster anywhere, but I wouldn't stand out in a crowd. I could persuade women to share my bed, but they never phoned me at midnight. And my job, whilst it still had a certain amount of glamour, wasn't in an expanding industry but a contracting one. My own paper seemed solid enough at the moment: but so had the News Chronicle and a hundred others once.

As I walked down Piccadilly it suddenly occurred to me how much I loved the city. I seemed to be alone in that love. All the married men in the office lived well out of it and were only waiting for the day when they'd be able to live still farther out. In the country, they'd say, the *real* country. . . . And the bachelors always seemed to spend their weekends in the country, doing whatever it was that people do there. I slackened my pace at the window of the Burlington Arcade jewellers, but I'd spent too long at the Albert Memorial. There wasn't time this morning to dream of a £360 watch or £50 cuff-links, much less to walk through the Arcade itself.

But I felt better for having been at least in the vicinity of the Burlington Arcade, and for having caught sight at least of the shops where shoes and shirts were made to measure, where all the goods were not only expensive but solid, the goods which weren't really part of the advertiser-consumer set-up because too few could afford them.

That morning I desired those things more sharply than ever before. Meeting Adam had reawakened all the old silly dreams of being really rich, of not merely having a good job, but of conspicuously having more money than anyone else. As boys Adam and I had always cherished the dream of being fabulously rich – but how exactly we'd attain this state was never worked out. As I crossed Shaftesbury Avenue I smiled to myself, remembering the Fukkadara V8, a limousine designed expressly for the purpose of fornication. The Fukkadara not only had an electrically-operated double bed and curtains but a shower and W.C. and a library of dirty books. That had been when we were seventeen and troubled by pimples and boils and sudden changes of voice.

And when we never had any money. The boys we'd been to the parish school with now had motor-bikes and new suits and girls and Continental holidays. We had ten shillings a week pocket money and our school uniforms.

I remembered complaining about this to Adam one summer's night when we'd just seen George Murphy, the dopiest boy in the history of St Chad's, flash past on a brand new Vespa with a blonde on the pillion behind him, show-

56

ing two inches of white flesh above the tops of her black stockings.

'Look at that for a glaring example of social injustice,' I'd said. 'If Pope Leo were alive, he'd write a special encyclical about it, by God he would. What shall we be doing this evening? Irregular French verbs, that's what.'

'You myopic moron,' Adam had said. 'And what will that stinking yob be doing ten years from now? Or five years from now, for that matter? He'll be married, living in a rotten little Council house, surrounded by yawling children and drying nappies, having one night out a week and being played hell with for it. And we'll be bachelors, living it up in London, never getting our hands dirty, using five pound notes for toilet paper. . . . And we won't be bloody bank clerks or school-teachers either.'

He had then glanced with some distaste at a group of adolescents outside Herman's Coffee Bar just outside the gates of the Charbury Memorial Park where we were at that moment going, ostensibly to look at the British Council Exhibition in the Institute, but actually in the vain hope of picking up some girls. Even if we had done, we'd have had to leave them early: the French irregular verbs were waiting.

They had yelled at us as we passed. We were both large for our age, and Adam had grown with extraordinary rapidity that year, so that his blazer was ridiculously skimpy. Mine was all too generously cut.

'Why don't you get yourself a job? Hey, big Nelly! Has the teacher strapped you today, then?'

It was Simon Deery, a classmate of mine at the parish school. I'd been friendly with Simon once, until I'd got to know Adam, who came to Charbury when he was ten.

Adam took no notice; when I stopped, he put his hand on my arm. 'Don't be a Dummkopf,' he said. 'They'll put the boot in as soon as look at you.'

'I can take any of that bloody lot on,' I said.

'Yes, in the school gym with gloves on and three minute rounds. But that lot don't keep the rules, because they don't know them. Let them have their fun. We'll have ours when we grow up.'

Out of earshot he said to me with a passionate and frightening earnestness: 'Christ, how I hate those bloody yobs. They think they're so bloody wonderful with their motor-bikes and their lousy cheap clothes that are out of fashion even before they wear them, and their nasty horny hands with their black fingernails and their lousy rotten teeth and their bloody fancy haircuts that make them look even more common than they already are. The vile sub-human bastards!'

'Steady on,' I said. 'They're not doing us any harm.'

'Yes, they are. They're battening on us. That's where all our taxes go, it's to keep those evil louts in free this and free that and free the bloody other. Do you think they ever worry? Not them. They pay hardly any tax, they get every damned thing free, and then they get council houses. All out of the rates my mother pays. My mother's never got a penny from anyone since my father died, and she's never bloody well asked either . . .'

I'd heard it all before from my own father when every month he went through the ritual of bill paying. But there wasn't the venom behind it that there was behind Adam's diatribe. Adam was, of course, worried. His father had died when he was fourteen, leaving little behind him but an unfashionably large old house filled with unfashionably large furniture and something like six thousand books, give or take a thousand. His mother had brushed up her short-hand and typing and had taken a job at Aisgills' Mills: there was just enough as long as she was working, but lately she'd been falling ill more and more often. Adam's university career – about which there seemed little doubt academically – was in the balance.

Walking through Long Acre amongst the smell of fruit and newsprint I remembered again that white acne-blemished face and that ludicrously tight blazer. And again I felt the same surge of pity; but not for long, since as I approached the office of the newspaper where I worked, I was inevitably going to be involved with a major problem of my own.

The name of the problem was Theresa Carndonagh. She was twenty-five, and for the last three months I'd been having an affair with her.

I still liked her; if only I hadn't, she wouldn't have been any problem. But sex with her now meant less than the first kiss I'd given her in a taxi returning from *The Prime of Miss Jean Brodie*.

Nothing since had quite matched that moment bowling along Kensington High Street, the words of the play still iridescent in the memory, and alongside the words the feeling that the play was specially for me, since, being a Catholic, I could understand it, could perceive that more than one kind of passion could inhibit the same heart, could understand too how in the end one might drive the other out, not rejecting it but simply absorbing it; as I kissed Theresa, rather clumsily, I was in my imagination a character in the play and so, I'm certain, was Theresa.

When we arrived at her flat in one of the streets off Napier Road, she'd invited me in for a cup of coffee. I'd followed her expecting to continue the love-making, already wondering pleasantly what she'd look like without her clothes and congratulating myself on my choice of play, feeling the tension mount between us. But when we went inside – pausing for a moment to kiss at the door – both her flat–mates were there sitting by the Magicoal in their dressing gowns drinking hot chocolate.

For one moment I felt sickeningly frustrated, almost betrayed; and then, sitting in the warm little room amongst a litter of pop art carrier bags, pieces of knitting, and books and gramophone records, breathing in the wonderful smell of healthy young women, I'd begun to be quietly happy. It hadn't been unlike the sort of domestic scene my sisters could create – cosy, secure, yet with a sense of life-and-death, womb-and-tomb mysteries in the background. And these girls weren't my sisters and somehow or other each one of them contrived to give me a glimpse of what was under their dressing-gowns (pink nylon, a deep cleft, blue cotton, wide apart but high) and in so doing acknowledged, not too portentously, that I was male and they were glad of it. I'd left the flat mysteriously full of energy and hope, satisfied in a way that had in one sense nothing to do with sex and in another everything to do with it.

Not long after that, in a rather matter-of-fact way, Theresa and I had become lovers. I had discovered that her hair was naturally black, I had discovered both that her breasts weren't as large as they appeared to be and that I didn't care what size they were. And I had discovered that she wasn't, despite five years in Fleet Street, in the least sophisticated, that though she was good at her job and likely to go far in it, what she really wanted was a man of her own whom she could mould into an image of her ideal.

And she was a Catholic – for which reason I'd kept her existence a secret from my mother. Once I'd let it slip out that I as much as knew a Catholic girl, my mother would have bombarded me with letters and phone calls, begging me to marry her and remove myself from the state of mortal sin in which she was absolutely certain I was living.

And Theresa was becoming more and more inquisitive about my mother who she already knew was Irish and devout, exactly like her own mother. And what would clinch the matter would be the fact that Theresa's father and the headmaster of St Theo's were first cousins, which to my mother would be the equivalent of having royal blood.

But as I walked past the Law Courts I firmly put her out of my mind. There was in any case a newcomer to the paper, Harry O'Toole, already hanging round Theresa. Harry was, from the sound of it, a much better Catholic than I was, and a member of the Keys and the Newman Society and the Knights of St Columba; when she at last understood that I didn't want to marry her or anyone else, his would be eminently suitable arms for her to fall into.

I looked at the Law Courts but not with any great affection. I liked that immense irregular Gothic exuberance, but there was a part of me which always rebelled against the grey, dusty, labyrinthine power behind it. It was Fleet Street that I loved, it was Fleet Street that, as I approached it, put an extra spring in my step, briskened my whole being with the promise of being at the centre of the real world of power, of having a reserved seat daily in the stalls and even a part in the play. I was never anything else other than starry-eyed about Fleet Street, it never diminished for me as other streets in London sooner or later seemed to diminish.

But that morning I found myself wondering, as I went by the Daily Telegraph and Daily Express offices, whether I shouldn't be thinking of changing newspapers. For the particular story I had a notion I was going to be engaged upon was bound to be tricky in a way I didn't like.

A scandal about a member of the Cabinet was coming to the boil. My paper had been trying to catch out this politician for a long time; which means that the proprietor wanted to destroy him for personal reasons. The politician had for the last twelve months been having an affair with a female novelist; he had taken great pains to be discreet, but the husband had at last found out, and had left home. And now it appeared that we had the politician on toast. He had only to be cited as co-respondent and his career was ruined. For he was something of a professional moralist, being especially severe upon those who made mock of the sanctity of marriage. The public can put up with, even appreciate, rakes; it can't bear a hypocrite.

What bothered me as I walked up the steps of the office under the massive entrance of a style best described as Triumphal Roman (it was very much at variance with the rest of the building which was Debased Gothic with the addition of three massive stonework balconies and a square clock tower, vaguely Norman) was that the proprietor was going to play it rough. We couldn't, if I knew him, be content to wait for something to happen. He would want to help matters along.

And as I got into the lift I was still running through the names of possible newspapers. The Beaverbrook Press? Not yet. One had to wait for them to ask for one's services. The Daily Mail? Still a bit too progressive. The Telegraph? The Mirror? They were like the Beaverbrook Press, but more so; they wanted only star performers, and I wasn't a star yet. That left only the Sketch and the Sun and the provincials and the Sundays. I didn't have any feelings for or against the Sketch, but I didn't fancy a Labour paper, I didn't want to run the risk of finding myself in the provinces again, and the tempo on the Sundays was too leisurely for me.

Going through the list of papers – already smaller than when I'd just entered journalism – reminded me of the fact that I was lucky to have a job in Fleet Street at all. Whatever compunction I might have at helping the proprietor – whom I had never met – to destroy a politician who was no better nor worse than any other politician, would have to be put aside until I was in a stronger position.

My desk was, as I'd expected, clear of everything except a typewriter. I sat down, took off my jacket, and lit a cheroot. People drifted in and out of the office; in the corner opposite Harry Rogers, a chubby young man who'd just come to us from the Telegraph, typed frantically away at what I knew was a think piece about Ghana. Janet Mor-grove, the film reviewer's secretary, was yawning as she thumbed through a pile of publicity handouts. There were only three of us in the big bare room with its twelve olive green steel desks; and only Harry was purposefully and urgently working. That was for me the charm of newspaper work; it wasn't always done in an atmosphere of frenzied activity with the editor yelling for the front page to be held back. There was an ebb and flow to it, there were moments when the office could be as quiet as a church.

I opened the desk drawer and took out an American sex manual that I'd borrowed from the Literary Editor's bookshelves. I was half-way through a description of a mechanical phallus – transparent with a camera in the tip – when my phone rang.

'Where've you been, you idle young devil?' It was the voice of Donald Barbury, the Assistant Editor.

'Here, reading a mucky book.'

'Bloody well stop it, then, I've got a job for you.'

'I'm coming over.'

Barbury's office – a cubicle with glass walls rather than a room – had a walnut desk and charcoal grey carpeting and in one corner a large walnut cabinet which I knew was full of bottles of liquor. Barbury was next in rank to the Deputy Editor and had, so it was said, been imported into our paper from another one in the group because he and the Editor hated each other's guts, the idea being that this hatred would keep them on their toes.

Barbury was dicating a letter as I entered his office.

'I trust that you will acknowledge that this new arrange-ment is to our mutual advantage,' he was concluding, 'And leave the superscription for me to write in, will you? He likes the personal touch . . . O.K. love, get it off straight away, will you?'

He looked at the girl longingly as she swayed out of the

63

door, at every step the short dress giving the illusion of shortening itself still further.

'Everything comes too late,' he said. 'I look at a bit of crackling like that now and I ask myself, is it worth the trouble and expense? Twenty years ago, I should just have gone ahead.'

'Don't you now?' I asked. I rather liked Barbury; after a lifetime in London he'd not lost his Yorkshire accent, though now I suspected that he exaggerated it for effect. And, though I had more sense than to trade upon it, I suspected that he rather liked me, seeing in me the young man he once had been when he first came to London from Warley, a small town not very far from Charbury, some thirty years ago.

'Don't be so cheeky,' he said. 'Anyway, I didn't ask you here to talk about sex. At least, not in connection with me. I'm going ahead with the Glenthorn story. They tell me he's on the bottle again.' He lit his pipe. Lean and nervous, with grey short hair and almost invariably wearing a rumpled navy blue lightweight suit, white shirt and a plain blue or maroon tie, he looked like an American general in mufti.

'On the bottle again? I didn't know that he drank at all.'

'Only wine normally. He's one of these bloody connoisseurs. But every now and again he tanks up on the hard stuff. I kept trying to get him yesterday, and his secretary kept saying he was indisposed. Well, I know this particular secretary, and so finally I asked him off the record just how indisposed the Minister was. As indisposed as a newt, the secretary said.'

'Anything there?' I wondered why Barbury hadn't asked the Political Correspondent to get in touch with Glenthorn, then recollected that the Political Correspondent was a friend of the Editor's.

'No, because the public wouldn't believe it. It's not in character, you see. And he's a tight-mouthed bastard, he

64

just locks himself up with a bottle of Scotch and doesn't speak to anyone. And the P.M. needs him, so he'll turn a blind eye. What with all these wild boys round him, he can't do without old Glenthorn. Glenthorn's still a patriot, and that makes him popular. But he's such a crashing bore that he'll never be any threat to our beloved leader. No, I don't think we can approach from that particular angle. All that interests me is that obviously he's worried. Judy Aviemore's husband must be kicking up quite a fuss.'

'Can't we do anything about that?'

'I wish we could. But I just don't know what the bastard's up to. He's turned a blind eye for years, having fish of his own to fry. Now he's succumbing to an attack of outraged honour. Rather inconsistent of him, seeing he changes girls as often as his shirts if not oftener.'

I grinned. 'Which of us is consistent?'

'Never mind that. Just go to see Judy Aviemore.'

I had come far enough now to see what it was he expected me to do. It wasn't my cup of tea; and my instincts told me that it wasn't the Editor's, or the Political Correspondent's.

'Are you sure we shouldn't just wait until the balloon goes up?'

'Do what everyone else will do? What the hell are you talking about?'

There was no jovial camaraderie, no aren't-we-all-jolly-journalists-together about his tone now. He was prepared to sack me on the spot, and to find a colourable excuse later.

'I only thought that perhaps she might see through it. She doesn't seem to give many interviews.'

'Because no-one asks her.'

'She does go on rather about how horrible the Press is. . . .'

'Because no-one asks her,' he repeated impatiently.

'Don't worry, she'll not refuse to see a paper with our circulation.'

'Is anyone else interested?'

'That's the nub of the matter, isn't it? I expect they all know and they're all being gentlemanly. But I don't want you to mention Glenthorn. Or her husband. Play it big. How clever she is, how outspoken on the telly, how shocking but how true her novels are . . .'

'Isn't she going to have a regular spot on *The Taste of Time* soon?'

'Yes, ask her about that. You've been to University, ask her if she thinks it'll be good for her prose. You know damned well what we want, Frank. Push Aviemore. We want everyone to know who she is when the balloon goes up. And even if the balloon doesn't go up, which God in his infinite mercy forbid, they'll ask themselves why the great interest? See?'

'I don't think there's any point in this at all unless you link her with Glenthorn,' I said.

'I'm coming to that. Linking their names is in fact what you must do. But you're strictly on your own. Don't you ever describe them as friends. And don't even say she has friends in high places. That's actionable too. But I'll see to that. Just a mention now and again that at her famous parties can be seen such prominent personalities as X, Y, Z and David Glenthorn. Or they could be seen somewhere else; they often are for that matter.' He scowled. 'Poor old Glenthorn. Going to all these bloody awful literary parties just to stare at Judy Aviemore across the room, holding it down with both hands . . . She's absolutely horrible, too. Triple Honours First Class Alpha plus at Oxford or some such qualifications. God knows what he sees in her. The bloody women have us by the balls as it is, even when they're supposed to be stupid. I remember when I was younger —' The phone rang. 'Tell him to ring back later,' he said, and put it down. 'When I was younger, I lived with a writer. Dead long since, poor bitch. Used to keep a note-book under her pillow . . .'

'Did you too?'

'No, you impudent young sod. I'm not a *writer*, I'm a journalist. She wrote novels. Ran off with a black man in the end. Well, this isn't getting my work done. Try and get something for me today if you can. About two sticks.'

'O.K.' I stood up.

He put his finger to his mouth. 'You needn't say any-thing to anyone about our long-term project. It's all extremely nebulous in any case . . . Understand?'

I nodded, and went to the next floor to see Theresa. She was frowning over a dummy with the Women's Page editor, Georgina Axmouth. Georgina was in her mid-thirties, with a big mouth and those harlequin spectacles which are supposed by the opticians to be madly gay, but which always to me give their wearers an appearance of determined malevolence. As they stared at the larger-than-life plan of the page with writing and pictures alike represented by scribbles, the faces of each were rapt with pleasure.

'It's *wrong* still,' Theresa was saying. 'It just doesn't look right. Can't we blow up the head a bit?'

She was quite happy, a child with a toy. Although I had no great interest in make-up myself, I knew that Theresa had a flair for it. When Georgina was off ill for a week in the summer she'd taken over, and in consequence the whole page had looked crisper, better-balanced, more harmonious typographically, though the matter itself was the same old flapdoodle about exciting breakthroughs in corsets, night-wear, colour, home cooking and all the rest of it. Theresa's suggestions wouldn't, I knew very well, be accepted now: though it was always possible that Georgina might advance them as her own at the editorial conference later in the day.

Theresa knew this, but I don't think she cared. Sooner or

later either she'd get Georgina's job or she'd move to another paper. She was, to use a favourite Women's Page expression, vibrant and aglow with self-confidence. She was wearing a shift dress apparently designed to express that happy state, bright red with a zig-zag pattern in white, with bright red stockings. It was exactly the right shade to bring out the darkness of her hair and its shape disguised her thinness and accentuated her best point, her legs. If only she'd been taller she'd have made a good model; but the rather flat face and the grey eyes didn't photograph. I would always forget when I was away from her what she looked like; she varied each time I saw her, the dress sense which one would imagine to be unerring in a person occupying her job being notably erratic.

She smiled at me in an abstracted sort of way when I came in. When Georgina had gone, taking with her a sheaf of photographs, she gave me a more thorough smile, one which made me remember briefly but in full detail our last meeting at my flat, and laid her hand lightly on my sleeve.

'Lunch?' I asked her.

'Honey, I have a business lunch with Miss Vaga at the Mirabelle.'

'I was thinking of sandwiches at the King Lud.'

'I'd much rather, but you know how it is. Vaga wants to tell me all about her fifth husband and how this is the real, deep-down, ultimate togetherness she's been searching for all her life —'

'The old whore,' I said.

'No, darling, you won't understand. She's been lost for so long, just like a poor little stray kitten out in the street on a winter's night. And now a door's opening for her, and there's light and warmth pouring out into the street ... That's what she told me last time anyway.'

'That's beautiful, it really is.' I was beginning to wonder

why I was against marrying her, wondering even why any-one as bright and attractive should want to marry me. Then I thought of Georgina and her harlequin spectacles and her habit of picking up sheaves of photographs and paper in order to appear even busier and even more efficient. Theresa wasn't the only girl in the world; but she was already beginning to show signs of aspiring to be the most efficient and self-confident girl in the world. 'I'll phone you this afternoon. Perhaps we can have dinner.'

She nodded. 'Fabulous, darling.'

Grand was the word when I first saw her. I hadn't liked that very much, but I liked the new word still less. I left her searching for a photograph of Vaga, wondering why she irritated me so much and yet why at the same time I liked her so much.

Back at my desk I phoned Judy Aviemore. The office was full now, each typewriter chattering away, the office boys marching in and out with cups of tea and memoranda and galley proofs; the atmosphere was beginning to thicken with tobacco smoke and there was an almost tangible ten-sion present. Later the tension would grow, seize everyone in the building; at the climax it would almost be sexual and yet it was always disciplined, being part of it set one off from the rest of the world which more and more lived by serving machines or following set procedures.

As Judy Aviemore's voice – cool, rather affected, with a Chelsea accent, basically a strangulated Cockney with the rough vowels toned down, basically, in fact, like Adam's – answered me, I wondered why I should be thinking so deeply about my job. If I'd thought about it before, it had been in strictly practical terms of salary and hours and holidays. Wasn't I, in fact, justifying my way of earning a living? Wasn't I, in fact, beginning to be envious of Adam?

Judy Aviemore could spare me an hour at four o'clock. I thanked her profusely, put the phone down, and went to work on the Harry Morgate piece, from long practice closing my ears to all the noise around me.

I finished at one o'clock, dropped the piece in at Barbury's office, and lunched at the King Lud off a ham sandwich and a pint of bitter. There was no other writing for me to do that day, unless war broke out, which just for once didn't appear likely; I sat in a corner with my ham sandwich and my beer, feeling quietly euphoric.

Whatever my feelings about the ethics of the job Barbury had given me, it was a step forward. And in addition I knew that the Harry Morgate article was pretty good – smooth without being insipid, astringent without being acid. And, somehow or other, I had managed to bring out a little of the real Harry who, I discovered as I wrote, was actually a rather lonely person. (Yes, all well-paid entertainers say this, but it doesn't make it any the less true.)

Here in the King Lud, as in any other pub in the neighbourhood of Fleet Street, I was completely at home. I was among fellow professionals, some of whom were national names; and there wasn't any reason why I shouldn't be among them one day. Looking around the bar, which at that hour was crowded, I could see no-one I knew: but eventually I should. This was one of my locals in the way that the Salisbury would be one of an actor's locals.

As I was ordering my second pint, Joyce Impington came in. As always, the glass-panelled door seemed to open itself for him. Impington, tall and thin with a nutcracker profile rather like Valentin's in the Toulouse-Lautrec poster, had come to the paper via the Foreign Office and the B.B.C. It was largely due to him that our paper was more often right than wrong on foreign affairs; according to one's politics he was alternatively described as a James Cameron with a head or a Peregrine Worsthorne with a heart. At thirty-five he was unmarried, but was known to like girls and, indeed, as they say in the Services, to poke

70

everything that moved, particularly if it were giggling, plump, and silly.

I waved to him, and he came over, giving me his rather cold and nervous smile.

'What will you have, Joyce?'

'Vodka and tonic, please.'

It was a drink very much in keeping with his personal appearance; he always wore white shirts with stiff collars, well-worn but well-kept dark suits of an old-fashioned cut, and dark silk ties of an unusual width, not kipper width but obviously manufactured at least ten years ago, before ties began to narrow. His light fawn reversible Burberry coat was, I think, the only one he possessed; but unlike other people's light fawn coats, it never seemed either to be soiled or to have just returned from dry-cleaning. And his straw-coloured hair, though rather long, was always of the same length, and never unduly long at the nape or over the ears. And he gave the impression of meticulous cleanliness without benefit of cologne or after-shave or talcum powder; I found myself admiring him because he was all that I could never be. Even his Catholicism was of a different brand from mine; he was of an old English Catholic family, and I was of Irish extraction on my mother's side.

'I didn't know you came here,' I said. He generally seemed to lunch at places like the White House or Rules or the Etoile, even, I think, when he was paying for the lunch himself.

'A whim,' he said. 'I was rather busy this morning. There's a certain amount of unpleasantness taking place in what used to be one of our far-flung corners of Empire. It will have the usual consequences: our friends will be sold down the river and our enemies will be put into power and eventually awarded huge sums in overseas aid. Which will instantly be spent on limousines and whores and huge meretricious monuments to themselves.' He ordered a beef sandwich, using exactly the same beautifully modulated emotionless tone. 'Let's sit down,' he said. 'Else I shall feel like a horse. It's bad enough actually to be a paid hack without physically behaving like one.'

'You sound annoyed.' In fact, it was impossible to tell whether he was annoyed or not, except by projecting his words before the mind's eye like print.

'I *am* annoyed. Incensed, enraged, full of choler. The bloody editor's been trying to tell me that a gang of bloody-handed terrorists are selfless and devoted patriots, and that this wretched Government's shabby and squalid betrayal of our friends is an act of far-sighted statesmanship.' He looked at me doubtfully, as if unsure of my allegiance. 'You do know what Tarband is, don't you? Some of his ideas are sound enough, but at bottom he's a Socialist.'

'The proprietor chose him.'

'Yes, because he fancies himself as another Beaverbrook. And Beaverbrook used to go out of his way to recruit socialists. They had fire in their bellies, they were rebels. And, when they'd been working for him for a few years, they changed. They didn't sell out; they grew up, because the old monster could make men grow up. But our proprietor can't. He's not a monster, just a gentlemanly old Tory.'

'Not so gentlemanly that he didn't bring in Barbury.'

'Barbury may well move on. He's a restless sort of character, and if our circulation ever drops, he won't want to be involved.' He was speaking in a less stilted fashion now, and there was feeling in his voice. 'You and he seem rather chummy,' he said.

'I'm reliable. I deliver my copy on time. And I rather like him. I wouldn't know whether he likes me.'

'Liking has nothing to do with it.' His voice had an edge to it. 'We get on with those who have the same opinions as us and we don't get on with those who don't.' Another vodka – a large one, I noticed – and another pint of bitter appeared. 'Those who have the same opinions must stick together. That's what politics is about.'

A plump young girl in a miniskirt and a short fur jacket came in; Impington glanced at her and waved his hand briefly, and for a second his face grew slack and foolish.

'It's a cause of confession,' I said, following the direction of his glance.

'If one has the name, one may as well have the game,' he said. I knew then why he'd come into the King Lud, and was for a moment saddened. He looked at the girl again; she smiled. 'You'll have to excuse me.'

He fished in his wallet. 'Look, here's my card. Give me a ring sometime, and we'll have a more leisurely talk. Incidentally, aren't you going to interview Judy Aviemore this afternoon?'

'How did you know?'

He waved the question away impatiently. His hands were long and thin, with tapering fingers, but the nails – the only flaw in his entire ensemble – were short and bitten to the quick. 'Take it easy, that's all. The bastards we're up against – and it's surprising how many of them are just that – are very cunning indeed. On the other hand, don't worry. It's the Lord's work that you're doing. Whatever embarrasses those evil idiots in the Government is pleasing in the sight of the Lord. Goodbye, and may Heaven bless you.'

He swallowed his drink and went over to the plump girl; she kissed him effusively and they left together after only a few minutes.

To stay at the pub after that seemed an anti-climax; I strolled back to the office and to my delight found the proof of the Morgate article on my desk. This delight never varied; I could never take for granted the smudgy strip of paper with my name and my words on it, words which, in only a few hours, would be seen by eighteen million people.

Sometimes my piece would be printed exactly as written. But this was very rare, not because I wrote over the required length, but because the needs of the paper varied from day to day and hour to hour. Today I had to cut out five inches; I had forty-five minutes to do the job in, and for five of those minutes it seemed impossible. Then I set to work, transposing, eliminating adjectives which had seemed only that morning uniquely and stimulatingly original, taking care all the time to cut at the places where it would have the maximum effect. To cut a line with one word on it is always preferable to cutting a full line; in journalism one cuts space rather than words.

When I look back I can see why that afternoon I enjoyed this task more even than I usually did. The piece was absolutely straightforward, a not unsympathetic portrait of a man in whom most of our readers were interested. It would be forgotten the day after it was printed. It wasn't going to alter anything.

Impington's words came back to me as I called over an office boy who was sitting on an empty desk reading a Superman comic. The boy had freckles like Jimmy Olsen (the Friend of Superman) who, because of his own foolishness, was being eaten by a giant mauve lobster. *It's the Lord's work that you're doing;* Impington hadn't been joking, he was entirely a political animal and had an absolute loathing for the Government. I didn't like the Labour Party, but my political beliefs, like my religious beliefs, were no more than conditioned reflexes. They carried me through life quite comfortably as they did my father. And that was all I wanted.

Now, I reflected as I put on my coat, I was in danger of going out of my depth. Why did the proprietor want to destroy Glenthorn? He wasn't really an important minister; his department had in fact been specially created for him since Wilson had gone and it was difficult even for the most

74

ardent Labour Party supporter to explain what its function was. There was no doubt as to Glenthorn's function personally; he was the Prime Minister's faithful friend, absolutely the only one in the Parliamentary Labour Party whom he could trust. He was, come to that, his only friend; it was said that the Prime Minister was the only man who had ever united the Labour Party because he was the only one whom everybody, Left, Right or Centre, hated without any sort of qualification. The public didn't care; indeed, it tended to accept the Prime Minister's own picture of himself as Honest John the People's Friend. Friendship, in fact, was one of his favourite themes.

He would have to throw Glenthorn to the wolves if Glenthorn was cited as co-respondent. If he didn't, he'd be accused of favouritism, if not corruption. But if he did, then bang would go the painfully built up image of the warmhearted universal chum, the non-political politician, the leader who put human relationships first. Either way, he'd be upset, a blow would have been landed fairly and squarely in his testicles.

I wasn't against that. I turned my collar up against the rain, enjoying the feel of it on my face. But soon it wouldn't be enjoyable; London rain had a way of turning sticky on the skin after a while, actually seeming to change its composition. I had been intending to take the tube to Judy Aviemore's house in Holland Park and charge a taxi to expenses. But there was no point in saving a few shillings and dripping all over her carpet.

I hailed a taxi and leaned back inside it; almost as soon as I'd entered it the rain intensified. For a moment I let go, my eyes half-closed, happy for twenty minutes or so not to have to take any decisions, maliciously pleased that outside Fleet Street was full of people who either couldn't afford a taxi or couldn't find one.

This was the way to live, as one of the privileged, going

by taxi to have tea with an attractive and intelligent woman, to meet a new person, to see someone else's home, to add to one's stock of experience, to add to one's collection of names. And perhaps to change the course of events, to have a small portion of power all for oneself, piping hot and tasty. And yet I didn't feel as I should, I couldn't deny that what I felt like was not a professional man doing his professional job, but a huckster with a line of goods he was beginning to despise.

three

It was Judy Aviemore's eyes which surprised me. The short beautifully cut skirt which she never tugged at, the long legs in the pink stockings, the deeply décolleté pink sweater, the gold bracelet watch and even her smell, almost stridently clean with undertones of some expensive scent with a civet and not ambergris base – all this one might have expected from a Cabinet Minister's mistress and not only a Cabinet Minister's mistress but the mistress at one time or another of at least a dozen prominent men. She had always said that she didn't believe in one morality for men and another for women; but not at the top of her voice, not messily and publicly. Her face was smooth, incapable of an ugly expression, with wonderful high cheek bones; it gave nothing away, it was a self-contained work of art.

The eyes, however, were vulnerable. Deep blue, widely spaced, they were clear, childlike, innocent. I began to understand why Glenthorn should be playing ducks and drakes with his career; if I had been older, or if I had been a little less sensible, I could have fallen in love with her myself, not because of her body, not because of her face, but simply because of her eyes.

The room she showed me into was untidy but expensively

and comfortably and – the word kept cropping up – *cleanly* untidy. There was a thick, mustard yellow carpet, bookcases lining three walls, a walnut desk with a cream Olivetti typewriter on it, three glass-topped tables littered with books and proofs and magazines, a pile of books on the floor, and a large coffee table with an assortment of bottles and glasses on it. One side was virtually all taken up with a French window which looked out upon a long and narrow garden. The garden was mostly lawn, with a narrow flower border. It could never be a blaze of colour, even in high summer, but there was enough living green there for it to have even at this season some sort of therapeutic effect.

It was warm enough in the room, and the books, mostly new, saved it from any danger of drabness or impersonality. But it was curiously austere: there was no attempt to spread out the two red Ercol armchairs and the grey and red studio couch so as to fill its thirty foot length, and the only trace of femininity to be seen was a huge stone vase full of chrysanthemums. There was no bric-à-brac, no attempt to commemorate the past.

She must have read my thoughts. 'I work here,' she said. 'That's the explanation.'

'I hadn't said anything, Mrs Aviemore.'

'There's scarcely any need. You have a rather expressive face.'

She was the sort of woman who can't rest until she has established some sort of personal relationship. I began to wonder whether it wouldn't be rewarding to build up that relationship. At twenty-seven one becomes adept at reading all the signs of sexual interest in women, and one of the first is any remark, no matter how outwardly innocent, about a man's physical appearance. What she was saying was *I know you have a body and I don't find that body unpleasing.*

Then I put the idea firmly but regretfully aside; it would

entail complications with which I would rather not cope. I contented myself with smiling and making a deprecating noise.

'Would you like some tea?' she asked. 'Or something stronger?' Her voice, I now began to notice, was a rather breathy contralto, slightly affected in tone but not in accent. I accepted a stiff drink of what was unquestionably a single-malt whisky, and as I sipped it I had to remind myself of my purpose in being there. I was relishing her company too much. I was, after only five minutes, restraining the impulse to pay her compliments, to make love to her with words.

'I thought I'd ask you a few questions about the new programme,' I said.

'I don't know how your paper came to hear about it.' She poured herself a drink of whisky as stiff as mine, and fitted a cigarette into a long holder.

'Now and again we do hear of something before anyone else. Though *scoops* aren't as important as you might believe.' I pronounced the word derisively: it always made me feel every inch the grubby hack.

'It may all come to nothing,' she said. 'I've been let in on the ground floor of too many world-shattering projects not to know that. But it does honestly seem a good idea. For one thing, it's live —' She paused. 'Aren't you going to take notes?'

'I don't need to.' It was perhaps my only extraordinary gift as a reporter; it kept my nose to the ground, which was a good thing, and prevented me raising my nose very high above the ground, which was a bad thing. I knew shorthand – which was more than could be said of many of my colleagues – but I never used it unless what I had to report was extremely lengthy and extremely boring.

'You really have absolute verbal recall?'

I nodded.

'I'll have to test you sometime.'

'I'm always at your disposal,' I said.

'I envy you,' she said. 'That's one of the difficulties in TV. Carrying it all in one's head ... You're not an only child, are you?'

'I have three sisters. I'm the eldest. How did you know?'

'It's obvious. You sit without fiddling. You're perfectly calm and still. Only children are twitchy.'

'You're an only child and you don't twitch. I've noticed when you're on television.'

'I'm so nervous that I daren't give way at all. Normally I'm terribly restless.'

We were on the right subject at last; so far one would have imagined that she was interviewing me.

'Don't you think that television is a waste of your time?'

'The money's useful. Besides, it puts me into contact with people whom otherwise I'd never meet. And this new programme is all about failures. Real, resounding failures. The awful thing is that one never never meets any of these in the normal course of events ... I don't know whether I'm looking forward to it or whether I dread it.'

'But don't you feel that television takes you away from your real work?' I didn't actually like her novels very much; they seemed to me to move much too slowly, to be too wincingly sensitive, too cryptically, portentously feminine. She was much better than what she wrote.

'I wish I knew. Of course it isn't really hard work at all. One's cossetted outrageously. Drinks, quite good food, a car and chauffeur to transport one ... And afterwards the solicitude's quite overwhelming. As if one had had a baby. And one's assured that one's marvellous, fabulous, a real professional, this was real TV —' She laughed, showing very good teeth which were all her own. 'Writing a thousand good words takes it out of me more than a hundred TV programmes. When all's said and done it's no more tiring than journalism, and a great deal more remunerative. One isn't wasting any material.'

'What exactly do you mean by that?' This was standard technique: one hadn't to ask questions which could be answered by a simple yes or no, but questions which drew the interviewee out.

'In journalism, even in reviewing, one's always in danger of drawing too much upon personal experience, even the sort of experience which can't be used again. And in print it's not enough to be facile. One's got to be original, and so one can waste really good metaphors for twenty guineas a thousand words. But on TV facility's everything, one's got to have on tap thousands of ready-made phrases. And a quite feeble joke goes down well, and an apposite quotation, no matter how hackneyed, strikes them dumb with admiration. And if by any chance one says something original there's no harm in using it later in print. The viewers won't remember longer than a day.'

'What does your husband think of the prospect of your becoming a television personality?'

I was watching her eyes. Her face displayed no emotion, but at the mention of her husband there was no doubt of her pain. She didn't seem as if she were going to answer at all: I elaborated my question.

'I mean, once a person's a familiar television face then the people around them personally tend to become rather shadowy. Perhaps a wife might be content to enjoy the reflected glory, but a husband very often isn't. Mr Aviemore's in the City, isn't he?'

'In a small way.' My information was that it was not only in a small way but a shaky way; I wondered whose money it was that had bought the house and was maintaining it in its present style.

'Martin never thinks about it. He's very sure of himself. Like my son. My son simply takes it for granted, though he now and again asks me for a hundred autographs. I think he swops them. A hundred of me for one Beatle would be about the going rate.'

'You undervalue yourself. But I wish I knew what your husband really thinks – that is, if he wanted to talk about it . . .'

'He's away on business rather a lot just now. Always going to rather glamorous places on unlimited expenses. I tell him I wish *I'd* been a businessman . . .' Her laugh was this time high-pitched and affected. I had gone as far as I was supposed to go or, indeed, wanted to go.

'Would you say yourself that authors are difficult to live with?'

She perceptibly relaxed.

'My dear, they're absolute hell. I've known a great many and I've known their wives and girl-friends and they speak with one voice. Authors aren't *there* most of the time. We're not human. We ought to be especially human, but we're emphatically not. And we're all terribly terribly self-conscious. We watch ourselves having emotions – how should we do otherwise? And as we watch ourselves, the emotion's gone.'

There was a genuine desolation in her voice. She poured me another whisky and one for herself.

'Do you like meeting people? Apart from TV?'

'I meet as many as I can. There's always the temptation, though, not to meet anyone, just to pull up the drawbridge and be cosy and safe . . .'

It was my day for being shocked; as she spoke I had a feeling that she was rejecting the whole of human life, that if there was a drawbridge there must be a castle, and in that castle there were dungeons and a torture-chamber. I wrenched my mind back to the job in hand.

'What sort of people are your friends?'

'Other writers. Painters. Stage people. The odd politician.

The odd parson or priest or journalist. But, you know, I always end up feeling envious of other people's jobs. I often wish I'd been a painter. I do paint sometimes, but it's always the same subject. Small figures running for shelter under a darkening sky.'

'You say you meet the occasional politician. Does that mean that you're actively interested in politics?' I tried not to think about the small figures running for shelter; she had put her finger on one of my private images of myself – indeed, of the whole human race.

'Only a few. I don't really *do* anything politically. I suppose that I ought to.'

'You were in CND for a while. Don't you care about that any longer?'

'I care about peace, but not about that particular way of achieving it.'

The story was that she'd severed her connection with CND because Glenthorn was against it. But how was I going to bring him into it? Unless, credibly and non-libellously, his name could be mentioned at least once, Barbury would spike the piece and put someone else on the job. And the atmosphere between Judy Aviemore and myself was changing. Soon it would be time for me to leave; she was beginning to be tired.

'You've not changed your beliefs at all, then?'

'They're the same as when I came down from Oxford.' She smiled. 'I'm not going to tell you the year I came down, either. You can jolly well look it up. I'm a socialist. I know that the present Government isn't perfect, but it's the only socialist government we've got —' She broke off. 'You're not on my side, are you? At least, your paper's not on my side.'

'We have a lot of socialist readers too,' I said. 'Besides, our proprietor's like Beaverbrook. He doesn't ask that we should be good Conservatives, just good journalists.'

'Yes, I've heard that one before.' There came into her voice a note of fervour which I found embarrassing. 'I've known people who want to work for your proprietor, young and full of ideals, as doubtless you are. They're not going to change, they're just doing a job. And then they become used to the expense account atmosphere, their salary goes up, their perks become more and more lush ... They're not asked to change their views, of course. They're not asked to conform. They needn't – they're not on the political side. And then almost without their knowing it, they have changed, they're like the rest – absolutely materialistic, absolutely corrupt, churning out their tailor-made pieces making little of everything decent people put their hopes on . . .'

She went on in this vein for some time, managing not only to express her detestation of my paper's proprietor – whom I had never met or even seen – but her deep, deep belief in UNO, the Welfare State, comprehensive schools and all the other issues upon which one is always being exhorted to stand up and be counted. When she began to run out of steam, perhaps aware that her voice when raised didn't sound very pleasant and aware too of my mounting boredom, I said in a carefully expressionless voice: 'You've given me something to think about, Mrs Aviemore. And I'm not saying that you mightn't be right.'

'You don't really care, do you?' she asked.

'It isn't that, honestly. But our readers would be more interested to know what your opinion is of the Government. The P.M., for instance?'

'No-one even knew he existed when Wilson was there,' she said. 'Least of all Wilson. But he was working away like a mole. And now he does just what he wants.'

'I wouldn't want to disillusion you any further,' I said, 'but when he went into politics, he tried the Tories first.

84

He's only Labour because Central Office wouldn't look at him.'

'You don't surprise me,' she said.

'What about the Foreign Secretary?'

'You're trying to make me say something unkind, aren't you? Well, I won't. He's doing his best. He's only the P.M.'s errand-boy, anyway . . .'

She was beginning to be bored; the intimacy which, however meretricious or transient, must be present for a good interview, was rapidly evaporating. I dropped a few more names quickly, then threw in Glenthorn's name.

'He's always struck me as being an honest man,' I said. 'Too honest for his own good. Don't you feel he's rather wasted where he is?'

'I'd better not say too much about him. He's a friend of mine. I met him at Oxford when he came to give a talk at my college . . .' She was clever enough not to pretend that he was merely an acquaintance and an occasional guest at her parties; but not clever enough, I reflected, to disguise the warmth which came into her eyes when she talked about him. 'He moves slowly, you know. But he's no right-winger. Oh, you're right, he's much too honest, much too loyal. He's a country boy really. I know his part of Northumberland very well, I was born and bred there . . .'

And then so smoothly that I couldn't discern just how it had happened, she was telling me about her childhood in a little village near Alnwick, the daughter of a doctor, and her voice was recreating her past, she was a child again. It was good stuff, I hadn't heard it before, I would have to use it, but it wasn't what I wanted.

'Enough about me,' she said, and stood up. 'I'm afraid I have a dinner appointment, if you'll excuse me.'

I stood up myself.

'I'm very grateful to you for giving me so much of your time.'

'Not at all. I'll only worry when the Press isn't interested in me.'

I went out into Holland Park with my head buzzing a little with the whisky. Her house stood at the top of a little street behind the park itself. The rain had stopped now and the sky had been washed a slate blue. I walked slowly though the park turning over the interview in my head, my nostrils full of the smell of wet leaves – fresh but slightly smoky, as if a fire had been put out. I was in London; this was a thought that would still come over me to illumine the most commonplace scene. But this wasn't commonplace; of all the London parks it was the most private in atmosphere, the one furthest away from the twentieth century.

I stopped at the Lyons on the Earl's Court Road and drank two cups of tea and ate a buttered fruit bun whilst reading the paper. The strong tea – the only drinkable tea in London – and the innocently exotic taste of the bun crammed with fruit, aromatic with saffron, were what I needed after what had proved to be an exhausting hour and a half with Judy Aviemore. The teashop seemed full of bent, muttering old women; I watched them over the cover of my paper, glad of a moment's leisure, grateful for the small treat I had arranged myself. There didn't seem to be any bent, muttering old men: Kensington is a widows' and spinsters' borough, curiously and drily sexless. This at least was my generalization at that time, when I still looked at London with the idea of writing a book about it. I started it all up then, livening my observations with instant sociology rather as in America non-alcoholic beer was spiked with ether.

I phoned Barbury from the Kensington High Street Tube station, though there was no need for me to do so. It was as well that he should be reminded that I was actually on the job and that I didn't keep trade union hours.

'I've seen Judy Aviemore,' I said.

'Got anything?'

'Glenthorn's a friend of hers. She met him when she was a student at Oxford. I haven't got any red-hot revelations, if that's what you mean. But enough to fire the first shots —'

'Fine. Let me have it about eleven tomorrow.'

'You don't want me for anything else?'

'No. I'm going to the theatre anyway. Promised to take my wife. Be good, Frank.'

'I'll try,' I said automatically, and went out into the street feeling vaguely let-down. I liked being at the news-paper in the evening: just as going to work at ten o'clock in the morning set one apart from other people, so did still being at work after six o'clock. Then I remembered Theresa and went back to the kiosk to phone her. 'She came in and out again,' a girl's voice said. It was Sandra, one of her flat mates. 'Is that Frank?'

'Yes, love,' I said. 'I've been working late.'

Sandra giggled. 'You do say *love* beautifully. Theresa didn't say where she'd be going. Perhaps she'll come back. I'll tell her you called.'

'Do that,' I said, and replaced the receiver, which suddenly seemed to have grown much heavier. The rain began again; I caught a taxi from under the nose of an old woman and leaned back with a cheroot, my eyes half-closed. The evening with Theresa, which I'd almost for-gotten, seemed infinitely, almost intolerably, desirable now that I'd been deprived of it.

But when I opened the door there was a woman sitting by the gas fire with a cup of tea. The sun was setting now and the only light in the room was the fire.

'I've only just made the tea,' she said without turning round.

'I phoned you,' I said. 'Do you want the light on?'

'It's nicer like this.'

I went over and kissed her.

'You smell of whisky,' she said.

'I've been interviewing Judy Aviemore.'

'I know.'

I poured myself a cup of tea. It was too weak, but it was at least hot.

'Everyone seems to know,' I said. 'Including Joyce Impington. It's extraordinary that everyone should be so interested in a routine interview with a lady novelist.'

'It's her friends you're interested in,' she said.

'I'm not interested in her at all,' I said. 'I don't particularly like her type. You should know that by now. It's Barbury —'

'The great man,' she interrupted. 'The great journalist whom you so besottedly hero-worship. That's a funny thing about you, Frank. You pretend to be so clear-headed and tough, but you're awfully soft. You admire people, and you can't see that they're just using you —'

'It's a job,' I said. 'A simple ordinary job. When I'm told to do a job I do it.'

'A simple ordinary smear job. The paper daren't come out in the open —'

'What, and be sued for £100,000?'

The conversation was beginning to bore me, just as Judy Aviemore's had. It was the old story, the high-minded waffle about integrity and honour and decency coming from people who never had had to dirty their hands.

'If Judy Aviemore and her boy friend don't want to be crucified,' I said, 'they'd better stop sleeping together. We don't fabricate scandal. If Glenthorn would only leave other men's wives alone, he'd have nothing to fear.'

'Maybe he's lonely,' she said. 'He's a widower.'

'Oh, Christ, don't make excuses for him. If he wants sex, it's easy enough for him to make discreet arrangements.'

'Perhaps he's really in love with her.'

'All the better. Makes him easier to destroy. We're out to destroy him and every other bloody socialist we can destroy.

Surely you approve of that? I may add that Joyce Impington does. Joyce is frightfully gentlemanly, but he knows that in politics you have to fight to win.'

'Maybe he does. But he's a political animal. You're not. You're not that sort of journalist, and the sooner you learn it the better. Besides, Barbury's wrong. One doesn't attack them that way. One attacks the poverty of their thinking, the stupidity of their policies —'

'Don't talk like a Guardian editorial, sweetheart. It isn't reasoned argument the public's interested in. Scandal, that's what they like. Sodomy, rape, adultery, bribery and corruption, public figures serving dinner in little leather aprons – that's the stuff to pull down a government with. Decency doesn't pay. It just doesn't sell newspapers. It's O.K. for you, of course. You're out of the battle zone. You always have been. You're doing the equivalent of serving char and wads in the NAAFI; it's poor buggers like me who risk our necks . . .' I stopped; she had turned away from the fire and was now facing me. 'I don't really care about politics,' I said. 'Do you?'

She smiled and came over to me. It was dark outside now and in the glow of the fire all the cheap furniture seemed to take on the lustrous dark red of the mahogany dressing-table, the whole room to become both more spacious and more cosy, a warm cave in the forest and a home fit for a rising young journalist to live in.

I went towards her but she pushed me away. 'You didn't phone,' she said. 'So I had to come to you.'

'I was working.'

She had changed into a high-necked grey shift dress with long sleeves and a white linen collar; but the hemline was well above her knees and she was wearing black stockings. She was a different person from the brisk and preoccupied fashion-plate I'd seen that morning: enigmatic, provocative, even a little whorish. I couldn't name her scent, which was heavy and almost palpably clinging, but that too she hadn't been wearing that morning. I was attracted by it – almost like a dog to a bitch, an observer in the back of my head sneered suddenly – and tomorrow morning the traces of it would, however briefly, rid the room of drabness. But it wasn't her, just as the short skirt and tarty stockings weren't her. My body, or one part of it would have its way; but what I, the reader, the listener to music, the walker through Holland Park who had occasional intimations of immortality, wanted was the top half, the demure half, and tea and conversation and gentleness and gradual discovery.

'You could have phoned,' she said. 'You know I go home early on Tuesday.'

I knelt down, taking both her hands.

'I'm sorry, love. It would have served me right if you hadn't come.'

'Harry asked me to go to dinner with him.'

'I thought you had when I phoned and you weren't in.' I disengaged one hand and lifted her skirt and gently kissed the flesh above the stocking top. Her hand pressed my head closer.

'Sandra and Denise knew I was waiting for your phone call,' she said. The words seemed to be dragged out of her.

I let her skirt fall and stood up.

'I love you.' I reached behind her and unzipped her dress.

'Don't you ever bother whether I love you?' Her voice was half-muffled by her dress as she pulled it off over her head.

'Of course you do.' Why was I whispering? I tried to take her in my arms.

'No. Close your eyes.'

'You don't love me?'

'Turn your back.'

She always refused to let me help her take more off

than her dress; but always until now she'd been insistent in her demands for reassurance that I loved her, and equally insistent in her protestations of love for me. I heard the faint rustle of her clothes dropping to the carpet and began to tear off my own clothes. On the first occasion we'd gone to bed together she in her impatience had helped me to undress; now she would wait under the bedclothes, her eyes bright, only her head showing. There would be a tussle, short but ferocious – *No, I won't let you into my bed!* –and then I would find myself looking at her naked body with the sharp little breasts and the long legs – longer than mine – and the surprisingly broad hips and the neat little dark tuft which she would always keep one hand over until the moment I would gently kiss it when the hand would fall aside and her eyes close.

I walked over to the bed, the lino cold and clammy beneath my feet as I left the carpet. It was perhaps this small shock, this reminder that I was living in a room no-one had ever given a damn about making comfortable, that made me, as I hurried to end what I wanted never to end, eager for her avowals of love, the barely coherent endearments, the final admission delivered in a scream like a confession from the rack.

But what she said, her legs still round my waist was, 'You dirty swine.'

'You don't mean that.'

Her legs tightened around me like a wrestler's.

'Yes, I do. You're a rotten cold-hearted swine.'

I laughed. 'You're joking.'

'No. No.' She rolled away from me. 'At my age I should be married and having lots of babies.'

'What about the population explosion?'

'Oh, fuck the population explosion.'

I looked at her in surprise. She didn't generally use four-letter-words.

four

I've been to a great many parties now; one blurs into another. I haven't entirely given up the hope at each one that somehow or other my life will be changed, that I'll meet the perfect mistress or be offered the perfect job; when I do give up that hope it will only mean that my prostate or my self-confidence (they almost amount to the same thing) has finally ceased to function. But my commonsense tells me that I'll drive home to Chertsey as usual, through long practice having drunk enough to be mildly ebullient but not so much as to go into a ditch.

But the party at Shalott House on the following Friday might have been held with the express purpose of changing my life. Adam would have given the party whether or not he'd run across me at the Salisbury; and its main purpose was business, as was the case with all his parties. It was, whether he intended it or not, a dazzling demonstration of a different way of living from any that I'd ever previously experienced. It was in fact my first adult party.

And it was the archetypal Shalott House party. There were no quarrels, no fights, no vomiting drunks, no fumbling under skirts in public, no gatecrashers; but there was plenty to drink, enough food to mop it up, and enough pretty girls to make the evening iridescent, to freshen the whole evening with their scent, to lighten the cumulative hubbub of a hundred voices with their chatter like bird-song.

But there was even more to it. There was – although I didn't realise this until long afterwards – a whole complex of relationships being built up. Other lives besides mine would be changed that evening. It was like watching a theatre-in-the-round performance in a foreign language; now and again one recognized a phrase, now and again one understood the play from the context of the action. And at any time one might be drawn into the action; Adam was apparently omnipresent, watching to see that no-one stood alone, asking the names of guests on the rare occasions he didn't know them. He couldn't bear his guests to be without a drink or without company; and on this occasion he'd hired not one, but two waitresses to attend to the business of serving drinks and washing up.

Not that anyone went to Shalott House parties for the drinks. He had then a rigid rule of serving only red and white *vin ordinaire* with ice and soda-water on the side. 'Most people don't know the difference anyway,' he'd say. 'And wine just livens people up. Spirits make them fighting drunk before they know where they are. And beer makes them pee all night, besides being dead common.'

But a handful of guests, by no means always the richest, were quietly taken aside and given whatever they fancied. Adam himself never drank anything but soda water until the last hour, when he and his inner circle were left. And at that hour too tea and coffee were made, and the serious preliminaries of business deals confirmed.

This is to see it too clearly, too long afterwards, to take what I'd call now the Chertsey view of things. When I arrived at Shalott House my first impressions were very different. Both a stained glass lamp over the door and two converted gas lamps at the bottom of the steps were switched on and the drive was full of cars. The moon was so bright that the light from the lamps seemed both pale and coarse, intruding ineffectually upon the whiteness that was almost blue and yet was soft and kind. There was an Aston Martin DB5, a new Rolls convertible, a Mercedes 230 SL, and an Oldsmobile Toronado, huge, boastful, and rather splendid, a well-founded statement on the benefits of capitalism. The rest were run-of-the-mill transportation, mostly Minis. That proved nothing; in London in particular, small cars are classless. But I was happy to see the proof in those four cars costing some £20,000 between them that at this party there were at least three of the people who are supposed not to exist any more, the indisputably rich.

I parked my Minor in a space behind the Toronado and walked up the front door steps slowly, the cold night air sharp and clean in my lungs, almost afraid to go inside for fear that the party wouldn't live up to my expectations of it. Shalott House seemed actually to have grown, the colour of its brick to have become warmer, the garden and the trees to have become groomed for the occasion. The house had even about it a certain brashness, a not unpleasing *nouveau riche* arrogance; it could well have recently been built, it could have been a private residence and not a block of flats.

Inside the feeling was even stronger. The Victorian dining table, for instance, had had two extensions put in and was laden with cheese, salami, ham, stand pies, pickled onions, pickled gherkins, hard-boiled eggs, potato crisps, sliced French loaves, salted peanuts, cheese and biscuits, and apples and tomatoes and celery. There were no sandwiches or canapés or sweet dishes of any kind, nor was there to be any given hour to eat. No-one had any need to go hungry; equally no-one need force themselves to eat if they didn't

94

want to. This buffet, I was to discover, was as invariable as the choice of wine.

The touches of luxury counted all the more: the size of the room itself, the vases crammed with flowers, an open fire in winter, and, I suppose, the girls. 'Enough to drink, something to eat, plenty of flowers, a roaring fire, and an abundance of young, firm breasts is the only party recipe I know,' Adam would often assert.

He could have added that there was always a nucleus of names, of public faces; their presence was not the main reason for the parties but an extra embellishment like the presents each child is given to take home after a birthday party. One never went away from a Shalott House party without at least one name to drop casually in conversation afterwards; I used to say to Adam that, given time, he'd work his way right through *Who's Who*.

When I came in Adam broke away from a black girl in a silver dress to come forward to shake my hand. 'Frank, I'm so glad you could make it.' His eyes were gleaming and his face flushed, though not with drink: this was his best moment, the party on its final plateau, the room and the guests each giving something to each other, the three big mirrors kaleidoscopic with the girls' dresses, everyone mixing.

'Meet Dolores La Souza,' he said. 'Dolly, Frank Batcombe. A journalist. Poor Dolly works for the BBC, Frank, surrounded by soulful Communists.'

'They are stupid bastards,' Dolores said. I noticed that she had a large diamond ring on her right hand and a gold necklace which from its design could only have been Andrew Grima. That would mean that she had a thousand pounds' worth on her person, excluding the dress.

'Why are they stupid?' I asked, taking a glass of red wine from the waitress.

'They are always talking about Apartheid. They mean

separate development, I think. I tell them I don't give a damn about Apartheid because I come from Jamaica and my father has plenty of money and they look at me all shocked and they say "Don't you care about the sufferings of your brothers and sisters?" and I say No, because my brothers and sisters have a fine time spending my father's money, how do they suffer? And they say, "we mean your brothers and sisters in South Africa." They can't bring themselves to say your black brothers and sisters in South Africa because they think that would offend me though as you see I'm as black as your hat. So I say I have no brothers and sisters in South Africa, though one brother has gone to New York where he's having a high old time laying all the white girls . . . Have you known Adam long?'

It always came back to Adam. 'I'm his cousin,' I said. 'It's a very remote and complicated relationship.'

'I know,' she said. 'I'm related to everyone in the West Indies, I think. My father is a most vigorous man.'

I laughed genuinely. I had never thought seriously about a black woman sexually before; even the law student at Leeds had in the end fulminated increasingly about the sorrows of her race. 'Not quite like that. We're both Irish on our mothers' side. The Irish are very moral. Booze and brawling are their only vices.'

She laid her hand on my sleeve.

'Are you rich? I'm a very expensive girl. Don't think you can fob me off with a visit to a discotheque and a glass of Coca-Cola.'

I could see that her tongue was in her cheek.

'I'm not rich, but like all white men I'm gay and child-like and enormously virile. I love to take away black men's girls. They can't hold them, you see, because they're too nervy and effete and over-civilized.'

She burst into a roar of laughter, which I could see

actually ripple all the way through her lithe body. After that I could do no wrong; I had just extracted her phone number from her when Adam appeared and laid a proprietary hand upon my shoulder. He had a short bespectacled young man in tow. 'Dolly, this is Toby Horsmoden. He's in films.'

She promptly switched her attention from me and I didn't talk to her again that night. Nor did I ever phone her. The moment at which I could have begun an affair passed as soon as I asked for her phone number instead of making a firm date. I don't feel any regret about this: in Chertsey one counts one's blessings. But I still find myself wondering what it would have been like, not only in bed with her but out of bed with her, how many new ways of thinking I should have acquired, how many old ones I should have rid myself of. But I went along obediently with Adam, to be introduced to, it almost seemed, everyone in the room.

Finally we sat down and he nodded towards the drink cabinet. 'You can have something else besides wine if you really fancy it,' he said. 'Damn it, you are my kith and kin.'

I shook my head.

'You seemed to be getting on famously with Dolly,' he said. 'But I had promised to introduce her to Toby. He says she has an interesting face.' He snickered. 'Toby, I said, what you're interested in is always kept in the same place, and it's a very simple and uncomplicated organ indeed.'

'No,' I said. 'It's like a gun with the casing off. And it's always different.'

What I was trying to say was that all women are different from each other, frighteningly so. I had found myself thinking of Theresa and was realizing that she wouldn't fit in here, and not because she wasn't clever or pretty

97

enough either. And that was another choice I was given that night and that I didn't take. It's easy enough to perceive it now; but then I was younger and, in the words of the poet, drunk with the variousness of things.

'Don't turn metaphysical,' Adam said. 'You always had a tendency that way. And sooner or later what it boils down to is asking in a bleating voice – he put on a Dublin accent – '*Joxer, what is the stars?* Bloody good, that, even though the sod is a Communist.' He jerked his head to the right where in the corner a short bald man in a dinner jacket was drinking whisky. '*There's* an arch-Lefty,' he said. 'Nuclear disarmament, aid to the under-developed countries, the lot.' I recognized him with some astonishment. It was Lord Mislingford, who had a minor post in the Government and much more political influence than the public – and for that matter the Labour Party Executive – ever suspected. Mislingford was a hereditary peer and had added to a sizeable inheritance by shrewd speculation. He was precisely the sort of socialist whom I hated and despised. (I was more given to violent reactions then than I am now.)

'What's he here for?' I asked. I was on my fourth glass of wine and inclined to be aggressive.

'Business,' Adam said. 'And possibly pleasure in God's good time.'

'What business?'

'It's very boring. It all depends upon other people. Besides, old Piers isn't so bad when you get to know him. I don't think that he's really a socialist. He's just backing the winning horse, which is forgivable.'

Mislingford was now listening with an air of infinite indulgence to a tall, thin, somehow moth-eaten man who was also drinking whisky. This was Jack Reaverhill, whom I'd frequently seen around Fleet Street, generally coming out of or going into a pub, his pockets stuffed with proofs and a bundle of books and magazines under his arm. Jack was a freelance journalist, fiercely Catholic and fiercely right-wing. He was even fiercely freelance; almost any paper would have been glad to have had him on its staff, but he wasn't the sort of man to accept even the mildest editorial direction. Later, I realized that he occupied the position, as far as any human being could occupy it, of Adam's conscience and, if this isn't too sentimental, his father. But then, new to Adam's parties, I was a little puzzled at his presence.

'Piers,' he was saying to Mislingford, 'you're a bad man. Never mind your personal morals. It's your public morals I'm criticizing. God forgive me for saying it, Piers, *but it would have been better had you never been born.*'

Mislingford chuckled and offered Reaverhill a cigar at least ten inches long which he accepted and cut very carefully with a gold cutter, which looked as if it had cost more than his stained and shapeless fawn tweed suit, grubby white shirt, and down-at-heel black shoes all put together.

'You never change, Jack,' Mislingford said. 'Full of working-class prejudice.'

'You're damned well right,' Reaverhill said. 'All my beliefs are working-class beliefs. Hang the murderer, flog the thug, jail the thief, distrust all foreigners, and keep Britain white.'

'That's why the working classes vote for us, of course,' Mislingford said, unperturbed. 'We believe the exact opposite from them. And we've never made any secret of it.'

'They vote for your lot, poor deluded devils, because they imagine you're going to give them more of everything. More jobs, more money, more wonder drugs, more roads, cheaper and stronger beer ... Poor stupid sods, their awakening won't be long in coming ...'

Mislingford laughed. It was a low and musical laugh if a

shade artificial. 'Come to lunch with me tomorrow, Jack, and I'll tell you just what we're going to give them next – or, if you like, not give them,' he said.

The lunch would not buy Jack, and there was no guarantee that the resulting article wouldn't take the form of a more than usually virulent attack. But Mislingford would be well aware that in his position almost any kind of publicity was better than no publicity and that Jack's name over an article was a guarantee of readability.

Reaverhill took out his diary.

'L'Etoile,' Mislingford said. 'One o'clock. Unless you prefer somewhere else?'

'You know bloody well I like the place,' Reaverhill said. He put his diary and pen away. I was amused to see the sudden change in his face. It wasn't obsequious because its harsh angles didn't know how to be but it was, in a word, neutral. This was business.

Adam caught his eye. 'Jack, this is Frank Batcombe. My cousin. Also a journalist. Piers, Frank Batcombe. He isn't on your side at present – in fact he makes Jack here look like a dyed-in-the-wool Communist – but he's quite human apart from that.'

'The New Right,' Mislingford said. 'Well, we can always do with some intelligent opposition. Which paper do you work for?'

I told him. Jack Reaverhill snorted. 'It's full of fellow-travellers,' he said.

'I know.'

'My papa left me some shares in it,' Mislingford said. 'Not a majority holding, unfortunately.' He took his cigar out of his mouth and scrutinized it as if it would advise him what to say next. 'It rather specializes in campaigns, doesn't it? Like its present one against David Glenthorn. I don't approve of all his opinions, but neither do I approve of what the paper's trying to do to him . . .'

'I don't determine its policy,' I said.

'But you carry it out. You're fully cognisant with the purpose of any campaign to which you're asked to contribute any item. Otherwise you'd not be much use as a journalist.'

'I'm *ordered* to do certain jobs,' I said, aware that I had to choose my words with some care. 'The final responsibility isn't mine. In fact, it's more yours than mine if you hold stock in the paper.'

'Better me than someone else,' Mislingford said. 'Are you married?'

I shook my head.

'Then you don't have any excuse.'

I was beginning to be annoyed. 'There's a good rule in journalism as in politics,' I said. 'If you don't like the heat, keep out of the kitchen.'

Mislingford replaced his cigar. 'Give the boy some whisky, Adam,' he said. 'That's a good answer.'

I took the whisky from Adam. 'It's what Truman said, not me.' I lit a cheroot.

'I'm very well acquainted with him,' Mislingford said. 'I'll tell you all about him some time.'

'He'll fill you up with lies,' Reaverhill said. His voice had traces of a Midland accent and was as harsh as his face. 'He's the most dangerous man in England.' He held out his empty glass to Adam. 'If I destroy him before I die, I'll be a happy man, and have a million days taken off my time in Purgatory into the bargain.'

'I can't compete with that,' Mislingford said. He smiled at me. 'Jack's absolutely certain that he has God on his side. I only have history in my corner.'

'The blind mole of history tunnelling away,' Reaverhill said. 'I heard all about it at Birmingham University.'

That was another direction, I see now. If I had decided at that moment that I was a political animal I might have begun laying the foundations for a different sort of career, my view of life might have been Westminster rather than Chertsey. I doubt whether either Mislingford or Reaverhill would actually have helped me change direction, but they would, without even knowing it, have made me take the decision. This was the best part of my youth and the reason why, until my dying day, I shall never find myself entirely accepting the Chertsey way of life. I have, as they say, my memories.

'That isn't what I meant, you old witch-hunter,' Mislingford said. He was looking round the room now; his gaze finally settled on a red-haired girl in a green crocheted mini-dress and green stockings. 'O whip the dogs away, My Lord, That make me ill with lust, Teach sulky lips to say, My Lord, That flaxen hair is dust ... The colour is different, but the principle's the same ... I wonder, Adam, if you might introduce me to that young woman?'

Reaverhill's face for a second was contorted with disgust, and he moved away without a word; he was fiercely puritanical as far as sex was concerned. Mislingford's eyes were shining.

'Nothing could be more simple,' Adam said. 'Excuse us, Frank.'

I was alone and as long as I had the whisky to prevent me from looking awkward, quite happy to be alone, to indulge in the simple and undemanding diversion of observation.

There was hardly any need for a host now; what introductions were necessary had all been made, the wine had flowed enough to charm away any shyness, the groups which had clung together initially were splitting up and forming into other groups, the men who, like Mislingford, had had their eyes on girls were now making their way towards the girls.

Some of the guests there I was never to see again. They

were friends of friends, they were strictly business contacts, they were the fulfilment of Adam's or Basil's social obligations. But for the most part they were Adam's friends, almost his family; though I didn't know it then, I should see them all again.

That evening the total of celebrities was unusually high. The odd thing here was that all of them were middle-aged. Adam's working rule for parties was, in fact, to invite no-one over thirty-five who wasn't a celebrity or very rich or both.

Jerry Knaphill, the novelist, for instance, wouldn't see forty again. Almost grossly fat, with short legs and long arms and gold-rimmed spectacles which gave him the look of an unsuccessful *Mitteleüropa* secret agent, he was more than usually drunk, his arm round a small pale girl in a black dress who was young enough to have been his granddaughter.

Jerry lived respectably and quietly in the West Country with his wife and five young children for two months out of every three and on the third month would rent a service flat in the West End, in order, as he said, to enlarge his experience. Enlarging his experience took the form of heavy drinking and intensive womanising.

He had a talent for the latter which his faintly grotesque appearance belied. Later that evening he would disappear with a woman – he had an instinct for discovering the most fervent admirers of his books – and would be found invariably at the Ritz bar the next day, drinking plain tonic water and feeling guilty at the top of his voice.

I didn't want to judge him too harshly – who could say whether I'd be any better at his age? – but I began to feel a certain compassion for the girl in the black dress. I was meditating intervention – she seemed too young and thin to bear his sweating bulk – when something about the line of her neck struck me as being familiar. Her publicity photos did her far more than justice, but it was without a doubt Pauline Yeavering, and if she was even remotely like the heroine of her first novel, it was Jerry I had to feel sorry for.

Jerry was a fully-fledged celebrity; Pauline had at least cadet rank. But the real ones, not so much because of achievement but because of public exposure, were Harry Morgate, Dick Sancreed and Saul Dykenhead. They were at the moment I surveyed the room, the centre of a small admiring group.

Harry in a midnight-blue dinner-jacket was evidently holding the floor; the other two were waiting their chance. They were the centre of attention, the party's main conversation-pieces, and each of them was fully cognisant of the fact. Harry was almost never off the screen, and was indeed due to appear in a recorded discussion about marijuana that very night. Dick Sancreed had just finished a series in which he figured as a battered but gentlemanly amorist. It hadn't been a very successful series; but everyone in the room knew that small neat face with the large melancholy eyes and the weak mouth of the kind described by publicists as almost feminine in its sensitivity. Saul Dykenhead, bald and bearded with narrow slanting eyes, closely resembled Lenin facially though not politically. His paintings were in what at first sight seemed an excessively old-fashioned style. It was only after a long scrutiny that their strangeness would penetrate the imagination hair-raisingly, that the meticulously detailed landscapes would fill up with ghosts. He too had just finished a TV series about, naturally, painting; I think that he had begun it unaware of himself as a physical presence but now his innocence had gone. Like the other two, he drew nourishment simply from being looked at.

The three of them looked uncommonly like a painting of the Soviet Realist school with Dykenhead about to reprove

Harry Morgate, type-cast as a capitalist with his dinner-jacket, frilled shirt, white well-brushed hair and thick black eyebrows and a cigar which was even longer than Misling-ford's, and to reassure Dick Sancreed who, painfully thin in a rumpled navy-blue suit and with a not very clean white shirt, looked more like a downtrodden factory worker than a professional actor.

The celebrities were important, they were the ingredient which gave Adam's parties the final and essential touch, the sherry in the trifle, the rum in the Christmas cake. But the hard core were people like Toby Horsmoden and Jack Reaverhill and Simon Cothill and John Axmouth and Nigel Binsey and Horace Tarland. The categories naturally tended to blur; the first three were almost celebrities, since they had names. The last three were more typical; Axmouth was in public relations, though not in Adam's firm, Binsey was a journalist, though not for my paper, and Tarland was an architect. They were all in their late twenties, all in the £5,000 a year bracket, all bachelors, and all, strangely enough, of the same physical type as Adam, tall and lean and inclined towards the young American executive in dress rather than either Savile Row or Carnaby Street.

They had the same political opinions – extreme right or, to be more accurate, derisively anti-left. But they could be relied upon not to express those opinions too vehemently, as they could be relied upon to hold their drink. With these friends Adam could relax; emotionally, they meant more to him, I now believe, than any of his girls. I've often wondered why Adam didn't ask any of them to share his flat when Gordon left; the answer, and one which I still don't find very palatable, is that they were too independent to live under anyone else's shadow, that though Adam may have seen them as his palace guard, they themselves would have declined the role.

The girls from time to time were rotated by marriage and

engagement. They would come back to Shalott House, but it wouldn't be the same. Women live in the present, sealing their past away in watertight compartments as in a ship.

Simon Cothill brought most of the transient girls (and also Carlos, a tall willowy youth in a purple corduroy suit). But certain faces were always there and it's these which I remember the most vividly. There was Maria Barrisdale, a platinum blonde model, Christine Berneray, a genuine blonde and occasional actress and model, Debby Framsden who changed the colour of her hair with her dress and who admitted frankly to living on men and occasional journalism. Elsa Marnhull, a rather astringent and tweedy publisher's editor with peat-coloured brown hair who was far too clever for me, Mandy Cassley, the red-haired girl whom Mislingford had appropriated and who was another model. There was Janice Glasbury, thin and drawling-voiced and dark, who worked for the BBC and who, like Elsa Marnhull was far too clever for me, and Abigail Pinmore, the last of the *débutantes*, a placid ash-blonde who was remarkable for nothing to my knowledge except an uncontrollable desire to take off all her clothes after a few drinks and a habit of becoming engaged every three months.

I observed them at the party that evening, standing there with a glass of whisky in my hand. I describe them physically as I observed them to myself then, a journalist quickly pinning down specimens. But even then it wasn't so simple; in a way I was in love with them all. Often now in the evening in Chertsey I contemplate visiting Shalott House again: I know that Adam will still be there, that the same girls will go to his parties. It's only twenty-five miles away by road, forty minutes by train to Waterloo, fifteen minutes to Hampstead. It might as well be a thousand miles.

Some of this was in my mind that evening. I felt that it

was all too good to be true, had even, I'll swear, a fore-knowledge of what was waiting for me, of pine trees at the bottom of the garden, of the unwinding with a gin-and-tonic before dinner, of the planning of a sun-room extension, of the building of a Wendy house.

But I was then not committed to any one way of life; I was even deluded enough to see myself as making preparations for conquest, as taking aim at a football. A truer image would have been of me as something small and metallic being drawn towards a huge magnetized sphere, priding itself upon being mobile and metallic and not grasping the fact that it was precisely this quality that drew it towards the sphere.

I finished my whisky and was making my way over to Debby Framsden, who that evening was a blonde with a glittering gold dress to match, when the doorbell rang.

Adam frowned and made a peremptory gesture towards Basil Staverton who had that evening apparently been appointed footman. What hour it was I don't remember; but it was the wrong hour, the gatecrashers' hour, too late for a guest and too early for anyone to be collected. Then his face cleared as a man and a woman entered the room. It was the man whom he was pleased to see; so much so that he rushed forward to him and shook him by both hands, the English substitute for an embrace.

'My dear Martin, I'm so delighted that you could make it . . .' He continued to hold both the man's hands, as if frightened he might try to run away. He turned to me. 'Frank, do meet Martin Aviemore. Martin, Frank Batcombe. A journalist, but human nevertheless. He's actually been interviewing Judy this week . . .'

He released Aviemore's hands; immediately Aviemore swayed forward, as if only Adam's grip had kept him upright. He was tall with good shoulders: when he swayed he swayed in one piece, retaining a military stiffness of bearing.

This discipline did not extend to his face, which seemed to sag both downwards and upwards in the direction of his heavy black moustache.

He grabbed my hand seeming to use it to push himself back to a rigid vertical position, which he succeeded in maintaining, rocking slightly on his heels.

'Delighted to meet you, old boy. Not that I do meet many of you chaps, that's more in my wife's line. Afraid my job's very dull, unless I were to take to pushing dud shares or something of that sort . . .'

He took a large white silk handkerchief from his sleeve and mopped his face. He was not incapably drunk, but he was enunciating his words with especial care. The rocking on his heels was developing into a sway.

'Angela,' Adam said to the girl with Aviemore, who had been standing a little apart, half-smiling, 'I didn't recognize you.'

'It's been four years, my sweet Adam,' the girl said. She was uncannily like Theresa, the same black hair but cut short, the same slim, if not skinny body, the same rather flat face. But her eyes were a vivid blue, rounder, almost doll-like, and her white open-work dress was a good inch and a half shorter than Theresa would have dared to go. She spoke in a deliberately affected drawl; it irritated me at first but then I realized that I wanted to go on hearing it.

'You haven't changed,' Adam said. He took a glass of red wine from the waitress.

'Is that why you didn't know me?'

'Probably. Frank's my cousin, by the way. Angela Guilsfield, Frank Batcombe.'

'There is a likeness.' I was inspected briefly; it was as if she were considering purchasing me, I thought resentfully.

'I'll get you a drink,' I said.

'Whisky with a lot of water, please.'

When I came back with the whisky Adam and Aviemore were talking with Mislingford. Aviemore was sipping brandy and smoking one of Mislingford's cigars. He seemed suddenly to be steady on his feet. The red-haired girl had disappeared and in the corner where the three of them stood – the furthest away from us – a space seemed to have cleared itself.

I offered Angela a cheroot. 'Do you smoke these?'

She took out a box of small Burma cheroots from her handbag. 'Not enough taste.' I lit it for her and she blew out a cloud of acrid but aromatic smoke; the smell, I thought, was more like incense than tobacco.

'Do you always prefer strong tastes?'

'That's the story of my life. *Non angeli sed Angela.*' She looked around the room. 'Adam's very grand these days.'

'Haven't you been here before?'

'I ran across Martin, purely by chance, and he invited me along with him. I've not been in England for a while, anyway. I'm by way of being a remittance girl. We haven't an Empire any more, so I mostly go to Tangier.'

'What about the travel allowance?'

She shrugged her shoulders, the small breasts lifting. 'I have remittance aunts and remittance uncles. Don't tell me you mind.'

'Good luck to you, love.'

'You come from Yorkshire, don't you? Adam used to talk like that.'

'I'm afraid so.'

'Oh, don't be afraid. It's very pleasant to hear it again. Daddy had a mouldering old house in Yorkshire once with a priest's hole, but he sold it.'

I had the sensation of being looked over for purchase again. On the face of it the conversation was commonplace enough but every word was playing its part in a plan, and a plan of her making.

'Was it your family house?' I asked.

'For about four hundred years.'

'Ours is a large Victorian villa in Charbury,' I said. 'My mother's family came over during the Famine.' It was becoming evident that she was a Catholic too, but of that most exclusive category of English Catholic. That would explain her air of cool arrogance, which was not unlike Joyce Impington's. I wondered when the word *recusant* would pop up.

'That's interesting,' she said. 'Our lot just hung on. Except one who went off to America, and became moderately prosperous. Which is nice for me, because I have some cousins there.'

She evidently was going to refuse the I'm-a-Catholic-too gambit. 'I'll get you something to eat,' I said. It was the easiest way of ascertaining her religion; it would have been cheating to have asked her outright. At the buffet she piled her plate with everything but meat, as I did. 'My Uncle Terry always used to say that bacon tasted best on a Friday,' I said as she looked at a veal-and-ham pie.

'It's about the only law of the Church I keep,' she said. For a few seconds I was overmastered by a strangely sad feeling, as if she were some other person than the person I took her to be, as if I were taking a mean advantage of her.

'I voted against the rule being abolished,' I said. 'Not that the laity should be allowed to decide. What the hell's the good of a permissive Church?'

'You're so right,' she said. 'We get enough of that at home.'

'What do you do at home?'

'I live at my brother's flat – he's in America, he just keeps it for the odd visit to London. But I don't work there. I have a sordid studio in sordid Notting Hill Gate. It's an awful dump. A family of six in the basement, a brothel on the ground floor, two queers on the first floor, an alcoholic poet on the second floor, and me in the attic.'

'You paint?'

'Very old-fashioned stuff. Do you like painting?'

She proceeded to put me through a brief but comprehensive examination on the history of painting designed for no other purpose than to discover whether I really meant what I said or was simply trying to please her. Angela told huge hurtful lies whenever it suited her; but she never told small lies, and no man had a chance with her who did so.

I glanced across the room at Mislingford and Aviemore. Adam had left them; Aviemore was sitting on the edge of the dining-table, his face braced up and sober, listening intently to Mislingford, who was telling him something, apparently of vital importance, in a harsh whisper.

'He's awful, isn't he?' Angela said.

'Which one?'

'Both, if you like. But in particular Martin. But is he more awful than Adam? I forgot, he's your cousin . . .'

'Never mind that,' I said. 'Why is Adam awful?'

'He's chatting up that rather nice little blonde now. He's finished being host and he's going to enjoy himself. He's so *cold*, so wonderfully deliberate. Oh, he's absolutely archetypal, the bright grammar school boy who's going to get on. Poor old Martin's awful too without a doubt, he's so vulgar and stupid, but there's this much to be said for him: your cousin could buy and sell him any day of the week. People like Adam are going to take over, and people like Martin are going to be left out in the cold . . .'

'And me?'

'Oh, you're probably awful too. Shall I give you my telephone number? You're going to ask me for it, anyway?'

I laughed. 'I wonder if you really like men,' I said lightly. She flushed. 'Don't you dare —'

'It's only a weak attempt at facetiousness,' I said.

'Facetiousness *is* a weak attempt,' she said waspishly. She gave me the number. 'Aren't you going to write it down?'

'I'll remember it.'

'I believe you will.' She kissed me lightly on the mouth. Her eyes were fixed on Aviemore.

'Can't we have lunch?' I asked. 'Monday?'

'I'm going to be busy.' Her tone was final. 'It's been very interesting talking to you, Frank.'

'I hope I was awful enough to please you,' I said. Mislingford had detached himself from Aviemore and was returning to the red-haired girl who was standing impassively her hands by her side.

'As Candida said, that's a good bid.'

'I take your point,' I said. 'But you don't really have to go off with that dilapidated bill-broker, do you?'

'Perhaps I like dilapidated bill-brokers,' she said. 'Besides, I feel sorry for him. He's married to a lady novelist.'

'I know.'

'Yes, of course. It's your *métier*. Phone me, then. Any time next week.'

The three big standard lights went off, leaving the room lit only by the fire and the two wall lights above the fireplace. Adam came over to me. 'Give me a hand with the carpet,' he said.

We rolled back the big Axminster carpet revealing the parquet floor.

'Enjoying yourself?' he asked. 'You seemed to be getting on famously with old Angela. Jesus, it gave me quite a turn when I saw her. Evidently she ran across Aviemore in a rather *louche* Soho drinking club he patronises, The Gearbox, or some such name. I think she likes him because he's so frightfully *seedy*. He shouldn't be, he's not as poor as all that, but let's put it this way. If he were a house, then no matter how many expensive improvements had been made, he'd be condemned.'

He switched on the tape recorder. 'Now for some nice smoochy music ... Did you get anywhere with Angela?'

'I got her phone number.'

'It's a beginning.' The room looked even larger now, the floor gleaming palely. The guests were beginning to thin out. Jack Reaverhill had gone, Dolores La Souza and Toby Horsmoden had gone. Mislingford and the red-haired girl had gone; and all the quieter, dimmer, more respectable guests had gone.

'Was Angela a real chum of yours once, then?'

'Believe it or not, never. She was a friend of Wendy's — somehow I never did anything about it. Incidentally, have you made your mind up about a share in the flat?'

'You've twisted my arm round. I'll move in next month.'

He slapped my back. 'Good. We'll have some more whisky on that. Mind you, we don't have parties like this every night. We live very quietly with the minimum of rules.'

'There's only one really,' Basil Staverton said, suddenly appearing at my elbow. 'Don't go in anyone else's bedroom if the door is closed.'

'Yes,' said Adam. 'And everything at these parties is off the record, unless cleared with me. Don't worry, Frank, I know you're not like these hacks from the tabloids. One sod slipped in one night and caused a divorce. But if you stick to the rules —' he lowered his voice — 'whatever my friends do they'll tell you first.'

'There's no need for you to spell it out,' I said. 'And I don't need any scraps of gossip. When I'm off duty I'm off duty.'

'Don't be so bloody touchy,' Adam said. 'I know you well enough to trust you. Believe me, I'd rather keep the room empty than have anyone in whom I couldn't absolutely rely upon. Never mind it now anyway. Let's consider it settled. What do you see that you fancy?'

It is here, and here only that my recollections of that evening grow hazy, if not fantastic. For I can only visualize myself as walking along a line of girls and finally settling for Debby Framsden. It can't have been as easy as all that; there must have been an introduction, there must have been a man to get her away from, there must have been at least a great many dances.

I remember the gold dress, I remember the gold stockings. I remember that at one stage the recording ran on into some Eddie Cantor songs and everyone stopped dancing to listen. It wasn't just the wonderful phrasing, it wasn't just the sheer unaffected richness of tone, it was the self-assurance, the innocence, the lack of awareness of evil; I remember fighting back the tears when his voice became the yolky clucking voice of an Italian mamma in *Josephine;* and as I finally let them flow I knew that I was weeping for a world I'd never known and that no-one would ever know again.

And I remember that though the party was a quiet one, couples, one of which was Carlos and Simon, were dancing more and more slowly, listening to some rhythm inside themselves rather than the music, and that couples were clinging together all over the room and that I knew – and it wasn't entirely the wine and the whisky – that I should never be so happy or so free again, with no responsibilities, no last train to catch, no need to look at my watch, no reality except my own pleasure.

And I remember standing on the steps of Shalott House flinging out my arms in the cold night air wanting to draw it all into myself – Hampstead, London, the world, and Debby in her big white fun fur coat with the golden stockings underneath.

'I'll take you home,' I said to her. But a part of me wanted to run about on the lawn in the moonlight shouting and singing, wanted to exult all through the night.

'No, I'll take you,' she said. And then I remember being in her Fiat 500 with the top down, the air in my face making me both more sober and more drunk, and then only her voice saying with unexpected sadness *You knew I wasn't really a blonde* and then abruptly, nothing, nothing at all.

five

'I think you're crazy to move,' Theresa said. We were sitting in the Chelsea Potter on the Thursday of the week after the party; it was full, as usual, of girls in miniskirts and young men with shoulder-length hair. Bells were being worn by both sexes – that was the last year of the Flower People – and every now and again a melancholy little tinkle would penetrate the hubbub. It was, as I well knew, an intensely parochial world, closed and barred to those who didn't belong to the right age group and wear the correct uniform.

Sitting there alone, I had often envied the habitués of the Chelsea Potter or the Markham Arms or the King's Head or indeed of all the pubs and bistros and coffee bars in or around the King's Road. They had some password I didn't possess, they were in and I was out. Now I had given in my notice at the World's End flat and would leave it without a pang. It was futile to try to make Theresa understand; nevertheless I made the attempt.

'I wanted a change,' I said. 'Chelsea isn't really me.' A girl was leaning over the next table to whisper something to a young man with a black Zapata moustache, hair in an old-fashioned tight permanent wave, a pink frilled shirt, and a mauve quilted silk jacket; I tried to look as though I were admiring the multi-coloured lampshades above her whilst at the same time watching her skirt ride up to show white flesh and, before she straightened her back, a flash of green underwear. Everyone, I thought, was very superior about the sort of pleasure that such glimpses gave men; but what harm was there in it?

'There are times when it seems to fit you like a bloody glove,' Theresa said. 'Stop looking at that damned girl. She should wear tights with a skirt like that, the horrid little slut. Probably full of drugs, anyway.'

'Not here. It's very respectable.'

'I'm not going to argue about it. All I'd like to know is why you haven't told me you were moving before now. Are you moving in with another woman or what?'

'Two chaps, actually. The leaseholder's my cousin, Adam Keelby.'

'Adam Keelby your cousin? You can't be serious.'

'I've told you, he's my cousin. And we went to the same school.'

Her face was white. She had an intensely clear Irish skin, as she had the intensely black Irish hair with red glints in it: her reactions were never difficult to apprehend.

'He's a bastard,' she said. 'The very worst sort of person for you to live with.'

I felt a sudden spasm of jealousy. 'May I ask how you come to know him so well?'

'I don't know him well. I've only met him once.'

'Once is enough,' I said. What was curious at this point was that at the same time I experienced the jealousy, I also experienced a febrile excitement.

'I interviewed him. We were doing a series on young bachelors in London. That was when I was working for "Vagina".' This was the name given by Fleet Street to the woman's magazine she had once worked for. 'Typical

"Vagina" stuff, of course. Very frank, very acid, very nonchalant.'

'That's your story,' I said. 'Why should they pick Adam? He's not exactly a big name.'

'That was the *raison d'être* for the whole series,' she said impatiently. 'Look up the files if you want. I remember Adam in particular because he was without any question the nastiest of a nasty bunch. Is he still at Shalott House?'

I nodded.

'It's a hateful flat. So adolescent – nude photos unretouched to show how broad-minded he is and a dirty picture next to his First Communion certificate. Oh, very very trendy.'

'Adam's a good Catholic.'

'It suits his purpose. It's just another gimmick.'

'Not necessarily a commercial gimmick.'

'Oh, no, you simpleton. Not these days. It's smart to be a Pape now ... Just as to be right-wing is smart. He's not sincere about it. He's not sincere about anything. That whole bloody flat's part of an elaborate PR set-up.'

'I find it amusing. I honestly can't imagine why you're making such a pother about it. Adam's not just my cousin, he's one of my oldest friends.'

'He's no-one's friend,' she said. 'If you went to school together, why haven't I heard about him before now? Why didn't you keep in touch?'

'His mother died five years ago. She was a widow. I think he just wanted to forget about Charbury.'

Her lips drew back. 'Oh, one of those. A mother's boy. I knew it anyway. I've never heard a man go on so much about furniture and carpets and pictures. *This is from my mother's house —*' she mimicked a man's voice – '*and it means a great deal to me* – why, the whole flat's just a wallow in the past. I bet he's looking for a father, isn't he?'

'Steady on,' I said. 'Queer is the last thing Adam is.'

'Oh, yes, I'm sure he has a lot of women. Trying to prove he's a man.'

'Christ, spare me the amateur psychology, Theresa. If a chap doesn't like girls he's queer. If he does like girls he's trying to prove he's not queer. I've heard it all before.'

'You've made up your mind, haven't you?' Her colour was returning now but she still looked ill. 'It's the same with Barbury. You think he's absolutely great, you'll do anything for him. And the moment you've exhausted your usefulness then – bang. He'll not want to know you. And if anything goes awry with his latest scheme who do you think will be thrown to the wolves? You, mate.' She spat out the last word. 'And you won't be told.'

'You may as well say *I'm* queer and have done with it.'

'You're not. You're just an old-fashioned hero-worshipper. Your trouble is that you have such lousy taste in heroes.' She lit a cigarette from the stub of its precursor. 'God, I could draw you a plan of that damned place, that damned *brothel*. The dinky little entrance hall, the great big drawing room, the cute little loo off the entrance hall. Oh, and the other little loo next to Basil's room. Real Edwardian period piece on a throne. And another loo in the bathroom. That's modern, though. Blush pink like the bath. There's a crucifix in each of the cloakrooms – did you notice that? And a shower room next to the bathroom – you use the same entrance. I bet there's many a merry confrontation when his lady friends are staying. And that folksy kitchen of his with the dish-washing rota pinned up. Did you see that? And did you also note that Adam's room is the biggest? It was the study originally, so it's got proper dividing walls. The other two are really one room divided by hardboard. You'll be able to hear everything that goes on. Oh, it's very matey.'

'For God's sake, what are you going on about?' It occurred to me, not for the first time, that the tone of our conversation was exactly that of an old married couple. 'I need a change. What could be simpler? Hampstead's much nicer than Chelsea and Shalott House much more comfortable than a glorified bed-sitter. Besides, Adam has all sorts of useful contacts.'

She laughed shortly. 'You poor innocent. Haven't *you* any contacts, any little bits of valuable knowledge? I've only met Adam Keelby once, and I sized him up in ten seconds flat. Believe me, you'll do more for him than he ever will for you.'

Despite myself I was impressed enough by her almost oracular seriousness to have a foreboding of misfortune which actually made the hair on my scalp bristle. Then reason asserted itself.

'I think you have hot pants for him, to be brutally frank. Else why should you remember him?'

'I wouldn't sleep with him if he were the last man on earth. And I'm not going to sleep with you at that damned brothel either. Have you thought of that? Any girl you sleep with there – why you might as well do it in Hyde Park in broad daylight with thousands cheering.'

'I've given in my notice at the World's End flat,' I said. 'So that's it. I'm going.'

'Get another flat, please.' I had recently seen *Doctor Zhivago* and its images kept recurring in my mind, boosting the commonplace as vodka does orange juice. Now Theresa, huddled into a big coat of grey fox fur that was ten years too old for her seemed like a *Zhivago* character, a refugee pleading with a Communist bureaucrat.

'Theresa, I can't have you running my whole life. It's so utterly ridiculous. We can still see each other —'

'You're so cold,' she said. 'You don't give a damn whether I live or die.' The tears began to trickle down her cheeks; no-one around us took the least notice.

'Don't cry,' I said. 'What's there to cry for?'

'I'm worried.'

'Your job?'

'Oh God. Frank, you're so *stupid!* I'm late.' She blushed. She very often alternated in this way, extreme shyness, following extreme outspokenness.

We could well have been, I thought, in a Charbury pub and I could well have been an employee of the insurance company my father worked for, which was typical of the jobs which had once been envisaged for me. I could well have been, I thought in my panic, an ordinary person in an ordinary job in an ordinary place. I saw Shalott House disappear, I saw my car disappear, I saw the hasty marriage and could hear, even in a newspaper office, the titters when one came out with the time-hallowed story of a premature birth. Fragments of my mother's conversation came back to me . . . *Dressed in white with her belly bumping her chin . . . A ten pound baby three months premature as if we couldn't count . . .*

'Jesus wept!' I exclaimed. 'Are you sure?'

'Naturally I'm sure. I'm like clockwork normally —'. She blushed again.

'I thought you were taking the pill.'

'It isn't infallible. Didn't you know that?'

'Christ, what a bloody time to have this happen! What a bloody rotten mess!' For the first time in my life I wanted to hit a woman. 'You did it on purpose, didn't you? You can't have been taking the things —'

'Oh, yes, I have. And don't think it's anyone else but you, either.'

'I haven't said that. What sort of sod do you think I am?'

'It's no-one but you. I don't care what happens now, I'll walk out of here and you'll never see me again. I won't ask you for anything, if you dare to say it isn't yours. Yes, you're the happy father, Frank.'

'I believe you.' And that was true enough. I couldn't imagine her climbing out of one man's bed into another and back again any more than I could imagine her lying. And I believed too that her own peculiar feminine honour would drive her out into the night if I said otherwise. And the unpleasant but astute observer·who seemed these days to have more and more authority over me pointed out, sniggering slightly, that a few words to her now would permanently rid me of her, that only an idiot would fail to take advantage of her unworldliness. She wasn't really good-looking enough for me, not even as good-looking a woman as I was a man, she was too domineering, she was too intolerant, she was, despite her lost virginity, a rigidly upright Catholic matron in the making. But apart from that, I didn't want to marry anyone. I was looking forward to at least two years in London, the new Shalott House London, before I finally settled down. I slowly and painfully pushed the observer out of my mind.

'What are you going to do about it?' Theresa asked me. There was something peremptory about even this simple request, as if I were an erring child or a defaulting debtor.

'I'll do what's right.'

'You will, won't you? You'll do what's right, with your face set like stone. Well, I suppose it's something to be grateful for.'

It was decided now; and what the observer had forgotten was that I had a good salary and £1,000 in the bank. I had always been a saver and my father had been all his life in the insurance business; he'd never been rich but he'd never been poor, and all his children were insured and endowed up to their eyebrows. Marriage wasn't the end of the world. 'I'm sorry,' I said. 'It was something of a shock.' I swallowed. 'I do love you.'

'Thank you. But even if you did, this isn't the way I'd have chosen to get married . . . Can I have a large gin?'

We both had a large gin, and then went into the West

End, finally dining at Chez Victor's on *moules marinères*, *steak Rossini* and *crêpes suzettes* with a bottle of *Moët Chandon* between us and brandy-and-Benedictine afterwards. I had wanted to dine inexpensively in Chelsea but Theresa had insisted upon the West End. I was glad of her choice when eating the food and drinking the champagne; and Chez Victor's in its comfortable dark brown shabbiness and its agreeably antique *décor* of huge bottles of beer no longer brewed and prints of Napoleon and its smudgy hand-written menu was what I needed to bring me comfortably down to earth and acceptance.

I drove her straight home afterwards. She didn't speak during the journey and when we reached the flat didn't, as I'd half-expected, take me up for coffee and to impart the news if not of her pregnancy, of her forthcoming marriage. But she clung to me for a moment, her cheek against mine. Her face seemed very hot, despite the coldness of the night. The street was one of tall terrace houses with stone porches supported by barley-sugar pillars; at each front door as far as I could see, was a row of bell-pushes each with a card underneath. There were lights in almost every window; perhaps because of the gin and the champagne and the brandy-and-Benedictine, perhaps because of Theresa's hot cheek, I thought of those lights not as signs of life but as signals for help.

'Thank you for a marvellous dinner,' she said. 'I'm tired, Frank. I'll see you tomorrow.' She kissed me on the mouth – quickly and lightly, her lips closed – and disappeared into the house.

When I reached my own flat it seemed to me for almost the first time a warm and certain refuge. I made myself a pot of coffee and took it and a bottle of brandy and a Stanley Ellin thriller *The Hanged Man* to bed, the gas fire turned full on, and sat up reading until three o'clock when my eyes began to close. It was a long time since I'd indulged in so simple a combination of pleasures; as I fell asleep I was completely persuaded that tomorrow was another day, that there was nothing more to be done about Theresa now, that it seemed more than likely that she was right about Adam and, finally, that I might do a great deal worse than marry her.

six

But it wasn't like that in the morning. The observer, the moment I awakened, began a vicious and well-thought out harangue, mostly centred upon the fact that Theresa had from the beginning to end manipulated me like a puppet. (I could actually see the puppet, a dangling clownish figure not unlike the Hanged Man on the cover of the Ellin thriller.) Theresa's pregnancy was, in fact, in my mind all day. It should have been a good day, since I was to have lunch with Glenthorn at the Ivy. Expense account lunches are not so frequent a feature of the journalist's life as most people suppose; it's fashionable to grumble about them, but I've always enjoyed them and so long as my liver and stomach hold out, always will. It's the one thing that sets one apart from the peasants, which makes success literally tangible. There's also the minor but important consideration of saving the money one would otherwise have spent on one's own lunch.

And I wanted to meet Glenthorn. I could have done to him what Barbury wanted doing without ever meeting him, as a pilot can bomb a town without ever walking through its streets or knowing a single one of its inhabitants. But Barbury wanted me to get to know him.

'He's human, Frank,' Barbury said to me that morning. 'He likes to talk about himself. And he doesn't trust any of that lot around him and he doesn't, unfortunately, like dear old Jackson.' Jackson was our Lobby Correspondent, and had been for twenty years; he would never be promoted because no-one else had twenty years' experience of the ramifications of Westminster. He was, in short, too useful where he was. And this was the reason why I'd always tried to steer clear of the political side of the newspaper.

'I didn't know that anyone disliked Jackson.'

'I think at some stage he let Glenthorn know what he really thought about the Labour Party. It's very odd, since I've never known him to upset anyone. But Glenthorn's a funny chap. He's discreet enough, he keeps the fire well banked down, so as to speak, then suddenly he flares up . . .'

'He's flared up about the Government's income policy, hasn't he?'

'*That?* Oh, it's simply a trial balloon. The PM arranged it, if you ask me. He's got to carry on with Wilson's policy for a bit, but he's aching for a change. You can talk about it to Glenthorn if you like, but I don't want to make an issue of it. It bores the pants off me, and I'm bloody sure it bores the pants off our readers.'

'The main issue seems a dead duck, though.' Aviemore had returned to his wife; our informant had added that otherwise everything was as it had been before – an armed truce rather than peace.

'That shows how damned ignorant you are. Aviemore and his wife may have patched up some sort of arrangement, but it won't continue indefinitely.'

'Supposing someone's been at Aviemore?' After some misgivings I told Barbury about the presence of both Aviemore and Mislingford at Adam's party; but he was inclined to make light of it. Mislingford, he said, was so far to the left of Glenthorn that if anything he'd give a hand in destroying him. I was, in short, being too clever by half.

'No. Glenthorn's got more enemies than friends. Besides, the whole thing still smells of trouble to me. Don't ask me to explain, because I'm not able to. Just go and give the bugger lunch and keep on digging away.'

I reached the Ivy early and sat for half an hour drinking Guinness under the oil picture of the fat man tucking in to his dinner with never a thought of coronary thrombosis. There was a sprinkling of celebrities, but there was also a family party – father, mother, grandmother, two little boys, and a baby – which was always an encouraging sign. It meant that the food was good enough for someone to pay for his own lunch, and that the service was flexible enough to meet the sometimes messy demands of babies and children.

I still have an uncomplicated feeling of happiness in a good restaurant, still digest all the better for being in the proximity of the rich and the famous; but then every new restaurant was a special occasion, and when I dropped the name in conversation afterwards it would roll from my lips with an especial sonority. The Guinness soothed away a faint queasiness which had for a while assailed me whilst talking with Barbury; and the half-hour waiting for Glenthorn passed with extraordinary rapidity. I succeeded, in fact, in not thinking of Theresa for a while; the most coherent thought in my head was a hope that someone who knew me, preferably someone from Charbury, would come in and recognize me.

Glenthorn kept his appointment on the dot and came straight over to me. Like all public figures he looked somehow smaller when seen in the flesh and, strangely enough, younger. He was renowned for his untidiness but on this occasion he was wearing a rather dashing pale blue over-check suit, black suède shoes, a plum red waist-coat and a plum red tie and matching silk handkerchief. The ensemble didn't go well with his craggy face and iron grey hair; he looked like a miner dressed up for a wedding.

He had never been at the pit face; he had been what in Northumberland was called a donkeyman. That is, he had been a fitter. For his hands, large and powerful but faintly pudgy, with very clean fingernails, had been a long time away from oil and metal filings. His accent was by now only faintly Northumbrian, soft in places where in all other accents it would be hard. But then he wasn't, as he told me over the *hors d'oeuvres*, a Geordie but an Alnwick (he pronounced it *Anneek*) man born and bred.

'Why isn't it true to describe you as a rebel?' I asked him in the operational period after the entrée – sole Colbert for me, it being Friday, steak-and-kidney pie for him.

'Because I want exactly what the Government wants. I want the country to be a going concern. But I also want to abolish the working-classes. I want everyone to get more, not less. You see, Frank, I've been to the U.S.A. quite a few times. And that's the real eye-opener. There they've got real trade unionism. They don't waste their time at union meetings talking about Vietnam or the H-Bomb or the public schools, they get on with the job of looking after their members' interests.' He scowled. 'Their *material* interests, for God's sake. I've heard them all, all these bloody crusaders, pulling their consciences out up there on the platform, and when they've finished, when they've had their orgasm, what have they done for the chaps they represent? Sweet F.A. I've told them time and time again to put their consciences away and zip up their flies and see to it the workers have more money and shorter hours. That's what trade unionism is about.'

'Some of your critics would say that's a narrow view, Minister.'

'Don't call me that. You sound like one of those TV bastards. It doesn't suit you, anyway.' He smiled at me with unexpected kindness. 'I'll give you a tip, Frank. Don't you ever try to be a real smarty, don't ever quite lose your Yorkshire accent. I know that you're a clever lad, otherwise you wouldn't be here, but don't make yourself really glossy.'

'Thank you,' I said. 'I honestly will remember that.' I wondered if he'd learned that trick of suddenly establishing personal intimacy from Judy Aviemore, or whether he'd been born knowing it, and decided that the latter would be the case.

'My name's David,' he said. 'Except in the Commons. That's another thing I learned in America. If a man's dignity won't survive the use of his Christian name, then he hasn't got any to begin with.' He sipped his hock. I'd noticed that this was his first glass, and that he'd refused a drink before the meal. Obviously he was off the bottle again and equally obviously he wasn't an alcoholic.

'But what about your critics, David?'

'Naturally they say I take a narrow view. To these sodding Communists everyone's narrow who doesn't agree with him. Dress up my language, Frank, but that's what I feel. I accept the Government's foreign policy and even if I didn't I wouldn't want foreign affairs to be mixed up with economic affairs . . .'

'Some say that they're inextricably mixed up.'

'Like hell they are. I'll tell you what are mixed up together, though. Communist foreign policy and the sort of foreign policy my critics would like. What matters for the majority of people isn't Vietnam or Apartheid or Greek political prisoners but having enough money to manage on and to do a bit more than just manage. Unemployment's a curse, it rots a man alive.'

'It always seems to hit the North-East first,' I said. 'What do you feel about that?'

'Like a bloody Judas,' he said. 'Sometimes I can hardly face the poor devils who voted for me. And sometimes I feel like clearing out of politics altogether. But if I do, who'll care for them?'

I began to like him more and more. And I could see now what attracted Judy Aviemore to him. She certainly wouldn't agree with him about Vietnam or Apartheid, to name only two issues; but to women it's always, no matter how they may twist and turn in the posh Sundays, personal relationships which come first. Glenthorn was absolutely sure of himself, absolutely masculine, which meant that he was strong enough to be gentle.

And he'd be able to keep up with her intellectually, too; bringing up the subject of his leisure activities over coffee, and half-expecting the usual excuses about having no time for anything but the local football team and the occasional thriller and political biography, I was surprised to find that not only did he like pictures and the theatre but that he'd read widely – so widely, in fact, that I abandoned my *viva voce* examination, fearing that he'd read more than I. But before we left the restaurant I inserted Judy Aviemore's name very delicately into the conversation, comparing her detrimentally to Brigid Brophy and Mary McCarthy; he swallowed the bait and, with almost the same kind of passion with which he'd spoken of the unemployed, defended and extolled her at some length and quotably.

I had what I needed. Nothing could be more innocent, indeed in a way more commendable than, for a politician to admire the work of a writer who was, after all, neither pornographic nor trivial. Nothing could be less actionable. And if in the same issue in the gossip column they were both named, along with half-a-dozen others, as guests of the same hostess, that too wasn't actionable. But gradually we were linking the two names or rather pushing them together in a certain way as in the game of spillikins. We would go a step backward for each two forward because the public memory is short, but nevertheless the job was being done.

When I asked the waiter for the bill he said firmly, 'Separate bills, please.'

'It's on me,' I said. 'Or rather on the paper.'

'Sorry,' he said. 'It's one of my rules. It's all right, Frank, don't look so woebegone. Anyone in Fleet Street will tell you, but I expect your editor thought you might as well try. My union gives me a very generous expense allowance just for this purpose. So if I'm ever bought, it won't be just for the price of a lunch. Nye Bevan's union took the same attitude.'

He was the professional politician again and the interview was at an end. I still liked him; as I said goodbye to him I couldn't help momentarily hoping that he or someone near to him would realize what Barbury was trying to do. He was popular in his constituency and in the country, he might even be of Prime Minister calibre if only he weren't so decent, if only he weren't so honest. Or was that his chief strength?

Back at the newspaper I went out of my way to call in Theresa's office, but she wasn't at her desk. Harry O'Toole was there, a proof in his hand, sitting all too casually on the desk lighting his pipe. He'd gone out of his way too, despite the proof. It was the copy boy's job to deliver proofs, not a senior sub-editor's. He looked at me coldly, as if to reprimand me: reprimand, I thought, was something for which his long dark bespectacled face was made-to-measure. The expression was of course jealousy; the way in which he looked at even the pens and yellow copy paper and hand-outs and photos and dress catalogues and the box of powder and lipstick container on her desk was testimony to his being in love with her. The desk was her shrine, the objects that she had touched were both titillating and holy; he was half-sad because she wasn't there and half-glad to wallow in the sensation of his love being absent.

'Theresa's off today,' he said. ''Flu.'

'There's a lot of it about,' I said, and went down to Barbury's office. He was drinking a cup of tea.

'Want some?' he asked.

'No, thanks.'

'Not after lunch at the Ivy, eh? Well, how did you get on? Manage to get him pissed?'

'He only had a glass of hock. Paid for his own lunch too.'

'No harm in trying to corrupt him.'

'That's more or less what *he* said.'

'He isn't a fool. But what did you get out of him?'

'A lot about unemployment. And he thinks trade unions should stick to improving wages and hours and keep out of politics. Some of it's pretty sound, actually. He's rather a nice man.'

'Bugger that for a tale. You don't become the PM's right-hand man through being nice. What about his whore?'

There were times when I didn't like Barbury or my job, and this was one of them. I didn't feel myself to be a professional man as I stood there before his walnut desk, my hand on the drinks cabinet. This was my senior, whose rank entitled him to the desk and the drinks cabinet and the bookcase and the fitted dark grey carpet, and I was his junior who had to answer his questions immediately. I lit a cheroot and sat down.

'I got him to talk about Judy Aviemore's books. He likes them. He likes them very much indeed. When I said she wasn't up to much he defended her very warmly indeed. He said that she knows more about love than any other living writer. He said she makes the others seem like sniggering adolescents. And also that in all her work there was truth, and tenderness, and an absolutely aching sense of compassion . . .'

'You sure you didn't make this up?' Barbury asked.

'I'll resign if you say that to me again.' I was surprised to hear myself saying this quite calmly; but he never would have respected me if I'd let it go.

'All right, all right, don't be so bloody touchy. I was only joking. It's only that it sounded too literate for a Labour politician . . . Is there any more?'

I told him. When I'd finished he got up, came round to me and shook my hand. Then he unlocked the drinks cupboard, half the space of which was occupied by a refrigerator. 'Scotch, gin, vodka, rum?'

'Scotch on the rocks.'

'I'll join you in that,' he said. I realized that he was completing his apology, and felt curiously touched.

'To think that I ever grumbled about having graduates on the staff . . . If you didn't have that English degree, you wouldn't have known what were the right questions to draw him out, would you? Well, three cheers for culture. We've got sex – same thing as love, after all – Glenthorn, and Judy Aviemore all mixed up together. Blended creamily and smoothly and in the best of taste.'

'Will you put it in tomorrow?'

'It's a question of space. We're a bit tight just now . . . still, a short piece, you could concentrate on the literary stuff and never mind the guff about unemployment. The public's bored with unemployment and I've no desire to build up the image of David Glenthorn the Poor Man's Friend, in any case. But I'll see . . . Bring me back about seven hundred words as soon as you can, will you?' He drained his whisky suddenly; I drained mine and the matter was settled; he turned back to the papers on his desk without a word.

I finished the piece within an hour, concentrating on the literary side of the interview with a few words about Glenthorn's university being the public library and the WEA class; if he'd only been forty-three instead of fifty-three, I said, he'd have almost certainly gone to a university and then what would he have been? Smoother, cooler, more mature perhaps, but perhaps with less fire in the belly, less of that understanding of the problems of ordinary people which is only gained through experience... But when I'd finished it I didn't take it straight to Barbury. If it became too firmly registered in his brain that I was a quick writer, I'd be turned into a sort of Stakhanovite with no extra roubles or vodka. The time to show him how quickly I could write would be a time of emergency; if I then wrote at my normal speed he'd imagine that I was putting on an extra spurt of effort especially for him.

I went up to Theresa's office again where Georgina Axmouth was as usual poring over a dummy page. Her glasses had slipped off the bridge of her nose, her hair was rumpled, but she didn't nevertheless look completely unattractive.

'I hear Theresa has 'flu,' I said casually.

Georgina laughed. 'It does sometimes go under that name,' she said.

'Your meaning escapes me.'

'When a girl begins to look extremely worried and easily flies off the handle and she hasn't even an engagement ring, I always know what's the matter with her.' She took off her glasses and rubbed her eyes; without them her eyes were revealed as strained and defenceless and peering, but her face was a woman's. 'She's a nice kid,' she said. 'Good at her job too. Frank, you're a selfish pig.'

'When gentlefolk meet compliments fly,' I said.

'Harry O'Toole now is worth ten of you, I never tire of

telling her. Apart from anything else, Frank, you've the sort of good looks that don't wear well —'

'You've noticed, then?' To my horror, I was flirting with her, aware for the first time that she was sexually attracted to me, and that she despised herself for it.

'That's part of my job. You'll get very fat, Frank, if you don't take care, and you'll wheeze going up steps, and your skin's the kind that soon turns red and blotchy. You're rather flushed now. Have you been lunching?'

'The Ivy,' I said with a certain triumph.

'Oh, my, we are going up in the world. It wouldn't be David Glenthorn you were lunching with, would it?'

'It seems superfluous for you to ask. Is he a friend of yours, then?'

'As a matter of fact he is. Quite genuinely. A friend of my husband's too.'

I raised my eyebrows. 'I didn't know you were a lefty.'

'I hate that bloody expression!' She rose as if to deliver the *coup de grâce*. 'It's a real McCarthyite term, a real smear term.'

I smiled. The more I smiled, the calmer I kept, the more I would annoy her. 'Prog then. Short for progressive. I didn't know you were a prog.'

'Some of us,' she said, 'care about other people. Some of us care about social justice. Some of us have to be in the rat-race because we've got to live and it's the only way we know how to make a living, but that doesn't mean we like it.' There was a slightly stagey throb in her voice which was beginning to embarrass me, but I was at the same time noting that her skin and teeth were good and her breasts firmer and more precise than I had ever noticed.

'We'll have a drink at opening-time,' I said, 'and you can tell me more. Maybe I ought to be reformed.'

It was becoming automatic; as soon as I met a woman who was even remotely bedworthy I set up shop, displayed all my goods to the best advantage. I didn't really want her, quite apart from her being married; but I had to prove to myself that I could have her.

'I'm going straight home,' she said. 'To my neat little house in Blackheath.'

'It'll still be there if you have a drink on the way,' I said. 'You see, I never had a chance. My father was a navvy who beat me every time he was drunk, which was every night. My poor old mother was sent out on the streets to earn his beer money. And I delivered newspapers and scrubbed the floors and made the beds and cooked the meals. Then he sent me out stealing. And it was reformatory after reformatory, and then prison. Don't blame me because I'm a rotten sod. Blame society. You are all guilty . . .'

She giggled. 'I don't take it back. You're still a rotten sod.'

'Then help me. Show you care. Have a drink with me at El Vino's. Or the Savoy if you like.'

'Some other time.' She put back her spectacles. 'Now bugger off. I'm busy.'

I smiled at her again and sauntered out, feeling her eyes on my back.

But at half-past five, as I was on the verge of going into the Cock, the reaction came. I was suddenly used up, empty, the traffic was too much for me, there were too many people hurrying past. I was only a body, a corruptible body, I was tired of putting food and drink into that body, I was tired of using my brain in order to get sexual satisfaction or the promise of sexual satisfaction. *Birth,* copulation, *and death – That's all, that's all, that's all;* the words which when I had first read them seemed so flat and prosaic now were a sonorous condemnation. But where was the birth, where was the new life?

I remembered that at St Cecilia and Anselm's there was

Mass at six o'clock, and turned and walked into Kingsway, my least favourite thoroughfare with its atmosphere of office ledgers and files and loose-leaf books and paper-clips – dry, clean, orderly, respectable, watching the clock from nine to half-past five.

It was very cold and raw; the cold was of the sort which depressed rather than stimulated, which made the nose run rather than the cheeks glow. I had put on that day for the first time that year my light overcoat; when I left the office it pushed away the cold easily but after five minutes began to let it in. It was dark by then, but the shop windows had little to show in this district. *Always winter and never Christmas;* but the world I was walking through had been put under an evil spell not by a beautiful young White Witch but by an ugly old Grey Witch, a reasonable and sensible witch with a certificate for shorthand-typing and money in the bank.

Help was near. I was going to the one place where the witch couldn't touch me, where I would neither be allowed to forget that my body was corruptible nor that my soul was immortal, where I would be with other people and yet not in competition with them, where I would be alone and yet not lonely, where I could be at home and safe. I walked faster and faster, nearly running; if the witch caught me, the commuters hurrying home wouldn't stop to help me. Or if they did stop because of the blood and screams they'd only stand there watching, their eyes glistening and their mouths wide open.

Inside the church I began to believe that I was happy. I didn't even touch the edge of a spiritual experience. And I couldn't know whether anyone else there – the rather smelly old man in a dirty raincoat fingering his rosary on my left, the middle-aged woman in a fur coat on my right, for instance – were actually breaking through the barriers of the flesh, knowing God face to face. But if only one person in the whole congregation achieved that, then everything I lived for was worthless, I was squandering the time that would not come again.

When I came out of the church I saw Harry O'Toole. I wasn't exactly uplifted, I had only the vaguest idea of changing my life, but I was more glad to see him than I would have been normally.

'Come for a drink,' I said.

He gave me a rather resentful look. 'Sorry, I must get home. I've had rather a lot of late nights recently —'

'You miserable sod,' I said, 'you can have what is termed a stirrup cup. I'm going home myself for the same reason.'

'I live pretty far out,' he said. 'The trains . . .'

'Will get you home eventually,' I said. 'If you miss one, you can catch the next.' I could see that he was a real commuter, a timetable expert, one who could discuss the virtues or defects of the Southern Region service for hours on end.

'I phoned Theresa,' he said suddenly as we walked in the direction of the Aldwych. 'But there wasn't any reply.' He looked at me reproachfully.

'Perhaps she's gone home.' He was wearing a black Homburg which put ten years on his age, and his overcoat seemed of blanket thickness and was of an unfashionable length. He had a woollen scarf on too, and as we walked along he put on a pair of woollen gloves. I knew without him telling me that he lived with his parents.

'I'm delighted to see you took your gloves off in Mass. My mother always told me that only murderers wore gloves in Church. Some pretty startling congregations she must have known . . .'

He gave a perfunctory snicker and then after we'd walked in silence for a few hundred yards said, 'You don't have Theresa's home number, do you?'

'I've got it somewhere,' I said. 'We'll go in the Waldorf, it's on your way.'

In the warm Edwardian opulence of the Waldorf bar I began to feel better. Harry O'Toole, on the other hand, seemed strangely nervous.

'Theresa's a wonderful girl,' he said.

'I think you're right. She has a tendency to be bossy, though.' I began to mull over Georgina Axmouth's words. Theresa was a good Catholic but she'd been out and about in the wicked world a long time; long enough to know where she could quickly and safely rid herself of her present embarrassment. If she had said outright she intended to have an abortion, I would have gone to any lengths to prevent it. But if I didn't know about it, then the sin would be hers. I was, in short, washing my hands of her without even having the guts to call out loudly for the bowl and the water. I have no excuse for myself, except that I didn't want to get married and that I hankered desperately after the new world of Shalott House.

'If you'll forgive me saying so, you completely misread her character,' I heard Harry say.

'Do I?' I took a large gulp of Guinness. Yes, after the wine and the whisky it did me good. I could swig it with no fuss and no connoisseurship simply for the effect it had upon me.

'She has very firm beliefs. And of course she's very good at her job. I don't mind telling you, I'm very fond of her.' He looked at me apprehensively.

'Why not? Here's her home phone number and address.' I wrote the address and phone number on an envelope and passed it to him. He put it carefully in his wallet. The wallet was pigskin with gold corners and as he opened it I had a glimpse of its neat interior with all the items in the correct compartments.

'Do you mind me asking for the number?'

'If I did, I wouldn't give it to you. Besides, there are such things as directories. Come to that, the office would give you the number.'

'I don't like all the girls knowing my business.' He blushed, which went rather oddly with his blue-black jowls and dark skin, making him appear murderously angry but with the brown eyes still mild and worried. He was a bit of a Herbert, but he was thoroughly decent; I even envied his simplicity.

'You're in love with her, aren't you?' I asked.

'How did you know?'

'It's not very difficult.'

He brought out a pipe and tobacco pouch and made a great show of fiddling with them. 'Are you serious about her?' he asked.

I hesitated. 'Harry, let me put it this way. She'll choose, not us. May the best man win. Why don't you send her some flowers?'

'I'll have to find out where she is first.'

'If she has the 'flu I don't think she'll have gone very far. I'd try her flat again first. She might have been asleep.'

'I rang for a long time.'

'There are such things as earplugs.'

'Poor kid,' he said. 'It must be awful being ill away from home.'

'I'd ring again if I were you,' I said. 'Her flat-mates should be home by now.' I was growing impatient with him; it was true that he was thoroughly decent, but he also seemed to be thoroughly ineffectual.

'I'll do that,' he said with an air of surprise at his own boldness. 'Thank you, Frank.' He shook my hand vigorously and hurried out leaving his Guinness only half-finished.

I sat there for about twenty minutes and had another Guinness, this time more slowly. If Theresa was as intelligent as I gave her credit for here was her escape route. Harry O'Toole would always be able to support her, and there was no doubt about him making her a good husband. And here was the escape route for me. I could let Harry take over, let the best man win. And if he had phoned before me, if he sent flowers and sympathy and I made no attempt whatever to get in touch with her, he would have a head start.

She was too bossy, she was too demanding, she'd bustle about my life dusting every nook and cranny, lifting all the carpets to sweep out all the dust, replacing my comfortably shabby sensualities with the correct and upright moral attitudes; she was, in fact, altogether too good for me.

I took out a packet of cheroots and pulled out a sheet of Debby's writing paper which she must have given me after I'd spent the night with her. She probably wouldn't be in, but there was no harm in trying. I phoned from the lobby; to my delight the rather squeaky little-girl's voice answered me.

'Frank! How fabulous! Where are you, dear heart?'

'The Waldorf. I wondered if you were free for dinner.'

'You lucky thing, I am. The bastard who was giving me dinner stood me up, and I shall sodding well ring him and tell him I'm going out with someone much nicer. Where will you take me?'

Chez Victor's, what with champagne and aperitifs and brandy-and-Benedictine and crêpes suzettes, had cost me the best part of nine pounds, it was time to economise.

'I thought we could go Chinese,' I said.

'Oh, you *are* a *sweetie*. That's just what I fancied. The outstanding and unparalleled bastard who stood me up loves Spanish food and it doesn't love me. I'll see you in about an hour, dear heart. The Lotus House. Au 'voir, angel.'

She had chosen what was among the most expensive Chinese restaurants in London and chosen in such a way that I had no option but to phone and make the booking. It struck me as I left the hotel and walked out into the Aldwych that it was a typical whore's trick. But then, I reflected, who was I to grumble about that? Hadn't she told me, within five minutes of our first meeting, that she was a whore?

And wasn't the price of a good dinner remarkably cheap for a night with a clean and pretty and willing girl?

And later in the bedroom of her flat off the Cromwell Road I acknowledged that it would have been cheap at double the price. Debby's great gift was that for her the sexual act was a physical enjoyment like any other; she didn't attempt to spice it with a sense of sin, nor did she have it, as it were, administered to her for its therapeutic value. And she was always happy, not laughing to hide the tears but laughing because she found everything and every-one funny.

'Dear heart,' she said as I lay beside her in her enormous four-poster bed, 'would you like a ciggie? Ciggies are all I've got.'

'They'll do,' I said. The cigarettes which she fished out of her handbag on the bedside table were squashed flat and tasted of powder.

'This is nice,' she said. 'You go on for quite a long time, don't you?'

'Did I when I was here last?'

She laughed. 'You maintained your honour, dear heart. But only just. Honestly, you were pissed out of your mind. You wanted me to pray with you.'

'Did you?' It was very warm in the big bedroom, all four bars of the big electric fire switched on. The red glow of the fire was just enough to make her hair into genuine new-minted gold.

'Of course. It's what they call a *frisson*. A new kick.'

'I'll write an article about you. Restless, discontented, always searching for a fresh sensation – what does the future hold for Debby?'

'I wish you would,' she said. 'Then the bastard who stood me up tonight would value me more highly. He'd love to feel that he has a notoriously wicked young woman for his mistress.'

'Who is he?' The floor of the bedroom was strewn with clothes – underwear, dresses, skirts, blouses, in neat piles or untidy heaps. The two wardrobes, the dressing-table and the chest-of-drawers were in matching white and gilt, with glass tops. The brushes and hand mirror on the dressing-table were gold-backed, and there was scarcely room for all the bottles of perfume and powder and hand lotion and hair-spray and, lonely in its brown utility, a large bottle of Milton. There was a white-painted bookcase full of new books; at least a dozen of these had found their way on to the floor.

'He's very rich,' she said. 'Do you know, I've never found a rich man who wasn't at bottom terribly sweet? But he can be *so* gloomy. He takes all kinds of pills, and he's always going on special diets. His name's Amroth, actually. He has a terrible inferiority complex because he isn't quite a millionaire. So his brother's going to make him a millionaire.'

'That's nice.'

'Yes, it is. Because though his brother's a millionaire, he doesn't really agree with him. About politics, I mean. His brother's Left, like that sweet old Mislingford, and R.A.'s very right-wing. I'm sure you'd like him.'

'You must introduce me.'

'Oh, I'm sure you'd get on together famously. R.A.'s very clever. He worries a lot about the country.'

'So do I.' I allowed myself to indulge in a political fantasy. The details weren't quite clear, but always resolved themselves in a cheering mob carrying me shoulder-high to Buckingham Palace. My eyes began to close.

'Do you want a drink?'

'A little one.'

She jumped out of bed and into a pair of black high-heeled shoes; as I watched her naked figure, slim but not with the skinniness of the professional model, disappear,

I breathed in the smell of the bedroom – tobacco, scent, clean linen, sex – in a haze of contentment. I moved over to her side of the bed and felt the warmth of her imprint, stretching on it like a cat. There would be no talk of shame, no need to tell lies about love. That would be the attraction for Amroth, who presumably would have paid for it all. That – and as I remembered now, he was in his late forties – the ego-enhancing pleasure of being seen with her. And her untidiness, her vast frivolous carelessness, would be another attraction; here he could, so to speak, let down his hair. Everything was permissible in this bedroom.

She reappeared with a bottle of Black and White and two glasses on a tray. We sat up in bed drinking and talking or rather she talked and I listened. It was a flow of soothing prattle – she lay in bed until noon, she shopped mainly at Harrods, she used to hunt, but she couldn't bear what happened to the poor fox, she loved to eat but not sweet things any more, she was pestering R.A. to buy her a Mini and she was going to have a psychedelic paint job done on it – she lived by her body, for her body, through her body, completely adjusted to the world of the senses, stroking each moment with whimpers of delight like a new mink coat.

Then she stopped and smiled. 'I believe there's a hubbub in the plaza, darling. Yes there is, there truly is . . .'

I almost screamed as the soft, apparently boneless hand touched me.

'Oh Christ. Wonderful. Wonderful.'

'We can't let it go to waste. Can we? Can we? Can we?' Her voice was rising higher and higher.

seven

Difficult though it may be to believe, I didn't make any attempt to see Debby again. That night had been too good to risk being disappointed by a repetition. And it had also been too expensive. I had a notion that she was genuinely the sort of girl – more frequently encountered than is generally supposed – for whom men ruin themselves. She wasn't, I think, deliberately a *femme fatale*, a sort of Kali the Destroyer with men's skulls round her neck; but I sensed the presence of danger.

And after her any other woman would have been an anti-climax. So for the next three weeks I lived in a state of surprisingly contented celibacy. I actually started work on my London book and did a great deal of walking round the London streets, discovering for the first time the difference between an aimless wandering and a purposeful itinerary. I still have the notes somewhere with an all too optimistic timetable attached.

I made no attempt to get into touch with Theresa either. If what I suspected was true, I wanted no part of it. And I couldn't bear seeing her if she were ill; I was afraid that a sense of pity might lead me into the very entanglement I desperately wanted to avoid, and cut me off from Shalott House for ever.

It was the day before I moved into Shalott House that she finally returned to the office. I came back to the office after a morning interviewing a survivor of a train crash; I was extremely good at this sort of thing, but the better I got the more I hated it. I found myself unaccountably delighted to see Theresa; she looked no different from when we'd last met, except perhaps a shade rosier and plumper.

'Come and have a bite,' I said. 'I've had an awful morning.'

'I won't have the time. I've a *mountain* of work to catch up with.'

'A drink, then.'

She looked away from me at the papers on her desk. 'No, Frank.'

'Come on, cheer me up. This bloody woman this morning nearly broke my heart. She pulled a little boy out of the wreckage and he died on her.' As I spoke, I felt the tears coming. She looked up.

'I didn't know you had a heart to break.'

'Please yourself.' I turned.

'Just a quick one, then.'

We went into Poppins. I had a glass of white wine and she had a gin-and-tonic. She looked at the wine and her mouth twisted but she made no comment. We sat for a moment in an awkward silence. I cleared my throat.

'Are you better then, love?'

'You don't really care whether I'm better or not. You've never taken the trouble even to phone.'

'Under the circumstances —' My favourite part of the pub was the top at the Fleet Street end; we were sitting in the far corner at the bottom for privacy, with the effect that I felt we were artificially isolated and everyone's attention was focused upon us.

'Under what circumstances?'

Her lips drew themselves inwards.

'You know damned well. I felt you might want to be – alone. You'd be too ill, or not looking your best —' I floundered on like this for a full five minutes longer, hardly knowing what I was saying.

'I'm beginning to get your drift,' she said. 'No, I've not been having an abortion. Do you hear that?' She raised her voice. 'I've not been jumping off kitchen tables or drinking gin in a hot bath, or drinking poison, and I've only used my knitting needles for knitting. Nor have I been to an exclusive nursing home to have my appendix out. I've been at my own home for nearly the whole of the last three weeks and I won't tell you what's been wrong with me but it absolutely hasn't had any connection with murdering unborn babies. But it does have some connection with me thinking I was pregnant.'

'I'm sorry, honey, I really am.'

'Don't be sorry, Frank, it isn't you. Some people have no more sense of guilt than the beasts of the field, and you're one of them. Besides, you don't need to marry me now. Isn't that nice? You're absolutely free. That's just as good as me having an abortion, isn't it? You can keep on poking that little tart you were seen with in the Lotus House. You see, Frank, London's a small place. One of my staff saw you there. Not that you'd have noticed her. You don't notice people very much, unless it's in the line of duty or you think you can get something out of them. Well, let me tell you something about dear little Debby. She's a high-grade trollop. She's been the other woman in two divorce cases and she was damned lucky not to be mixed up in something bigger, much bigger than the Profumo case, last year. Or maybe she wouldn't have thought herself lucky. Maybe it would have increased her market value. These creatures have their own standards.'

I rather admired Theresa at that moment. Her face was flushed but her voice steady and she spoke with extraordinary fluency. She knew what was right and what was wrong; and I was relieved, even delighted, that she hadn't had an abortion. I would even have been relieved if she'd been in the position where she needed one and hadn't had one. And I knew that even now if I told her all this, if I told her exactly what I felt, then everything would be as it was before, but better. Then I thought about Shalott House and felt a positive hunger for what it represented.

'You're not exactly full of Christian charity,' I said mildly.

'Christian charity doesn't mean toleration of sin,' she said. 'You should know better than that.'

'She's as God made her,' I said. 'She may well have her own sorrows.'

'Go on, feel sorry for her. You did sleep with her, didn't you?'

'Why should I tell you a lie?'

'I wouldn't want to touch you with a barge-pole then. Not after her. But that's OK with you, isn't it? You needn't marry me, you needn't come down to earth and live as ordinary people do, you can go ahead and move to Hampstead with your double-doored cousin and I hope you have lots of affairs with the bloody old scrubbers who infest the bloody old brothel he calls his home and I hope they spend all your money and break your heart, that is if you've got one.'

'Double-doored? Adam isn't double-doored. My God, has it reached the stage where one can't be friendly with one's own sex? I might as well accuse you —'

'All right.' Her voice was becoming more and more tired. 'But for all that, he's very thick with Simon Cothill. You told me so yourself.'

'He's doing a PR job for him or persuading him that he needs one done. For heaven's sake, Theresa, don't lash about so wildly.' It was that fatigue in her voice and in her face that I couldn't bear; and now that I knew she wasn't pregnant there was no reason why we shouldn't see each other from time to time. (Did I work it out as coldly as all that, I now ask myself incredulously.)

'Look, let's have dinner tonight. Chez Victor's again if you like. You know I'm very fond of you —'

'No. I'm going out with Harry O'Toole. Harry isn't as clever as you, Frank, and no doubt he never will be. And he's not as good-looking. But he sent me flowers and he came to see me and he wrote to me. He's kind and he's decent.'

'I'm sure he is.' Although I'd been quite gaily prepared to hand her over to Harry, it was a different proposition when it came to the point, at Poppins in cold daylight, of having her prefer him to me.

'You're sneering. It's written all over your face. Strangely enough, he thinks you're bloody wonderful. Your copy doesn't cut easy and you're a good Catholic too. That's because he caught you going to Mass one evening when it wasn't a Holyday of Obligation. I must admit that it surprised me. I always had the impression that you were strictly a Sunday Catholic. Couldn't you bear yourself, or what?'

'That's my business.'

'No, it's God's. That's just where you're mistaken.' She looked at her enormous wrist watch with the Union Jack face. 'I'm going back now. You needn't get up.'

'Don't be silly,' I said. I felt that when she left some sort of certainty would leave my life. I was sure I didn't want to marry her; I was equally sure that she possessed something which I desperately needed.

She sat down again. 'Perhaps I could have persuaded you to marry me. If only I could have told you a few lies . . .'

'You wouldn't do that.'

'You don't know much about women. Or about journalism either. Don't worry; you'll learn a lot more about lying on the lousy rag you're working for now.'

'You work for it too.'

'Not on your side. Not on the smear side.'

'We're both against the bloody Government, aren't we? Don't you believe that you fight to win?'

'Not in that way. I've warned you before, Frank, because I know you're a good journalist, and it really isn't journalism that you're doing now. I'm looking for another job, so it doesn't matter to me.'

'Another job? The Mirror? The Express —'

'Women's magazines or maybe TV.'

'That's all right, is it? Nice and clean?'

'It's different and you know it is. Anyway, there's no future in it, is there? I mean for us. Thanks for the drink, Frank. No, this time I'm really going.'

I didn't watch her go out but bought another glass of white wine and sat by myself for a moment brooding before moving to the other end of the bar in search of company. Now that it was all over I had never found her so attractive. She was honest and she was tough and no-one, least of all myself, would ever be able to use her. Perhaps it was simply that she was too good for me, that I could never live up to her standards. But most of all, I felt, with a comfortably wistful sadness, it was a question of her being the right person met at the wrong time.

As I left my seat two young men entered. They were laughing a great deal and though not exactly hand-in-hand gave the impression that they'd like to be. One was Carlos in a grey nylon fur topcoat and a grey astrakhan cap; the other, with a platinum blonde *bouffant* hairdo and a long Capone style blue overcoat and a broad white tie and navy blue shirt, I hadn't seen before. I noticed them only because they weren't the kind of customers one expected to see in Poppins. I suppose that was the reason for their choosing it.

Carlos's heavy-lidded eyes flickered in my direction and he said, 'Hi, Frankie boy.'

'Hi, Chuck,' I said, having a notion that he liked that variation of his name as little as I liked Frankie. But I didn't stay to chat with him; apart from disliking him I had no taste for being seen in the company of queers, particularly in a Fleet Street pub.

I thought nothing more about the encounter, though I mentioned it casually to Adam some time after. Yet it was another working part of my future that was fabricated at that moment. Whatever I did at that period, whatever happened to me, no matter how trivial, *counted*. And I never knew what the machines all round me were making, or to put it in another way, I was too stupid to realize that I was walking blind through a minefield, laying and detonating mines almost simultaneously.

eight

For the next day I moved into Shalott House. I ceased to think about my future. I imagined that I was already there. A new sort of comfort began, based on old-fashioned but efficient central heating and constant hot water. This is more important than most people suppose; I started thinking in a new way.

It wasn't that I'd not bathed or, indeed, been especially uncomfortable at the World's End flat. But the chilly little shower compartment and the shilling-in-the-slot gas fire were a far cry from the arrangements at Shalott House. The bathroom there was huge and almost stiflingly warm, and full of expensive colognes and talcs and bath salts and, when I moved in, several jars of a French bath oil which Adam's firm was helping to push, retailing at about five pounds for half-a-pint with a smell that was half herbal, half medicinal. The flat itself was always spotless and warm; Adam had the knack of getting the most out of not only the furnace in the basement but the menials (as he described them) who came to clean the place and do the odd jobs around it twice weekly, whenever, he would say disgustedly, the bastards weren't being ill.

'The difference between us and the working classes,' he

said to me one evening when we'd both been working late and weren't for once going anywhere, 'is precisely what the middle-classes have always said. They're always being ill and they enjoy being ill. It's the only time that they feel important. And, trite though it may be, they smell. Do you know why I never see any of my poor relations? They smell like polecats, that's why. Jesus, at my mother's funeral I was hard put to it not to spew. Even bloody foreigners aren't so bad, at least they wash their feet and private parts. But I don't think my Uncle Mick, for instance, ever has a bath, but literally. You can smell the old sod before you see him coming. That's why I stopped going to St Chad's when I came home from Oxford. The smell of the faithful put me off my prayers. St Felicity's now, wasn't so bad because it was a middle-class parish. In fact, some of the women there put me off my prayers in a different way. They smelled too nice.'

'You're an impious old bugger,' I said. 'You should accept these minor mortifications for the good of your soul.'

'Never mind my soul,' he said. 'The very first thing to remember, no matter how obvious it may seem, is that what marks one off from the peasantry is that one doesn't stink. It doesn't of course matter very much sexually, because women aren't over-fastidious. But the chaps you do business with care very much. They hate you anyway, because you're going to take some of their money off them. But they'll hate you still more if they have to put their handkerchiefs to their noses when you come into the office. You've got to be well-dressed, that goes without saying. Clean shirt, not second-day shirt, good suit, good shoes, good watch. Or else you look as if you need money, and naturally they won't want to do business with you. You'll only get any of their money out of them if you look as if you don't need it. But above all you've got to be clean. And we've got to be doubly clean because we went to a grammar school. Sometimes – because what school you went to is the first thing that interests the silly sods – you can see the customer sniffing away. And that's another thing. Either don't use cologne and all the rest of it or use stuff that you can only get at Floris or Trumpers or Harrods. And wear a different suit and tie every day. Hell, you can afford it. If you can't now, you'll never be able to . . .'

To a certain extent, he was telling me only what I knew already. It was all old stuff, a gallimaufry of pre-war middle-class attitudes with psychedelic paintwork. But I always liked to hear him, to be reminded of how far we'd come, how much we had that other men in our age group would sell their immortal souls for. I expect too that the ties of blood and religion counted for something; like me, Adam could no more have changed his religion than changed his ancestry. 'We need it more than those Confraternity types,' he'd say. 'The Church is for sinners just as much as for saints. And chaps like us, who don't believe in change, do far more for the Church than a thousand bloody progs like Pope John. Not that the new Pope's any better, sucking up to these bloody blacks. And then there's these bastards who have dialogues with Communists. Dialogues with Communists! I know how those end. In a monologue from behind a machine gun . . .' We even one night over a couple of bottles of Burgundy, a perquisite like the French bath oil, invented the Society for the Propagation of Reaction, Arrogance, and Stubborn Prejudice, to be known by the initials RASP. Cardinal Ottidudni was the chaplain, the president was Barry Goldwater, and the executive committee comprised General Franco, Ian Smith, Dr Salazar and Mr Vorster. The slogan, to be used at all times, was Basil's war-cry, *Down with Oxfam*.

This is the sort of *jeu d'esprit* more common to undergraduates than to grown men; but it's one of the reasons why, even now, I can never think of Adam otherwise than with affection – indeed with love. Part at least of Theresa's indictment of him was true – he was selfish, he was hard, he used people for his own ends, he didn't really give a damn for me or for anyone else. But he gave me back, however briefly, something which I thought I'd lost for good, a kind of irreverent high spiritedness. He never used the chilling expression *But seriously*; it was impossible to tell whether he was ever serious or not. It was one of his sharpest weapons in the game that he called Prog-baiting; sooner or later, when he said that there was a great deal to be said in favour of Apartheid, or that he fervently supported inequality of opportunity, the progressive he was baiting would cry, outraged: 'You can't mean that! You're not serious!' And Adam would smile contentedly and assure the Prog that he did and go on to say, looking his victim straight in the eye, that he would pray for him that very night. 'Jesus loves you too,' he would say, 'just as I do.'

I'd never been happier in my life. Yes, there can be now visitations of happiness of a depth and intensity I could never have experienced then. But they have to be paid for in the hard currency of duty. I paid for happiness at Shalott House in the softer currency of time and money; we did exactly as we pleased.

There were a few rules, however. The drawing-room and the kitchen, unless notice was given well in advance, were common property. The girls who visited the flat in a never-ending stream were common property too. And the cost of drink and food for parties was entirely the responsibility of the person giving that party; they were mostly Adam's parties because they were mostly business parties. And I, like any other journalist attending these parties, was supposed to keep my mouth shut about what went on there, unless specifically requested to interview someone. In return, the guests would give information – births, marriages, divorces, new jobs – to me first. I didn't always use this information myself, not being a gossip columnist, but when I didn't do so I would pass it on to someone else at the newspaper. So the parties were business parties for me too, a fact which I'd acknowledge by occasionally bearing the cost of one. And Basil would throw one himself even more occasionally; his guests, surprisingly enough, tended to be far grander than ours. His family was what is called a very old one – decaying in fact, he would himself say, or else he wouldn't have been a mere solicitor – and all his guests seemed at least to have an entry in Burke's.

It all worked out very well. I loved my job, I was advancing my career even in my leisure hours, I had enough money for all my needs, and the invitations kept rolling in. There were periods when the problem was which function to attend, when we could have gone to two different ones each night of the week.

And I began to know London and especially Hampstead, for the first time. It's the cruellest city in the world to be poor and lonely in, the cruellest city in the world for the married on a low income. But for bachelors like ourselves it was perfect, it belonged to us uniquely and completely and intoxicatingly.

Do I regret Shalott House, though, or do I simply regret my own youth? Harry Morgate once said to me in a moment of unusual candour: 'You know, dear boy, one always imagines that sex and boozing become better as one grows older. *They don't.*' I'm nowhere near that stage yet, but I'm at the stage where the domestic fireside gradually becomes more appealing, where one's head isn't quite as hard or one's stomach so cast-iron lined, where one notes girls' telephone numbers but never telephones them. And I can envisage, as I could not at Shalott House, the bald patch and the increasing girth, my children's weddings, my children's children on my knee and Extreme Unction and the Requiem Mass.

It was all as if for the first time when I lived at Shalott House; again and again it occurs to me in these terms. Food, alcohol, sex, travel, the procession of new faces – and at any moment my whole life could have been changed. And there was never anything shabby about our lives; when sometimes I had to go through Soho I'd look at the sad-eyed or stony-faced men outside the pornographic bookshops and strip clubs with a real pity.

I went home to Charbury occasionally, but now it seemed dingy and boring. I had no violent feelings against it, and I was glad to see my parents and sisters, but two days were long enough. Everyone had gone away or got married; there was nothing to do but eat far too much and go for walks on the moors and wait for opening time. Basil went home to Berkshire every other weekend, but to Basil the weekend was an institution, he indulged his country pursuits like hunting and shooting and fishing. To me and everyone in Charbury the weekend was simply a time when one didn't work.

Weekends at Shalott House were a different matter. It was then that I discovered a taste for solitude. (I've been alone in Chertsey since then during rare intervals of grass widowerhood but after a couple of hours the house seems large and empty and the worrying about the safety of one's wife and children begins.) When I was alone there I made for myself a special routine. On the Saturday, I'd lie in bed until ten, breakfast off coffee and a doughnut in a coffee bar, and wander round the shops buying what little I needed. Wandering round the shops, looking at the crowds, always cleaner and brighter and younger and more prosperous in Hampstead than anywhere else, I would be alone and yet not alone, there would be no demands upon me, and yet I could dream of this girl or that girl, white or black or yellow or brown, of possessing this or that house, American ranch-style or Georgian, or ornately Edwardian, of nudging one's way past the Toll House in a Lancia or Rolls or Mercedes, of being a rising politician or business-man or novelist. For I knew that within a five miles radius of Shalott House there lived at least fifty examples of each category. One of the advantages of being a journalist is that one's like the giant Asmodeus who could lift the roofs off houses and peer inside.

And if them, why not me? In fact, I was one of them. I would have a sandwich and a pint for lunch, generally at the Spaniards or Jack Straw's Castle, and sit there until precisely five minutes before closing time in a state which, allowing for the difference on the scale of being between myself and, say, St John of the Cross, was not very far from a direct apprehension of the nature of existence. Three pints would suffice me; the state was too precious to be risked for the sake of any artificial euphoria. Sometimes I'd feel the need to inform someone that I was one of them, that I belonged there, that I didn't live on my tod in any wretched bed-sitter, that I was, in short, a rising young journalist; but I resisted the temptation.

Occasionally I'd meet someone whom I knew, but Hampstead, for all that it was predominantly left-wing and presumably dedicated to the Brotherhood of Man, was no more warm and neighbourly than any other London borough. The kinship I felt for the rising young men around me had nothing to do with friendship and everything to do with the certainty that one day I should do better than any of them.

And in the afternoon I would go down into the centre and visit art galleries and museums. I didn't do this out of any desire to acquire culture, or even to fill in the afternoon; I did it simply because I enjoyed it, working my way through the National Gallery a section at a time, then on to the Tate, and so on. And I have this now to remember too, when once home in Chertsey I can't face travelling into

London again, when I only see pictures and *objets d'art* in reproduction or occasionally at some dealer's party when they are virtually never anything else but the same dreary old fashionable rubbish. Whatever London has to offer I took with both hands; and now in Chertsey it's more and more the paintings in the National Gallery which I remember, particularly the Dutch seventeenth century landscapes. I try to bring them out now before my mind's eye; water, weather, light through water, clouds and ruins and quietness and losing oneself in the best way, ceasing to compete, staring at the same picture for hours at a time. Sometimes now I visit the National Gallery, always in the end drawn to Van Ruysdael's *Pool surrounded by Trees*, but it isn't the same, I have to keep looking at my watch, there's always an appointment to keep or copy to write.

When I was a bachelor I wouldn't leave the gallery or museum until closing time and I would go to the theatre or the cinema, even sometimes to a party. (But I noticed that Adam and Basil always seemed to contrive not to go away for the weekend when there was a party on a Saturday. If they were at Shalott House the whole pattern of the day would change.)

Sundays had a different colour and shape. They were best of all when I worked, returning at about eleven-thirty to find Adam and Basil there.

This is what is strange: I don't remember best the Saturdays when I brought a girl to Shalott House with me, spent the night with her there, and all the morning too, not going to Mass until the evening. I remember best sleeping alone in the flat on a Saturday night, waking up a little frightened in the small hours, brewing myself a pot of tea and saying my prayers again, and drinking the tea in bed whilst reading one of Adam's books. *Doctor Doolittle's Zoo* or *Swallows and Amazons* or *William's Happy Days* or *The Wind in the Willows* – with which the large bookcase in his room

159

was entirely filled. They all had the original covers, the series were all complete; I used to borrow them with a slightly guilty feeling. At that hour, with the place empty, the central heating and the woodwork would make rustling and groaning noises not always the same twice, not always immediately identifiable, and I would have in my mind vague pictures of all the people who had lived there before me. I would not be afraid of death, having said my prayers; what I was afraid of was starting to think, deeply and honestly, about what was not material, about what was – why should I be so shy of saying it? – spiritual. The children's books kept such thoughts away, all the more effectually since the best of them represented to some extent the author's rejection of ordinary life, of hardness and coldness and sensuality. I would fall asleep, warm and snug, rather complacent at my intellectual courage for allowing myself a wallow in childish pleasures, allowing the faceless ghosts to cry unheeded.

And in the morning I would rise late and walk over to St Mary's in Heath Place for eleven o'clock Mass. It's a small church, made smaller by an abundance of pillars inside and a little over-ornate for its size. Its charm for me was its approach up the narrow steps off Heath Row past the small expensive period houses glossy with paint like new toy soldiers. Hampstead is one of the few places in England where one can't feel Sunday in the air, but in the vicinity of St Mary's at least I always could, and was always reassured.

After Mass I would leave St Mary's in the other direction, past the churchyard, and would always have a drink in the Three Horseshoes in Heath Street, the taste of the Eucharist – always to me slightly meaty the second before dissolving – having left my mouth. I would sit there with all the Sunday papers, staring from time to time at the green and gold wallpaper, perfectly contented, then at one o'clock return to Shalott House and grill myself a steak and drink half a bottle of wine with it. After a cup of coffee I would drive down to Fleet Street along half-empty roads into an empty London. Inside the office would at first sight be as busy as an ordinary day; but there would be a holiday feeling, as if everyone were working for diversion rather than for their daily bread. There was in actuality rather less to do and a greater willingness to sneak out for a beer or a coffee; but simply to be there on Sunday used to charge my system with extra adrenalin. It was all needed by eight o'clock when the pace quickened and the big stories always seemed to come in and the whole make-up of the paper had to be altered, the advertisements being the only items to remain constant in size and content. At about half-past ten the paper could be finally put to bed; there was very rarely any need for me to stay past half-past nine, but the longer I stayed the more I learned. Mouth dry with too many cheroots, head aching slightly, I would drive to Shalott House, my spirits always rising when I saw Basil's Renault and Adam's Minibrake parked in the drive and the lights on in the drawing-room.

This was the almost unvarying shape of my Sundays. My whole existence, in fact, seemed to have come as near to complete fulfilment as anyone's can this side of the grave. Then one frosty Sunday night early in the New Year, returning from Fleet Street as usual at about eleven-thirty, I heard a woman's voice from behind the drawing-room door. My first feelings were of slight resentment; I felt too tired to set out the goods in my shop window. I had that day written two articles at Barbury's special request, and my stock of charm was running low. But my interest in women wasn't, and I had no taste either for Basil or Adam taking a woman to bed in the flat and reminding me that all that week for one reason and another I'd been sleeping alone. I straightened my tie, ran my hand over my hair,

and went in to see Angela lolling by the fire in a lavender
tweed trouser suit, Adam and Basil standing over her. She
looked more sunburned than ever and more dashingly
unattainably fashionable; her black hair had been cut even
shorter, and the cut of the suit was, as they say, severely
masculine. She looked no more, even much less, feminine
than a queer like Carlos; there was a second when some
instinct repelled me and then she smiled at me, the round
china-blue eyes opening wide, and I wanted her thin,
narrow-hipped body more than anything else on earth and
I knew that she was coolly and amusedly aware that I
wanted it.

'You remember Angela Guilsfield, Frank,' Adam said.
'We ran across each other at Nordhover Hall, so I gave her
a lift home.' He seemed anxious to explain the innocuous
nature of the encounter; looking at him more closely, his
face seemed strained. Nordhover Hall was a country mansion where from time to time there were held musical
weekends; the Squire wanted to put the whole operation
on a more paying basis and had asked Adam's firm to help.
'Bloody wonderful place, the Hall. Terrific ballroom, good
acoustics for once, fifty acres of parkland. I'll arrange an
interview with the Squire if you like. A nice ride to Sussex,
smashing nosh – he's got a French chef – and apart from
anything else he's a damned interesting chap. Pilot, racing
driver, ex-Colonel of Gurkhas, but really knows about
music —'

'He's an old goat,' Angela said in her high clear voice.
'He kept putting his hand up my skirt all through dinner
last night.'

'I'm sorry about that,' Adam said in a worried voice.

'Don't be,' Angela said. 'I quite enjoyed it.' She left her
armchair and came over to me.

'Why did you never phone me, Frank?'

'You weren't in when I did.'

'Well, I'm back now. God knows why.'

Adam opened a bottle of Vieux Ceps which had to my relief replaced the Spanish burgundy. He seemed to have recovered his composure. 'Is Tangier too hot to hold you, love?'

'Good God, no. I don't know what one has to do to be thrown out of Tangier. That's its chief attraction, frankly. Have you ever been there, Frank?'

'Not yet.' We sat down on the sofa together. Adam looked at us with a strangely complacent smile and remained standing by the liquor cabinet; Basil took the chair that Angela had vacated and closed his eyes.

'I'll take you sometime,' she said. 'Perhaps you can work it with the paper, and I'll go as your secretary. Or I'll do some sketches and you do the commentary.'

'Why not?' I took her hand. 'You're cold.'

'My blood's thin,' she said. 'I can't bear this weather. You're nice and clean, aren't you, honey? Those two over there, now, they're decadent. How do you come to be here?'

'Adam's my cousin.'

'I remember. There is a likeness. You'll either go much further than him or else you'll be nothing. You *watch* a lot, don't you?' She squeezed my hand. 'I'm not sure whether I like that. Adam watches too, but only long enough to make the kill.'

'What kill?' Now she was sitting so as to display the shape of her small breasts.

'Any kind of kill. Mostly business. He was talking business all weekend. When he wasn't talking about it he was thinking about it. Isn't that so, Adam?'

'I have to live,' Adam said.

'One of my buddies in Tangier used to be in the Gestapo. A very sweet little man. He always says that.'

'Angela is trying to needle Adam,' Adam said.

'I don't think I could.' She squeezed my hand again.

'Now I could with your cousin. He has a full set of emotions, all in working order.' She looked at me like a child with a new toy. 'Haven't you, Frank?'

'You'll have to find out.' But she was still looking at Adam. I felt that I was somehow being made a fool of, that he and she were playing a complicated adult game and I was a kind of shuttlecock between them.

'What have you been doing today, Frank?' It was as if she'd asked me if I'd had a nice day at nursery school.

'Working. At the newspaper. It's just been put to bed.'

'You like that, don't you? Adam says you're a real old-fashioned romantic newspaperman. Is that true?'

'I expect it is. Does it matter as long as I enjoy it?'

'All of it?' She was looking at Adam again, her eyes narrowing. Basil yawned. 'Excuse me, my dear friends. I must retire.' He left abruptly, a small dapper figure in thornproof tweeds and brogues which gave him an air of masquerade.

'You've embarrassed him,' Adam said.

'Nonsense. He's simply tired. You're always looking for explanations of the most commonplace —'

The doorbell rang loudly again and again.

'Bloody old Simon, no doubt,' Adam said. 'Can't sleep for thinking of his disgusting sins.'

'I'll answer it,' I said, glad of the excuse to disentangle my hand from Angela's, which was surprisingly strong and now beginning to hurt.

The girl who stood with a hand against the wall was Wendy, whom I'd last seen in the Salisbury in September.

'Adam?' she said thickly. 'You're not Adam. Where's Adam?'

'Come in.' I took her arm; her red hair was dishevelled and dirty, she smelled of vomit, her blouse was unbuttoned to the waist, and there was a deep cut on her left cheekbone.

She slumped down into the armchair by the fire. 'My

164

lovely old Adam,' she said. 'My lovely old swine of an Adam. How well you look, Adam.'

'You look bloody awful. I told you not to come here.' I had never heard his voice sound so ugly.

'But I've come just the same.' She started to cry, then her eyes focused on Angela. 'Bloody Angela. Bloody bitch Angela. Angela in the beginning and Angela in the rotten end.'

'We ran across each other purely by chance,' Adam said. 'You're no-one to talk, are you?'

'Give me a drink, you bastard.'

He poured a little brandy into a glass and deluged it with soda.

'That's not a drink.' She began to laugh. 'Dear old Angela, dear old buddy and more than buddy Angela.'

'You'd better have some coffee,' Angela said. She was cool and sober, a faint smile on her face. 'You know, Wendy, you're absolutely wrong about Adam and me. He's telling the truth. It was purely by chance we met. For the second time in four years.'

'Second time in a pig's arse. Frank, listen. Frank, that's your name, isn't it? Well, listen to me, Frank. These two are absolutely the last word in rottenness. They're un – believable. Un – believable. I thought I was wild until I met them. But they're the wild ones. The wild wild wild ones.'

'You really had better let me clean you up,' Angela said.

'Get away from me, you dirty bitch. Frank, you look like – like a human being. Take me home. I can't stand the smell in here.'

I half rose.

'No, Frank,' Angela said. 'Wendy's going soon when she's had some coffee and washed her face. She's going to have that face washed now. It's a really nasty cut.'

She took Wendy by the hand; to my surprise, she followed her meekly, as if her outburst had never taken place.

'Sorry about that,' Adam said. 'I'm afraid poor old Wendy's rapidly becoming a real alcoholic. But Angela will cope. Bloody good girl, old Angela.' He lowered his voice. 'It's interesting in a way, isn't it? I mean, Wendy's barely thirty, every advantage, et cetera. One husband already written off, another husband soon to be written off – or to write her off – and about her only hope is her career. If she keeps on knocking back the hard stuff, there won't be any career, either.'

'No children?'

'These people don't go in for children, Frank. They're frightened of spoiling their figures and having to cut down on their social life. That was one of the bones of contention between us – I mean, I don't see any point in being married if you don't have any children. Christ, what a decadent country this is, all the middle-classes frightened to breed, and even the working-classes getting the Pill and abortions on the National Health. There'll be no-one breeding soon but the niggers and the Pakistanis, and who the hell will close the dollar gap then?'

I held back a yawn. 'You seem to be terribly worked up about our black brothers. You ought to go in for politics.'

'Maybe I will, but not until the Tories have had a thorough house-cleaning. We have a Tory M.P. do business with us sometimes. He's as thorough-going a lefty as anyone in the Labour Party – you know, all for prison reform, racial integration, overseas aid, sanctions against Rhodesia, comprehensive schools and all that crap . . .'

I laughed. 'Your starry-eyed idealism is truly inspiring, Mr Keelby. We are grateful to you sir, for your lucid exposition of your aims . . .'

'I expect I do go on a bit,' he said. He looked in the direction of the bathroom. 'Christ, I hope Wendy hasn't passed out. I once had to send the dear old family doctor to her with a stomach pump, and that was when we were engaged and she had, as they say, everything to live for. And she's more or less out with her family now.'

'I think I'd better go to bed.'

'No, no. Angela will take her home. I've had enough. Her coming here is absolutely the last straw.' He rummaged in his pocket and took out two green pills, washing them down with wine. 'Don't look at me like that,' he said. 'They're quite safe, guaranteed non-habit-forming. I only take them when I see Wendy.'

'Is she an old friend of Angela's, then?'

I was mystified by the effect of this innocuous question upon him. He looked first of all uncontrollably angry, then uncontrollably sad. He didn't answer me immediately but seemed to be using all his energy to bring his face back into a state of indifference.

'They were buddies once, as much as women ever are. I think that Angela once dabbled with the idea of acting, then took up this painting lark, and got control of some money and started to travel. You seem quite interested in Angela, don't you?'

'You're not jealous, perhaps?'

'Not of Angela. Our relationship is purely platonic. Makes a nice change.'

When Wendy returned with Angela she seemed to have recovered herself almost miraculously. The cut was seen to be more in the nature of a scratch, her hair was brushed, her face clean, her blouse fastened up, her stockings tight, her mouth properly lipsticked and her face powdered. She sat down primly whilst Angela phoned for a taxi, drinking three cups of black coffee, the cup rattling against the saucer.

'Some people are so shy,' she said after her first cup of coffee. 'Some people do the last thing one would have suspected.' Then she sat silent until the taxi came. Angela too was silent, sipping her coffee, a half-smile on her face. I helped her take Wendy to the taxi, each of us taking an arm. When the cold air outside hit Wendy she gasped and went limp; we half-dragged her to the taxi.

'Phone me tomorrow at ten,' Angela said. 'Neither before nor after. I'll be free all week.' She gave me her telephone number again. 'I've remembered it,' I said. I stood at the top of the steps watching the rear lights of the taxi disappear out of sight between the pine trees bordering the drive. Under the pale moon I saw the lights of London and the huge blackness of the Heath, made huger by the roads which disappeared into it. The air seemed positively to crackle with cold; I breathed in deeply, to find it warm within my lungs. I wondered why it was that all the women I was attracted to and who found me attractive should be not only of the same physical type but of the same disposition, efficient, calm, self-opinionated, masterful if not down-right domineering. One side of me didn't like Angela at all, preferred even poor boozy Wendy because she was human enough to be weak, to make a mess of her life; and the other side, not able to deceive itself because of that view, because of the wonderful cold air and sense of great height, knew very well that I would phone Angela tomorrow at ten o'clock, neither sooner nor later.

Adam was half asleep when I returned to the drawing-room.

'Thought you'd gone off with them,' he said.

'It isn't my day for being gallant. I was just having a breath of air.'

'You're a great one for that, aren't you? When we were kids you used to love it. Bus to Bingley, bus to Dick Hudson's, over the moors to Ilkley, and you'd always stop at the highest point.' He poured me another glass of wine. 'It's funny, you know, you're always supposed to miss that.

The curlew saying *Go back, go back,* and the wind in the heather and all that. I don't miss it, I miss people, and the people I miss most I'm never going to see again anyway.'

'I know.'

'Yes, you do. Not like these sods I meet in the way of business, who've no more imagination or sympathy than their office furniture. Witherslack Inc. and I aren't exactly going to part company, but I'm a bit fed up of doing the lion's share of the work and knowing full well that even if I did it all I wouldn't get any further. Oh, I'd get a new title on the office door, maybe even a new office with a bit more carpet, maybe a thousand more a year, which is only worth five hundred anyway. But the real money only goes to people called Witherslack. And that's what I want. The real money, the capital gain stuff, whilst I'm still young enough to enjoy it.'

'Doesn't Wendy have money?'

'Her parents have. It isn't the same thing. I don't say that no-one ever marries money, mind you, but it doesn't happen very much outside of books. I couldn't have married her anyway. We just weren't cut out for each other. And there was – well, woman trouble. I was young and couldn't understand —'

'I thought you said that you and Angela had a platonic friendship?' I had been adding together all that had been said that evening and remembering particularly Wendy's reaction when she saw Angela.

'You're jumping to conclusions. There's never been anything between me and Angela. I give you my word. Why should I tell you a lie?'

'I don't know why you should. But that's not to say you're telling the truth. Frankly, sometimes you puzzle me. Why do you put up with Wendy?'

'I'm sorry for her. That's all. I wouldn't ever go to bed with her again, if that's what you're thinking. She's too loony now, it might just push her over the edge. And I can't marry a divorced woman, either. But – well, I'm no saint, but I suppose somehow I feel a certain responsibility for the poor bitch.'

'Now you puzzle me more than ever. For once you're practising Christian charity.' And I didn't intend the statement to be ironical.

nine

When I found myself alone in Angela's flat with her I couldn't help, through force of habit, looking around me for signs of her flatmates. It seemed far too large a flat – the drawing-room wasn't much smaller than the one at Shalott House – to be occupied wholly by one person. For, I'd thought to myself throughout the whole evening, so easily arranged over the phone at ten o'clock, neither earlier nor later, there must be some catch somewhere. Sooner or later I'd be sent home, having spent £7 upon her at the Trattoria Terrazza, with a warm thank you and a kiss upon the cheek. And she had very firmly refused to return to Shalott House with me.

I'd been looking forward to that. Yes, Adam had merely told me the truth about their relationship; but for me to parade my conquest under his nose would, I felt instinctively, cause him considerable frustration, would take him down a peg or two. It's one thing to have a platonic friendship with a woman and another to have one's friend go to bed with her. This wouldn't have mattered with any other woman; it did matter with Angela. I didn't mistake her for a vestal virgin – in fact, I knew that she'd have slept with a stranger picked up in the street if her whim had taken her that way – but I was sure that her standards were high.

I had sprawled myself out in one of the biggest armchairs I'd ever seen. The springing was luxurious, the gold brocade covering dully resplendent; the matching sofa was a full four-seater, the green fitted carpet was ankle deep. Everything else in the room – the new mahogany side-board, the pieces of china on the wall shelves, the large glass ashtrays, the walnut cocktail cabinet, the gilt nesting-tables, the ornate black-and-gold clock on the marble mantelpiece – was new, heavy, expensive, but the total effect was somehow drab and impersonal.

Angela came out of the bathroom. 'Don't look round too closely with that trained observer's eye,' she said. 'I've been away for months and however well one treats the menials, they tend to take advantage. Can I give you a drink?'

'A very small brandy.'

She poured me a small measure of Courvoisier and a larger one for herself. The room didn't look in the least untidy; it would perhaps have been more cheerful if it had. The only signs of her occupancy were a white negligée on an armchair in the corner and a big Way In carrier-bag from Harrods.

'It's really my brother's flat,' Angela said. 'He's big business. But he's really American now. Can't stand the climate here. Don't look frightened. He's not the type to descend upon us without notice. Not that it would matter if he did. He only uses the place about four times a year. And there are four bedrooms. And Mummy and Daddy come here once in a blue moon – they're either buried deep in the West Country or gallivanting round the world.'

'The rent must cost the earth.'

'In Montagu Square? You're damn well right it does. But Perry's firm is really American, so that doesn't matter. Perry never did care about money, anyway. He makes so much that he literally doesn't know how to spend it. Not that I know much about him. He went away to school before I was born, and even during the holidays he generally didn't stay at home. Stayed with his friends, as they used to do in the school stories.'

She poured herself another brandy and gestured towards me. I shook my head. 'I have the oddest family, Frank. They scarcely know whether I'm alive or dead. I visit them occasionally and it's all the same to them whether I stay a day or the rest of my life. Papa's terribly open-minded, the E. M. Forster type liberal, you know, but he's somehow missed that bit about connecting. And Mummy's in a permanent trance. Inside the trance I'm sure she's enjoying herself no end, but that's just my surmise. I expect in your family you connect like anything, don't you? Adam told me you had three sisters.'

'I'd have connected more with brothers.'

'Well, naturally. But I mean that you'll all recognise each other as people, you will be a family. You'll be *our* Frank. Oh, you're so lucky, you've no idea.'

'Don't romanticize me,' I said sharply. 'I'm very ordinary.' Though not particularly sensitive about such things, I sensed in Angela the growing sense of patronage, of her stooping down, as it were, to stroke a large and beautiful St Bernard, a being of another order.

'You're not ordinary, my dear. You're very fresh, you've lots of vitality, you could become anything, anything at all. And you've got a career and you work hard at it. Adam told me that too. Now I just waste my time swanning around the world but mostly Tangier because no-one there gives a toss who you are or what you do and now and again I sell a few pictures, which makes me feel useful, one of the world's workers. But I'm just a layabout really.'

'I don't see any of your pictures here.' There were a few pictures – still lifes and landscapes, competent but dull, which appeared as if ordered with the rest of the furniture and fittings, bought unseen.

She smiled. 'How clever of you to know. But I only keep a few here. The rest are at the studio in Notting Hill Gate. I can't stink up my brother's flat with paint and turps, he might come here unexpectedly and then I'd have to get a flat for myself.'

As she talked about her studio she seemed to change. I had a notion that it represented what was real to her as far as anything was real to her; standing there in her green mini-dress, her eyes bright with alcohol, she seemed wilder than I'd thought. I'd been listening to her; I should have concentrated upon looking at her.

'Why Notting Hill?' I asked. 'It isn't you. Why not Chelsea —'

She laughed shrilly.

'How do you know, Frank? On the contrary, I like the place. It's like Tangier, a free port. No-one cares.' She swallowed her brandy. 'Well, what are we waiting for? Don't toy with your brandy, you fool. Come and look at my etchings.'

In her bedroom — my mouth dry now, my breath catching my throat, I could only take in the large new bed with the brass rails and the white silk eiderdown and the big black crucifix with a black Christ over the bed. She pulled off her dress and threw it on the floor. She punched me hard in the belly. 'You're nice now,' she said, 'but you'll have to take a lot of exercise. Else you'll become a mountain of pink wobbling flesh.' She was wearing now only a pair of pink tights; her sharp little breasts seemed to distend as I looked at them. She pushed me away as I moved towards her. 'Tell me what you think of my pictures.'

Stacked against the walls, they were the last sort of work I should have expected; realistic, glossy, almost academic in conception but for the violence of their colour and the faces of the models which, how I could not quite fathom, were subtly distorted. There were two female nudes, one standing, one lying down; the pudenda were meticulously detailed; two male nudes and – by now I was breathing painfully hard – a naked man and a naked woman by a bed, obviously about to make love. And lastly there were two naked girls, their bodies intertwined. When it came to these three pictures I abandoned the technical terms. They weren't pornographic but there wasn't in their composition one iota of idealism.

'That's pure pastiche,' she said. 'Or impure pastiche. Courbet-and-water. It was a labour of love for those two girls, I assure you.'

'You're a professional,' I said, taking off my tie and jacket and shirt almost in one moment. 'You know about form – look there in the first one, and see how that vase on the chest-of-drawers helps the whole conception along – and you know about colour, but not enough about orange – is this a bloody examination?' For my processes of thought, now that she had moved closer to me, were ceasing to function.

'I'll help you,' she said. 'Examination over. Because you really do know something about it, you see. If you hadn't, if you'd given the wrong answer, if you'd just said they were absolutely fabulous I'd have sent you off –' her hands were busy with my trousers – 'yes, even with this. You'd hardly have been able to walk, would you, darling?'

I moaned. 'You hate the flesh,' I managed to say. 'Really hate it.'

'Yes, I know.' She peeled off her tights.

In the big new bed with the brass rails and the white silk eiderdown – immediately flung off – I submitted myself to a completely new experience. For Angela treated me on the first time that night exactly as if I'd been a male whore, shouting commands which grew more and more outrageous. It was as if she were determined to discover exactly what extremes of pleasure could be achieved from every possible combination of the male and the female body. It was a frenzy that assailed us, but not a divine one, not a visitation of Eros. For even when screaming her delight, dragging my head down to every part of her, writhing in the last, the very last wave, the great one, the identity-shattering one, the drowning one down to the sea bed smothering and driven upwards again, I had the feeling that, writhing as she was as if being burned alive, the china-blue eyes staring, she was taking notes, it was the shapes our muscles took, the expressions on our faces, that interested her, that we were life models, not servants of Eros, not simple animals coupling, not, above all not, a man and a woman making love.

And when the wave had finally subsided, instead of lying quietly by me she suddenly hit me across the face and then bit my hand, drawing blood. I took hold of her shoulders and shook her hard then hit her hard across her cheek. 'Goddam you, you crazy bitch, don't do that again. I can't bear being hit. Do you hear me?'

She sprung at me, her hands clawing, but I threw her back, her head hitting the brass rails. Then she smiled. 'I'm sorry,' she said. 'It takes me that way sometimes. But you'd be surprised how many men like that sort of thing.'

She padded across the room to the built-in wardrobe – painted shocking pink to match the walls – and flung me across a dressing-gown and put one on herself. My dressing-gown was bright blue silk with a padded lining; I could see through the open doors of the wardrobe at least a dozen others.

'Let's have a drink,' she said. 'A nice strong one.'

'I'd rather have coffee.'

'All right, we'll have coffee.'

'Your brother has a lot of dressing-gowns,' I said.

'Perry's the last of the big spenders. He always buys things by the dozen and then forgets about them. Are you enjoying your coffee?'

Angela made coffee in about five seconds, as far as I could see by tossing a handful of coffee into an earthenware pot and pouring on boiling water. I have never drunk better coffee before or since; the truth was, I think, that she had the visual artist's knack of being on good terms with the non-animate world.

'It's good,' I said. 'But I couldn't imagine you making anything tasteless.'

She put two cheroots in her mouth, lit them, and brought me one over. Sitting at my feet now, she said – her voice for the first time that night showing tenderness – 'It's marvellous that you don't always need alcohol. Most of the men one meets do. Or pills. Or drugs. Or pot.'

'Jesus, what a fine lot you must know.'

'They are one's friends and that's that. They're the people one meets, and keeps on meeting. You don't choose your friends, any more than you choose your parents. You hang together or hang separately, that's all.'

We returned to the bedroom; for a split second it seemed to me as if, having already proved myself, I was re-entering the arena. This time, however, it was even better; there was even a moment when it seemed as if we might actually meet as human beings, might actually share, might indeed be unable to avoid sharing, but we stayed apart, our coming together was a contrived coincidence and not a fusion, and then one minute later we were both suddenly asleep.

I awoke to find her standing over me with a cup of tea. She was fully dressed in a red dress and red woollen stockings and a perceptible air of brisk good health.

'My sodding parents have decided on the spur of the moment to drive up from the Cotswolds,' she said. 'They're frightfully broadminded, but you'd better not be around.

So off you go into the cold grey dawn. There's a shower in the bathroom, but you've no time for a bath.'

I tried to pull her into bed but she broke away. 'I wouldn't have bothered getting dressed if I'd wanted that,' she said.

'It's only eight o'clock for God's sake, Angela. I don't have to be anywhere until half-past ten —'

'No,' she said. 'They'll be here by lunch time, and they'll be staying for a few days. And the bedroom reeks of you. They're not so old that they won't know what it is.'

I found myself outside in Montagu Square with an aching head and a feeling of emptiness. My face smarted from my hurried shave with Perry's electric razor, an unfamiliar make with enough controls on it for a jet bomber. And under my shirt my chest was stinging with her bites. I felt vaguely let down and at the same time wildly elated. I had never had an experience like it; and when I came to think of it, never in such exclusive surroundings. The square – or to be more accurate – oblong – was shrouded in mist; it was too large for charm, but it did have a certain grandeur. If I had been risking my immortal soul (these thoughts persisted in coming to me) I'd been doing it in style. I said a quick act of Contrition and climbed into the Minor.

When I parked the car outside Shalott House I saw a woman running up the steps. I quickened my pace and saw that it was Judy Aviemore. She ran into the entrance hall and up the steps to Simon Cothill's studio. I was going to speak to her, feeling that I'd be an idiot to miss any opportunity, however small, of helping the Barbury campaign along, when Angela's bites simultaneously began to itch along with my belly rumbling. It was time enough to begin work when I interviewed my latest subject, yet another provincial novelist who'd hit the jackpot, in his new home on Christchurch Road at 10.30.

I went into the flat, grunted at Adam, who was wearing a battered woollen dressing-gown and looking bad-tempered and had a quick shower. I hurried into a new grey check suit and a clean white shirt and then began to feel better. Angela's bites still smarted, but I could feel them now as honourable scars rather than as mere annoyances.

Adam had made a pot of tea and buttered a pile of toast when I went into the kitchen. The electric fire on the wall was switched on and a wave of warmth met me along with the smell of toast. I had an hour before I saw the provincial novelist and through the yellow Venetian blind I could see that the sun had come out.

I took a slice of toast, wanting to delay the wonderful moment when I first had a drink of strong tea.

'Didn't she give you breakfast?' Adam asked.

'No. Wouldn't even give me time for a bath. Mummy and Daddy were coming, she said. Damned nearly threw me out naked.'

'I didn't know she had a Mummy and Daddy. She's not a girl for talking about family matters.'

'Apparently they're very vague. And her brother is absolutely rolling in money. Keeps this huge flat in Montagu Square to use about once every million years.'

'I knew about dear old Perry. She talks about him so damned much that I wonder if he's not doing something for her.'

'I should think she's normal enough.'

'None of that lot is. How the hell could they be? They never really see their parents, they never see their brothers and sisters, they're left to the tender care of nannies and au pair girls and cooks and matrons —'

'Come off it, Adam. That's just what you'll do with your kids when you get married.'

'I know, and rotten decadent little sods they'll turn out to be, too. You must learn to be more logical, Batcombe.'

I took another piece of toast. 'What did you do last night, then?'

'Had Jack Reaverhill and his wife in. And Joyce Impington. I thought it was about time that Jack got himself a staff job. He's not getting any younger, and he spends every penny he makes. I know damned well your paper would like to have Jack. But it was no good. I could tell it was no good. Joyce and he got on famously, but whenever I tried to point out the advantages of a steady job to Jack, he'd change the subject.'

'Perhaps he doesn't like having his life arranged for him. You no doubt mean well, old china, but you're inclined to be domineering. I wasn't aware you even knew Impington, by the way.'

'I know a lot of people.' He spread out his hands and assumed a foreign accent. 'You vant contacts. I have them ... Never mind, it was a good evening. Jack came up with an idea for breeding Progs as domestic animals. The purpose is to have a creature about the place you can thoroughly despise and give all the most lowly jobs to. After a hard day at the office you come home and kick the Prog and then set it to cleaning out the cesspool ... They wouldn't cost much to keep. You could feed them on mealie porridge from South Africa, of course, and great buckets of cheap but nourishing soup ... He's a card, is old Jack.'

'I'm sorry I didn't stay home,' I said. I lit a cheroot. 'Incidentally, I saw Judy Aviemore here this morning. Evidently going up to Simon's flat.'

'She doesn't know it, but we're going to have old Mislingford breed a fine litter of Progs upon her. She's not past it yet.'

'But what was she doing here?'

'She and Simon are doing a book together. All about the downtrodden suffering poor and the rotten old swinging rich. But never mind that. The great question is last night. How was it? Did her cry of physical exultation rise before the altar?'

This was a private joke from the time when at the age of twelve we'd been unbearably excited by the description of the seduction of the boss's wife in an empty church in Cronin's *The Stars Look Down*. I was touched that Adam should remember; pouring myself another cup of tea, I began to tell him all about it.

ten

The first party of Adam's which I ever attended was important to me as the prototype of all the others, and as the occasion on which I was aware, however vaguely, of the number of opportunities with which one is presented at a certain time of one's life. But it was at my fourth party at Shalott House that, though I didn't know it, I was finally wound up and firmly pushed like a clockwork soldier irrecoverably towards Chertsey.

We knew it afterwards as the New Year's party, though in fact it didn't take place until the end of January. It wasn't an absolutely typical Shalott House party; although most of the regular guests were present, there was an unusually high proportion of journalists. Besides Jack Reaverhill and Joyce Impington and Nigel Binsey and myself, there were Don and Linda Warlingworth and Wilfred Tilstock. The Warlingworths and Tilstock and Nigel Binsey were all from different papers and all on the gossip column side; they weren't positively objectionable, but they weren't important or amusing enough to be invited in their own right.

And there were two photographers, one from my own newspaper. In one sense their presence was a triumph; the party was officially news. There was a sense of expectancy, a feeling of occasion; but to my mind there was also a feeling of strain. And because of the fact that journalists on the job demand hard liquor the nice distinction between one kind of guest and another had to be abandoned, with the consequence that there was a great deal too much heavy drinking.

The ostensible purpose of the party was a little private PR job for Dick Sancreed. In fact, Adam said to me beforehand, it was hardly going to show any profit at all. But if he could push Dick a little, he'd also be pushing himself. Could I – this was the first time he'd asked me a business favour – do my best for the poor old sod? And because it was always best to ask for the hell of a lot whilst one was about it, he did most earnestly implore me to note the existence of another poor old sod – literally a sod too – – Simon Cothill.

With some show of reluctance, I made Adam the required promise, adding that it wouldn't be easy since both Dick and Simon were at present something of a drug on the market. But I would do it out of friendship; there was nothing in it for me. I was actually doing it because I knew that both Judy Aviemore and David Glenthorn were to be guests; though when Adam had mentioned this fact, I'd taken care to display no satisfaction.

'Do your best,' Adam said. 'That's all I ask. And on this occasion the house rule is suspended. If there are any faces smacked or knickers pulled down, you print it. Everyone knows what to expect with all these journalists here.'

Barbury was delighted when I told him. 'Don't worry, Frank. We'll have a good chap there, ready to snap Glenthorn the moment he looks down Aviemore's dress or better still, gives her a feel. Anyone else there besides?'

'Mislingford. Dick Sancreed. Simon Cothill. Saul Dykenhead. Jerry Knaphill. You might do something for Sancreed and Cothill, by the way.'

'Sounds like a music-hall juggling act. I doubt whether either rings a bell any longer. It's a funny thing about names. It's only about five years ago that those two names were, you might say, valid currency. Now –' he jabbed his thumb downwards.

'The party's really for them. Or Dick Sancreed anyway.'

'Any birds there?'

'Lots. There always are.'

'Adam Keelby's giving it, so you don't surprise me. His firm has a reputation for providing company for clients.'

'Don't they all.'

'Not all, and you know bloody well they don't. It's all right, I expect, until someone gets a dose.'

For the time it took the long second hand of the black-and-gold Swiss clock on the shelf behind him to go round the dial I seemed through my mind's eye to be seeing corruption – rashes, pustules, ulcers, a girl's face smiling and revealing a mouthful of black broken teeth. I redirected myself with an effort to the business in hand. 'You'll pass it if I have something put in about Sancreed and Cothill, then?'

'O.K., O.K. The more names the merrier. That slob Knaphill's always good for a quote if he's sober enough.'

'Why don't you come yourself?'

'God, I've enough on my plate as it is. I know all too well what happens when I look at a young bird. It costs me money. I just have to smile at them and the big spending starts. And my bloody wife always finds out and then I've got to bring her a peace offering. It was a dishwasher last time, but next time it'll be a bloody mink coat . . .'

Our Glenthorn campaign was still progressing, but rather as the British campaign in the Somme did, about an inch a day in the mud. We knew that Judy Aviemore's husband was still technically living with her, we knew that she and Glenthorn were still lovers. But there were no signs of any public scandal, nor of any other politician taking advantage of the situation. But we were at least reaching the point where the public would couple the two names together without knowing why; and after the party we would have trudged another inch forward.

If Judy Aviemore had not been so obviously and firmly attached to Glenthorn (when they weren't actually together each discreetly scanned the room looking for the other) I think that I would have tried to get her for myself. In an ankle-length, high-necked kaftan stiff with gold brocade, she easily dominated all the other women there. It was her face and dark hair that one looked at, not her breasts and legs; but the stiff brocade, falling straight down in ceremonial folds, was a more disturbing guarantee of the naked body underneath than was, for instance, Debby's new dress, which was so cut as to reveal the beginning of the cleft between her buttocks.

The photographer, grinning, took pictures of Debby first; she would probably make a better picture than Judy Aviemore, bottoms having a more immediate effect than gold brocade. Then he moved on to Judy Aviemore, trying to take a picture of her and Glenthorn together; but, her eyes looking incessantly in the direction of her lover, she spent most of her time with Simon Cothill. I was puzzled about this until I remembered that they were collaborating on a book; what could be more natural than for them to be talking together?

Simon, who seemed noticeably more subdued than usual in a quite respectable dark blue six-button double-breasted worsted suit, camp only in the matching tie and handkerchief and gold identity bracelet, was being watched hungrily by someone else. Carlos had pointedly not been invited ('Don't bring that drug-sodden bum-boy of yours,' had been Adam's exact words to Simon) but he had made his way in just the same, resplendent in a gold brocade Regency frock coat with a high-collared white frilled shirt and tight black trousers and pointed black boots. He had changed his hair style to a straight fringe and altogether looked less girlish than usual. Growing tired of yearning after Simon (or of not being noticed by him) he introduced himself to Jack Reaverhill and turned upon him the full battery of his charms. As Simon often used fondly to say, there was more to Carlos than a pretty face; he also read books and newspapers and remembered what he'd read for as long as twenty-four hours.

'Oh, I did so *adore* your article this morning,' I heard him say to the glowering Reaverhill. 'You're an absolute paladin, you're so brave. Why should we subsidize these frightful blacks?'

'There's a bit more to it than that,' Reaverhill said, perceptibly thawing.

'Of course, my dear. I'm an absolute idiot myself, but that doesn't mean that I don't appreciate *brains* . . . Even when I don't understand you, I feel that I ought to . . .'

'Socrates about to be seduced by Alcibiades,' said Mislingford, sidling up beside me as I was drinking a large whisky. 'Jack has got brains too. It's a shame that he's so wrong-headed.' The small but keen blue eyes examined me. 'I think we met at another party of Adam's. Frank Batcombe, isn't it? You're a journalist.'

'You've a good memory, my lord.'

'No, no, none of that. My name's Piers, as I remember I told you the last time. I only remain involved with this mediaeval flummery to help my Party. Which isn't, since you're a friend of Adam's, yours.'

'Not by a long chalk.' I didn't altogether relish being classified as a faithful follower of Adam, but there seemed no point in explaining exactly what my opinions were.

'I like that. By Jove, I like that. We must have lunch together some time. You're not too old to be saved.' On this occasion he was wearing a lounge suit of a cut and pattern which was fashionable in the thirties and which now with its bold white stripe against deep chocolate brown was, though I don't suppose he cared, fashionable again. 'You see, Frank, I'm always being agreed with by young men. Are you quite sure you don't think that I may be right about *something*? I take it that you know my beliefs?' He pulled out his notebook, as if about to read them out.

'Yes, I do, Piers. They're all wrong. Some of them disastrously wrong.' As I watched his face, I could see that this was what he wanted to hear.

'That's the spirit.' He smiled. 'You're a tonic, my dear chap.'

'I'll look forward to it, then.'

He rubbed his hands; white and plump and manicured, with a big gold signet ring on the left hand, they were the hands of a rich and powerful man, they were as greedy and sleek as his face was twinkling and avuncular.

'So will I, my dear young friend . . . Tell me, who's that young lady over there?' He indicated Debby. I wondered how it was that although, like Glenthorn, he was a widower, nothing ever appeared in the Press about his succession of young girls. It was because he had too many interests, because he knew too much about too many people. I wondered if perhaps he was the true instigator of the campaign against Glenthorn, then decided that it was better not to be too inquisitive beyond a certain level. The fact was that he gave me the creeps and, between one sip of whisky and another, taking him over to Debby, I felt that everyone there gave me the creeps.

I would just as soon have been with Theresa, being gently nagged as the price of being regarded simply as a person, a man, a potential husband and father, not simply a phallus in search of an orifice, a hand in search for money, a brain in search for power.

I took another sip of whisky and went over to Judy

187

Aviemore and Simon, feeling both like a pimp and a virgin in a brothel and pleased with myself for having such a wide range, and knowing that another glass of whisky would bring me back to the party again, another happy pig at the trough.

'How lovely to see you again,' Judy Aviemore said, kissing me lightly on the cheek. 'Simon and I are being very naughty, you see, and just talking shop.' There was a flash of a photographer's bulb, but it wasn't ours. Glenthorn was moving nearer, deep in conversation with Joyce Impington.

'What exactly is the book going to be about?'

'Contrasts. All this –' she waved her wrist, the diamond bracelet glittering – 'and the world where they live ten in a room. It isn't original, but what is? It's a job which has to be done afresh every generation –'

'It's a challenge for Simon.'

Simon pulled a face. 'My sweet old Yorkshire pudding, it's completely and revoltingly and drastically depressing. The *smell!* Smelly old-age pensioners, smelly young children with *rotten* teeth, smelly streets, smelly cities; even, I give you my word, smelly casualty wards.' He lowered his voice. 'You didn't know, did you, that when they've had an accident, lots of people shit themselves or spew their guts out?'

'I did, actually.'

'Well, it's all right for you, you're more *robust* than I am. But I'm prostrated, I'm soaked in other people's sufferings, and we haven't even *begun.*'

'The artist must suffer,' I said. Glenthorn left Joyce Impington in mid-sentence and came over to us, swaying slightly. The grey hair was a little dishevelled, the eyes beginning to be glassy. As a journalist I was pleased; but at the same time I didn't want him to be vulnerable, to be lolling naked in his tent, I wanted to respect him.

'You know that Mrs Aviemore and Simon Cothill are doing a book on social contrasts, David,' I said quickly.

Where the hell was our photographer? 'Why don't you send them up to the North-East? Deserted pit villages, unemployed miners ... You know all the right people to introduce them to ...'

Simon was moving over to Judy Aviemore to come between her and our photographer whose eye I had just caught.

'Certainly I'll do that,' Glenthorn said. 'Delighted to be of assistance.'

'There's never been such affluence,' I said. 'The sexes becoming blurred, men dressing in brocades and bright colours – look at Carlos, for example.' I virtually dragged Simon away from his place in front of Judy Aviemore which wasn't too difficult, since he instinctively turned his attention towards Carlos, who was fetching Jack Reaverhill a brimming glass of whisky, and himself another, moving with the special gliding gait which betrayed his original vocation of waiter. The flash went off, and then another; I held Simon's arm firmly with my hand, which I think he rather enjoyed.

I released his arm and relaxed. The photographer could go home now. And in addition to the picture of Glenthorn, appearing unmistakably dissipated, a glass in his hand, his eyes almost pathetic in their hunger for Judy Aviemore, there could be a respectable little paragraph about his promise to show her and Simon the black spots of the North-East. Even in his social moments the Right Honourable David Glenthorn never relaxes ... He is telling Judy Aviemore, whose work he so much admires, about the forgotten men of the North-East ...

I went to the phone in my room to unload the who what where and when before the whisky did the job for me. As I was going out Jerry Knaphill and Pauline Yeavering came in; his face was glistening with sweat and there were dark patches under the arms of his light grey suit. She looked younger and frailer than ever, all legs and not very well-brushed hair and eyes with too much blue on the lids; she had hold of Jerry's hand and it was difficult to tell who was leading whom. This was more than a one-night stand; as my Uncle Terry used to say of every destructive phenomenon from floods to H-bombs, someone was going to get lamed.

It was no business of mine, though I would pass it on to the proper person at the office. Pauline was a clever little bitch and would know exactly how to butter Jerry up. She would get him, and her entrée into London literary society such as it was, and material for at least a dozen highly sensitive and throbbingly feminine novels, and who would care if his five children ever missed their father?

When I returned to the drawing-room Jack Reaverhill had somehow got rid of Carlos, who was sitting by himself near the fire pretending to read a book, his lower lip pushed out and trembling. As he put down his book and put a cigarette into a long diamanté holder I could see that the party was now forming itself into a collection of charmed circles, into which neither his impudence nor appearance could gain him admission and, what was more, that he knew it. Sex and shop, or sex and shop combined in the case of Jerry Knaphill and Pauline Yeavering, were forming the circles; they would open up to let the right person in for a little while but at the end of the party they would close up again. Simon Cothill was still with Judy Aviemore and David Glenthorn and now Toby Horsmoden had joined them; but I knew who would sleep with Judy Aviemore that night. I contemplated joining them; but I had had enough of Judy Aviemore and David Glenthorn for that evening. Whatever they did – and Glenthorn now, his face red, had his hand on Judy Aviemore's shoulder – I didn't want to know; I had filed my copy.

Instead I joined Jack Reaverhill and his wife, who were explaining his Prog-breeding scheme to Saul Dykenhead, who was making more and more outrageous suggestions as to likely couples to breed from. I had heard it all from Adam at secondhand; but Jack made it sound better, bringing to it a steadier, more savage, and more controlled wit. Jack's wife Betty watched Jack and his whisky consumption with a slightly worried air. I liked Betty; she was plump and fifty and I had no physical desire for her, and that was in itself a recommendation.

'He does enjoy himself so much at these parties,' she said. 'He's the happiest man I've ever known.'

She had met him at the University when he was twenty-one and she was twenty-two; they'd married when he graduated, had had seven children, and, I was convinced, had never as much as thought of anyone else. There were times when I wondered if that wasn't the secret of his enormous output and unflagging intellectual energy, just as it was the secret of her unlined skin and clear blue eyes.

'Haven't you ever tried to persuade him to take a staff job?' I asked her.

'It's no use, Frank. He knows the Lord will provide.'

'I could get him a good offer. He's entitled to some security now.' I wasn't thinking of Jack as I said it, but myself; listening to him there, so fiercely and arrogantly and unself-consciously his own man, I was thinking of how much I'd like to work with him, hoping that if he did, perhaps some of his qualities might rub off on to me.

'You're not very happy, are you, Frank?'

'Happy enough,' I said, catching sight of Christine Berneray in a short feathered dress and golden stockings to match her hair. She was sipping a pale green drink and looking rather bored, on her own as I was.

'Aren't you friendly with Angela Guilsfield?' Betty asked.

'More or less. She's in Florida just now, trying to sell her paintings.'

'We used to see a lot of her once,' she said, rather to my astonishment. 'She had a period of great devotion; in fact, we used sometimes to wonder if she hadn't a vocation. And then she just seemed to disappear.'

'She still does.'

'I wouldn't care to be a young man who was in love with her,' she said. 'God forgive me for being uncharitable. But she's a strange girl. The whole family's strange.'

'One has that impression.' I still couldn't digest the idea of Angela as a possible nun; it seemed to make me merely an incident in her development. It was shocking too; if she could be subject to this arbitrary and random spiritual conscription – as if God picked people's names from His hat – then so could I.

Betty took her husband's whisky away – he had put it down on a nearby table to allow himself more freedom to gesticulate – and filled it up with soda. 'He won't notice,' she said. 'Once he's in full gallop he'd drink cold tea and not know the difference.' She put her hand on my arm. 'It's not easy for a young bachelor in London,' she said. 'Not that it'll be loneliness that'll be your trouble here. Phone us any time and come and have a meal.'

She didn't add *Come and see a Catholic home, be at your ease in a Catholic family,* but that was what she really meant. But it was not until long afterwards that I took her up on her invitation, desperately though one side of me wanted to. The atmosphere of that untidy house on Highgate Hill, crammed with books and dogs and cats and young people and gramophone records and galley proofs, smelling always of coffee and roasting meat, might well have made me change direction before I did; but even now I'm unregenerate enough not to regret too deeply having the run for my money that I did, having acted out all my desires, having wasted none of my youth in merely hankering after forbidden fruit, having indeed made it my daily bread.

Jerry Knaphill came over to us, temporarily without Pauline Yeavering. He stared owlishly at Saul Dykenhead. 'By God, you're the spit-and-image of Lenin. Has anyone ever told you?' Alcohol seems to expand most men, to make them larger than life; with Jerry the effect was to wizen his round face, to elongate the long arms, to take a couple of inches off the already short legs.

'When you come home at the end of the day,' Jack Reaverhill said, disregarding Jerry completely, 'it'll be *Down, Walker, down!*' He cuffed the air at the level of his thighs. 'Useful beast, this, you'll say to your visitors. Not beautiful or lovable, but *useful . . .*'

Jerry circled Saul Dykenhead. 'By God, it's uncanny,' he said. 'Old Ully – ully – vitch himself. Or is it Ulyovanitch?'

Saul Dykenhead gave him a strained smile.

'I know I look like Lenin, Jerry,' he said. 'You've often told me. The fact is that every man with a bald head and pointed beard looks like Lenin.'

'Not as much as you,' Jerry said. 'I went to Russia once. Bloody marvellous. At the Cathedral of the Sacred Blood there's niches all round the walls and a stone Christ in each niche. And at the foot of each Christ a woman flat on her face on the stone. Praying. I remember a lot of things like that. I'm fat and ugly, but I do remember things.'

'Yes, you do, Jerry,' Saul Dykenhead said gently. 'Why don't we have lunch tomorrow and discuss it? We never see you these days.'

'I'm always rushing around,' Jerry said. 'Never do what I want to do . . .'

Jack and Betty Reaverhill fell silent; on their faces were the same expressions of solicitude as on Saul's. And I understood that the solicitude was not so much for Jerry personally as for Jerry as the caretaker of a genuine talent. I bitterly envied him, grotesque though he was. If I had been drunk in the same way, they wouldn't have been so tolerant; my talent was too commonplace, I had no option but always to mind my p's and q's.

Pauline Yeavering appeared and joined the circle, linking her arm possessively in Jerry's. She belonged in the circle; she had a genuine talent, she was on their level too. I made an excuse, which I don't think anyone heard, and went outside to stand on the front doorstep and breathe in the cold sharp air. The flat did not belong to me, the view did not belong to me, the future did not belong to me; tears stung my eyes.

I stayed there until I began to shiver and as I began to shiver my self-confidence – or perhaps my illusions – returned. I had to take what was available for me; and what was available was Christine Berneray who was, when I came back gratefully to the warmth of the drawing-room, talking to Carlos.

The party was thinning out now; Saul Dykenhead, the Reaverhills, and Jerry Knaphill and Pauline Yeavering had gone, Mislingford and Debby were going as I came in; the party wasn't over but this was the hour at which the baby-sitters had to be taken home, and at which the need for bed, alone or otherwise, began to manifest itself.

I took Christine's hand. 'I've been looking for you all evening.'

'I haven't been very far away.'

Carlos shrugged and returned to his book.

'Big oaf,' he muttered.

I felt a need to hit him. 'What's that, Carlos?'

'Nothing, dear. I'm quite happy and contented, dear. I'm on my tod, and I don't care.'

'Don't care was made to care,' I said. I was puzzled at my violent hatred of him; until that evening I had had no feelings about him at all: he was merely a standard model pretty boy wondering whether it was more profitable to be butch or queen, a creature whose life couldn't impinge upon mine. And yet as he sat there, frightened yet expectantly excited, all the signals in my brain were set at danger.

'I've something I want to tell you,' I said to Christine.

'No prizes for guessing,' Carlos said. 'Don't you go, love. Stay here and tell me where you bought that pretty dress.'

'Probably the same place as you buy yours,' I said, then realized that he was controlling me and sniggeringly overjoyed to be controlling me. I abruptly took Christine into my room, springing the latch behind me.

'You're the most beautiful girl here,' I whispered. I was appalled to discover that my lust was all in my head, and only in the vaguest way at that. Perhaps that had been Carlos's intention. I breathed deeply and looked round the familiar room, lit only by a table lamp. It was only, of course, half a larger room and, lit only by the small table lamp, it appeared now as tall as it was long. But the dark red fitted carpet was almost brand new, purchased by Adam at cost price, and my white sheepskin rug by the three-quarter divan bed looked more in place there than ever it had done in Chelsea. And my pictures, particularly the Picasso *Mother and Child* kept the off-white walls from bareness, in fact made any sort of wall covering superfluous. A walnut Victorian davenport, a small office desk and office chair, and a basket chair and a round bedside table completed the furniture; it wasn't the most luxurious of rooms, it gave somehow an impression of monasticism, and yet it was part of me. I would think of it at the office as being the home I'd be glad to return to. And as I stood there with Christine the lust gradually left my head and took its proper place.

'Do you hear what I say?' I asked her.

'I'm the most beautiful girl here.'

'You are, aren't you?'

'Yes.' She had a slight lisp. 'I expect I am.'

I gently stroked her glittering blonde hair. 'It seems silly but I'm already a bit in love with you. You're on my mind often. In this room, all alone in that very bed.'

'That's very nice. I like to be on people's minds. You're very nice too. Some girls like much older men; but I don't see how they can, do you? I mean, there's Debby with that horrid old Mislingford, he must be sixty if he's a day. But I expect he's very rich. Are you very rich, Frank?'

'You know bloody well I'm not.' I kissed her; her mouth tasted of gin and garlic and I didn't mind, in fact enjoyed it. I wouldn't have done if her teeth had been bad or if she'd been sick, but what I was tasting was the breath of a healthy young woman who'd been eating and drinking.

She pressed her body hard against me; I could feel her breasts, but less as protuberances as relaxations of the muscle in the hard skinny little body. I ran my hand under her skirt and heard her gasp. 'I like that,' she said.

I tried to manoeuvre her towards the bed.

'No,' she said. 'Someone might come in.'

'It's my room, and the door's locked.'

She giggled. 'They'll know what we're doing then, won't they?'

I explored her flat belly with my other hand. 'How do you take them off?

'It's a body stocking, silly. I'm not going to take it off.'

More and more it was like reliving one's adolescence, when every detail of a woman's clothing was almost menacing in its mystery, perplexingly different from what the girls in the pin-ups wore, so much more part of them, so much more creased and wrinkled, no matter how clean, so much less gaudy and so much more disturbing.

Her hand moved to my belly. 'All hard,' she said. 'Not just a bit of it. Pauline likes that horrid old Jerry Knaphill. I don't see how she can, do you? You'd think he'd overlay her. But Pauline adores older men. It's not just because he's rich and famous. I think it's kinky, don't you?' The long nervous fingers worked their way to my fly; I was all sensation now, rising to meet her hand, I pushed her to-wards the bed again and she withdrew her hand and disengaged herself from me.

'Christine. I love you. Stay here.'

'I love you too.' I believe that she said this to salve her conscience, to glamorise the stark act of sex. 'But we needn't hurry-skurry-boo, need we? Let's go and have a quiet drink.'

As it turned out, there was little that was quiet about the final stages of the party. Adam had turned on the tape-recorder and the room was throbbing to the sound of the Twist and I and Christine were in it; I was still at the age when I could fling myself into the most violent activity late at night without paying the least penalty the morning after.

The music stopped for a moment whilst Adam changed the spool, but Abigail Pinmore kept on dancing by herself, listening, I can only suppose, to some music inside her head, the long ash-blonde hair falling nearly to the middle of her back. There weren't many people left in the room now, only Adam's oldest friends, his steadiest girls, the ones who dropped in the most often, the ones he phoned the most; those who comprised his family, the nearest thing to a family he was ever likely to have.

Judy Aviemore and Glenthorn were still there; from time to time their hands touched, but now they weren't watching each other but Abigail, the same rather greedy expression on their faces. Abigail pulled her black dress over her head and threw it to Adam, who caught it and put it neatly across an armchair; the same wing-sided armchair, I now re-called, that his father always sat in.

Adam put on *Boris Godunov*; the obvious choice would have been something far more Eastern but this was better with its thunderingly ecclesiastical note, its smell of incense, its thundering reiteration of the godhead in power always about to batter its way through to God, taking the Czar's crown as the next best thing; the room expanded to accommodate the sound, all the colours deepened, black was midnight blue and the yellow glow of the standard lamp which was now the only light in the room, the fire having died down to a few red embers, was gold, real gold, and I could taste still the gin and garlic from Christine's mouth. Abigail threw off her slip; I caught the wisp of pink nylon, still warm from her body. Gin and garlic; juniper berries and the charm against vampires. I knew then what the world has to offer, I knew then what is to be seen from the high place.

It was no more than can be seen at any Soho strip club, but Abigail wasn't doing it for money nor, though she'd had a lot of wine, because she was drunk. The breasts which were now being bared, fuller and richer than those of professional models like Christine, the surprisingly wide hips, almost grotesquely functional, almost clumsily female — these were shown as part of a sacrament, sex was part of it, but not the only part, she was dancing now for herself as much as for us. This was the flesh, this was the here and now and there didn't have to be anything else, this was enough; I apprehended perfectly not only her naked body but everything and everyone in the room and, above all, the room itself, its high ceiling, its deep skirting boards, its solid picture rail, its coved ceiling, the planks on the floor which I now noticed were dovetailed. I didn't desire Abigail physically nor even, at that moment of perfect apprehension, Christine, whose thin hand was now surreptitiously stroking my thigh. But I was never so deep in mortal sin because I was nothing but a body and a body that had forgotten, that couldn't even conceive the idea, that it must die, and everyone in the room must die and even the room itself crumble away into dust.

Then Maria Barrisdale joined in and the dancing became more and more frenzied, leaving the music behind. But

Maria was more self-conscious, more sexual, she danced too well, the eye was drawn too compulsively downwards to compare the dark brown with the platinum blonde mane falling over her face. Her slim body too much the model's to look complete without clothes.

Adam's face was impassive, but his eyes never left Maria. The photographers had gone long since, and now Judy Aviemore and Glenthorn were slipping out of the room. Carlos, his back to the dancers, was drinking sherry from the bottle. He put the bottle down and, his hand cupped over the match flame as if outdoors in a howling gale, lit a cigarette. There was a bitter but sweetish smell, reminiscent somehow of autumn and bonfires; I sniffed at it for a while, disentangling it from the smell of tobacco and perfume and the remains of the cold buffet and the smell which pervades a room occupied by a great many people, no matter how clean, a smell not noticeable until the room begins to empty.

Adam stopped the music; the girls scampered out of the room picking up their clothes on the way. He strode over to Carlos, grabbed the cigarette from his hand and threw it into the fireplace, his face distorted with rage.

'Simon,' he shouted, 'take this filth away.' He took hold of Carlos by the shirt – I heard a button pop – and shook him violently. Carlos went limp, an expression appearing on his face which was almost ecstatic. 'Don't ever come here again, you degenerate shit. You bloody well know you weren't invited in the first place. And if you do show your face here again, I'll split on you to the coppers, I swear to God I will. They're longing to make an example of bastards like you.'

Simon appeared from the background. 'Adam dear, I'm terribly sorry. He really is a silly little bitch. He's very young —'

'Old enough to go to jail,' Adam said. He released Carlos

as violently as he had taken hold of him; Carlos staggered, then began to tidy himself, his hands trembling.

'You think you're very clever, Mister Man. But I know things about you—' He cowered close to Simon as Adam raised his fist.

'Nothing I can be jailed for,' Adam said. 'That's the difference, isn't it? Take him away for Christ's sake, Simon, before there's a scene.'

I began to laugh helplessly. 'You're a card, Adam. What's that if it isn't a scene?'

Adam joined in my laughter as Simon and Carlos left the room. 'It's all very well for you to laugh, Frankie boy, but you can be jailed just for allowing your home to be used for pot smoking. It just needs one phone call, one reefer in an ashtray, or even the smell of the bloody stuff, and we're all in it up to the neck. Ask Basil, if you don't believe me.' He yawned. 'The party appears to be over,' he said. 'Or perhaps it's just beginning. You and Christine seemed to be missed during some part of the evening.'

Christine giggled. He winked at me; and as he winked I realized that he had slept with her once and was now, so to speak, recommending her.

Basil came into the room, his hand in Abigail's. 'We're making coffee,' he said.

Adam threw himself into an armchair. 'There's nothing I need more. I take it you're giving poor little Abigail shelter for the night?' He yawned again. 'Of all the hours of the day, my dear friends, this is to me the most precious. All our guests have gone home though not, I think, all to their own homes, and we're free to relax among the débris.'

I was now in the smallest, tightest circle of all, relaxing among the débris; there was something almost domestic about the six of us as we drank our coffee, not needing to talk very much, not again referring to the fact that Abigail would share Basil's room, Christine my room and Maria, who padded in wearing Adam's dressing-gown, Adam's room.

There was after the last cup of coffee had been drunk and the last cigarette smoked, a certain amount of awkwardness about the bathroom, which everyone seemed to need at once. Then, like characters in a French farce, we each made our way into our respective rooms.

What followed wasn't like a French farce. Christine was as violent in her desire, as impatient of preliminaries, as Angela, but her demands were less complicated, her whole reaction noisier and healthier. There was no sense of sin – always present though never spoken of with Angela, the sharp sauce to spur the appetite. But always, ritually, at the moment of climax, the long legs round my waist, there were the endearments, the magic words to make the act more than coupling – *I love you, darling* again and again, but always addressing me as darling, never by my name. She wasn't clumsy but she was greedy in her roughness, a child demanding more sweets even with its mouth crammed full and like a child too when she said towards morning, suddenly sad – 'I wish you'd say you loved me with more *feeling.*'

We awoke first and made morning tea. The girls seemed all to dress and be away with extraordinary rapidity, each in their own cars, glancing all the time at their wristwatches, as if the night had been part of a long-planned, tightly-packed programme. Basil too after helping in a desultory sort of way to clear up the mess the party had left in its wake, drove off home to Berkshire. At twelve o'clock we put out the last empty bottle and Adam unplugged the Hoover.

'The next women we have here are going to be domesticated types,' he said. 'Not one of the bitches can so much as boil an egg or sweep a floor.'

'I know,' I said, and poured myself a glass of wine, the

first drink of the day. 'They only want us for the one thing.'

'Our bodies,' he said. 'Our beautiful white bodies.' He sighed and looked round the room with satisfaction. 'I love this flat, but it's the hell of a place to keep straight. You can't get menials to come on Saturday, that's the trouble. It's their sacred day, they want time and a half for it, and double time on Sundays, the hypocritical bastards, just as if they were Christians. How did you get on with Christine?'

'Strenuous but fun.'

'Maria isn't quite as spirited in the pit as one would think. Still, they do say it's good for the complexion . . . Did you note and inwardly digest old Glenthorn and Judy last night? Christ, he's going to come a fearful purler if he doesn't watch out.'

'Nothing would surprise me less.'

He rose from his chair and began to pace the room restlessly. 'Look, Frank, you won't plant too many dirty thoughts in the public mind about him and Judy, will you?'

'It's out of my hands now. But as far as I'm concerned, I went off duty when the photographers left. I can't answer for anyone else.'

'That's good enough for me.'

'I'm afraid you don't have much option. You did say it was every man for himself last night. You do the Argus a favour, the Argus does you a favour. You can't have your piece in about Dick and Simon if you don't have something in about Glenthorn and Judy.'

'All right, Frank, there's no need to spell it out . . .' He straightened the First Communion Certificate. 'I don't really blame the poor old devil,' he said. 'I could fancy Judy myself if she weren't married, but to keep off married women is one of my few rules. Are you going to the office tomorrow?'

I nodded.

'I've said it before and I'll say it again; sooner your job

than mine. You *make* something. I just intrigue and manipulate and bloody well pimp. Hell, what else do these sods like Mislingford come to my parties for?'

'You don't pimp for Simon.'

He laughed. 'Well, I don't provide boys yet. But if a customer — I always say customer not client — wanted one, who knows?'

'It would be rather superfluous with dear old Simon.'

'That bloody Carlos. That bloody horrible little menace. Tell me, what was the pub you saw him in?'

I told him. 'It's not where you'd expect to find anyone like Carlos,' I said. 'They're very particular in Fleet Street.'

He looked past me through the window. The sun had broken through the morning mist and the grass and the trees were sparkling with frost.

'I'll fix Master Carlos,' he said. 'Yes indeed. I'll fix him up good and proper. Come on, Frank, let's walk over the Heath and get some fresh air.'

As I followed him it struck me not for the first time, that there was about him an extraordinary relentless streak. I was grateful — naïve as I was — that he wasn't against me. And for the first time I was sorry for Carlos.

eleven

'Poor old Wendy!' Adam said. 'God, what a way to go!'

'I don't suppose she knew what she was doing.' It was a month after the party, a raw February night when I was glad for once to come straight back to Shalott House and sit by the fire with a glass of wine before planning where I was going to eat.

I wasn't going out with Angela that evening; I had been at her flat all the night before and if not precisely in a *post coitus triste* mood was not sorry about the prospect of sleeping alone.

'You can say that again. It's not so long since I saw her — you remember that night when she came in absolutely soused? Well, she kept on getting soused, and then she went into this private looney bin. She'd already fallen into the hands of the Living Psychiatrist, and then she met a new one, with the consequence she was soon so full of pills she rattled when she walked.'

'How did you get to know all this?'

'I've been phoning around. I should have done sooner, anyway. I might have known things were even worse with her than usual. But I didn't bother, you see. Too wrapped up in my own piddling affairs.'

'Oh God,' I said, 'don't go all guilty. It's not your fault she committed suicide.'

'Isn't it? The poor silly bitch used to always feel she could come to me, and then for some reason she felt she couldn't. Did I bother to find out what was the matter? Did I hell. I was damned glad to have her off my back, to tell you the honest truth. I thought perhaps she had a new boy friend or even that she'd pulled herself together. And I knew, I *knew* she couldn't pull herself together, not ever.'

'It might have been an accident,' I said.

'It was no accident. She wasn't such a fool that she didn't know what sleeping pills and alcohol do together. God, Frank, you know me, I've never pretended to care about Vietnam or South Africa or any of that crap. But I've always said I cared about people, private persons. Evidently I don't.'

'You're actually blaming yourself? You must be sick, Adam.'

Despite my fatigue I was interested; I hadn't imagined before that he thought of women as anything other than bodies to be used. I was so young then for my years that I couldn't even begin to imagine what had driven Wendy to her death; I knew something of the flesh, was beginning to be more and more drawn into the world of the flesh, but of how savagely the flesh could turn – the domestic animal turned killer – upon those who lived by it I had as yet no conception.

He didn't seem to hear me.

'Do you know *Cecily Parsley's Nursery Rhymes*?' he asked.

'It's a long time since I looked at it.'

'When I was a kid I used to look for hours at the illustration to *This little pig cried Wee! Wee! Wee! I can't find my way home.* And there's that pig with its little shopping basket weeping at the crossroads. It's night, because there's an owl on the top of the signpost. And in the background there's the woods.

You can't see anything there but you can be sure there is something there and what's there either doesn't like little pigs or likes them a great deal too much. You can be sure that that little pig never did find its way home. That was Wendy. *Wee! Wee! Wee!* I can't find my way home. So she ran into the woods.'

This is exactly what he said, shivering as he said it. He wouldn't, I honestly believe, have said it anywhere else except in Shalott House, which was so much part of himself, or said it to anyone else except me. And if ever occasionally now I feel bitter towards him I have only to remember that once at least he trusted me with the revelation that he too, as much as Wendy, couldn't find his way home.

And that evening, trembling all the time, speaking more quickly than ever I'd heard him speak before, but always coherently, he tried to justify his whole attitude which to some extent I'd learned from him, the attitude which instinctively Theresa had rejected so violently.

'It's a game, you see. Work's a game too, but you can't work all the time. It's the best game in the world as long as you recognise it. Do you know that Dave Berry number, The Crying Game? *And before you know where you are you're saying goodbye* – that's it, that hits the nail on the head. And it's fine as long as you know it's not serious. Wendy tried to make it serious. Not with me, she knew it wouldn't work with me. But with others, with all the others. She got the game mixed up with marriage too. It isn't the same thing. Of course, how could she know it, poor bitch, being an absolute pagan?'

'All your girls seem to be pagans,' I said rather waspishly.

'Of course, you idiot. As you well realized with Theresa, you've got to *marry* a good Catholic girl.' He had stopped trembling now and was sipping his wine rather than swigging it. The moment for confidences was over. 'Plenty of time to think about that. I've news for you. First of all, I've definitely got rid of Carlos. As you'll know, he hasn't got any better, and last night when you were locked in the arms of whoever you were locked in the arms of –' he grinned – 'there was the hell of a row. Simon returned unexpectedly from some hell-hole in the North and discovered Carlos and a friend throwing a little reefer party. Christ, the screaming and shouting! Simon asked me to come up and give him some support – the friend looked a real deadeye. But he was merely a paper tiger, and stupid old Simon was nearly at the point of forgiving all when I fortunately remembered what you told me about seeing him with this chap at Poppins. Then he threw Carlos out.'

'How do you know it was the same chap?'

'He was a platinum blond.' He grinned. 'But does it matter? I may have embroidered it a bit. The crux of the matter was to inform Simon that Carlos had been making a fool of him for a long time, which I did.'

I wasn't concerned with what happened to Carlos, but as Adam talked I began to see about him a ruthlessness which didn't even have the saving grace of masculinity. He had used a piece of information which I'd given him, and not blurted it out immediately but waited for the moment when it would have the most effect.

'I don't like it,' I said. 'You seem to have stirred it up still further. In fact, it's bloody squalid. I know Carlos is horrible, but who wants to get involved in these messy quarrels? You leave them alone. And keep me out of it too.'

'You're too squeamish, Frank. For one thing, we live here, and I'm not having any dirt dragged into my home. I don't give a damn about Carlos being queer, any more than I give a damn about Simon being queer. But as I've told you a thousand times, Carlos is pure ivory from the neck up, and he's heading straight for a big scandal. When it happens, I want it not to happen here.'

'It'd be publicity for Simon, wouldn't it?'

'Not the sort of publicity I'm aiming at. But if it happens here, then we're all tarred with the same brush. And right now I don't want to be touched by the least breath of scandal . . . The fact is, I'm looking for capital. And capital scares easily . . . No, don't look frightened. I'm not asking you. I've got several people in mind already. I'm going into business on my own account.'

'You mean that you and Witherslack Inc. aren't seeing eye-to-eye any more?'

'No, no. In fact, they'll give me some accounts. And I can have the use of an office there. I've been thinking this over for a bit: I want the chance to earn some real money. I'm wondering if you'd like to join me.'

I had never thought very much about money until I'd met Angela; I had, indeed, always had more than enough. But her scale of living,—based upon a free luxury flat and a sizeable allowance plus what she earned from her paintings —had sent up my expenditure alarmingly. And life at Shalott House was by no means as cheap as at the World's End. For the first time I was beginning to worry about money, to make calculations before I wrote a cheque, to cut down my smoking, to use the Tube rather than a taxi, to become too dependent upon fiddling my expenses. But somehow I couldn't bring myself to accept Adam's offer immediately, perhaps because the cooler side of me, the side that observed Adam rather than hero-worshipped him, told me that it was wisest not to appear too eager.

'There's only one drawback,' I said. 'I'm not a PR man. It's the last job in the world I'd be any use at. Are you sure you know what you're doing?' I looked pointedly at the bottle of wine by his side.

He laughed. 'I haven't drunk all that much, Frank. Believe me, it's entirely for my own devious ends that I'm asking you. The technical side of it – there just isn't any. There may be degrees in Public Relations in the good old

U.S.A. of course, but not here. As long as you can read and write – and I have my doubts about our Managing Director in that direction – you're in.'

I looked up at the chandelier in the centre of the ceiling; it was an exceptionally large one with four rows of glass beads, a genuine Victorian piece which Adam's father had bought in the Lanes at Brighton at a time when there was no vogue for the period. And I realized that gradually, even in the short time I'd been at Shalott House, Adam had been making the room still more Victorian, adding a small inlaid walnut table here, wax fruit under a glass dome there and, only last week, a horsehair sofa. As in his career he pushed further and further ahead into the bleak plastic-and-alloy wastes of his own era, so in his leisure he retreated further and further into the past.

'You make it sound very easy,' I said.

'It's the easiest way of living without working that was ever invented. There's always an answer to every problem in PR. You know, there's a bloody good SF story I read once about a PR man who has to sell to the whole earth, no less, the idea of an alliance with a race of creatures from another planet. These creatures have just had a ferocious war with the earth, they're absolutely hideous, they've used human children as laboratory animals, and on top of it they smell indescribably vile. Well, the task seems hopeless. He can't find any way of making these beings attractive or even tolerable because there isn't any. Then he realizes that there is. He's only to find someone or something for people to hate more than these big-eyed monsters. He does; it's he himself. What makes him a PR man is not so much having the *nouse* to work this out, but the guts to put it into practice. It isn't the same thing as advertising, which is comparatively civilized.'

'I might prefer a civilized way of earning a living.' But I didn't then take him seriously. His whole approach seemed to me melodramatic, more strongly influenced by novels and films than he would have cared to admit.

'Your present employers are hardly civilized, are they? You can't deny that they're doing a pretty clever long-range smear job on David Glenthorn, for instance.'

'He's a politician. They're there to be shot at. Anyway, it's not my responsibility. I'm just one of the poor old foot soldiers, not a general.'

He shook his head.

'No. Practically an A.D.C. Definitely full lieutenant. They couldn't do this sort of job without people like you. Because you're a damned good journalist. That's part of the reason I want you in with me. But most important of all you've got – hell, one hardly dare use the word – integrity. In short, I can trust you.'

'That's very handsome of you.' I was touched despite myself.

'Think nothing of it. It happens to be true. You can keep your mouth shut, you wouldn't even know how to slip the old knife into a friend's back, and you can get on with people. It's only about once every million years all these things go together. Anyway, think it over.'

'I'll do that. I can't give you an answer now —'

'Of course not. In any event, things won't begin to move for a month or so. It isn't easy to start up on your own under this present Government, malignant moronic bastards that they are —'

There was a knock at the door, then the bell rang. It kept on ringing, and the knocks became a fusillade.

'It's the secret police,' Adam said, grinning.

'I always said you'd go too far. I shall point you out as the traitor, naturally.'

'The fascist bourgeois traitor, don't forget. Christ, he's going to batter the door down in a minute. See who it is, will you?'

It was Carlos, his face white. He brushed past me, and went up to Adam, who didn't move from his chair.

'You told rotten lies to Si,' he shouted. 'You bloody shit-house! You want sorting out, you do. We was friends, Si and me, and you can't bear that, your kind can't bear that, can you?'

Adam rose. 'Get out,' he whispered. 'Or I'll smash your face in, you nasty little whore.'

'Don't you call me a whore!' Carlos screamed. 'I know about you. Trying to alter Si's bloody image, because you say he's camp! Well, he is camp, and you can't alter it, Mr Cleverhead. I know about you. You think just because you like women, that makes you perfect.' He looked at me; I was annoyed to see an expression of pity on the soft little face. 'Don't you trust him, mate,' he said. 'Don't you trust him. He doesn't know what friendship is —'

Adam hit him in the mouth, then in the belly. I had often, particularly in Charbury, seen the consequences of violence, had even more often seen it in two dimensions on the films and TV; and it was cosy enough to read about in the pages of Ian Fleming tucked up in bed on a winter night with front and back doors locked and bolted. But I'd never before witnessed it at close quarters; it was much uglier, and at the same time much more fascinating to watch than ever I had imagined. Carlos doubled up moaning, a stream of blood running from his mouth; the sound his breath made when Adam hit him in the belly was like an exploded balloon, curiously disproportionate to the force of the blow.

'Steady on,' I said to Adam, who seemed to be preparing to hit Carlos again.

'Don't worry, Frank. Carlos is a pacifist. Marched to Aldermaston once, the bloody little idiot.'

'I'm not worried about *you*,' I said. 'You're enjoying yourself too much.' I was feeling a little sick now. Carlos was as tall as Adam, but he was thin and small-boned, willowy rather than wiry; I'd attended too many coroners' inquests not to be aware of how easily a man can be killed with bare fists, and had been a journalist for too long not to know what a juicy story all the newspapers, mine included, would make of Carlos' death.

'Don't come here again,' Adam said as Carlos put his handkerchief to his mouth.

'Maybe some of my friends will,' Carlos mumbled, going to the door.

Adam grabbed him. 'If ever they do, if ever you come within ten miles of this place again, you'll be up on a drugs charge. And it won't just be pot either. And don't think Simon will save you. Go on, get out. It makes me sick to look at you.'

When Carlos had gone I found myself unable to speak for a moment. It wasn't the sort of scene I'd been brought up to think of myself as even remotely part of; something harsh and dirty, unthinkingly brutal had been brought into the room and, against all logic, I felt that I was somehow to blame. If ever now I become restive, if ever I find the Chertsey way of life too constricting, I have only to remember that scene.

'Was all that really necessary?' I finally managed to say. 'Goddam it, you didn't have to hit him.'

Adam patted my shoulder as if I were a child. 'There's no other language they understand in the end. It's nothing to do with Carlos being queer; he's one of the low, that's all. You can't call the bugger working-class because he doesn't work. He's been to Borstal – petty thievery, that's all – and of course he's been in the hands of the psychiatrist and that's completely balled him up. He thinks he's important, he thinks his squalid little sins significant. All these toffs talking to him about his sad case and never even making a pass at him. Approach Carlos as if he were a human being and he just thinks you're a fool. Hit him in the chops and he respects you. Why, I've done him the world of good —'

I burst out laughing. 'No-one would have thought it,' I said.

'That's my boy. Always sees the funny side of things.' He rubbed his hands. 'Well, let's have a quick fry-up here for once and then see if we can't have a bit of company in.'

We had ham and eggs and later Saul Dykenhead and Jack Reaverhill and Joyce Impington came in for drinks and we talked and drank wine until two in the morning. Joyce had recently returned from Vietnam and his experiences provided exactly what the occasion needed if it were to be something more than a sharing of opinions, a banding together in face of the common enemy. There were even times during the course of the evening when I believed myself to be on an intellectual level with the others; and even when alone in bed on the verge of sleep I acknowledged that this wasn't true, that I was actually no more than their feed man, someone to admire them, and laugh at their jokes, I was still grateful for having experienced what I should have experienced at Charbury University but never actually did. For not only was there always a last bus to catch, but the people there who talked into the small hours were the left-wingers, who always seem to end their symposiums by voting to organise a demonstration. And the few Conservatives at Charbury liked drinking better than talking and horses, dogs and cars better than ideas.

That evening was the best I ever had at Shalott House – better than any of the more obviously enjoyable evenings which after all in the end only boiled down to alcohol and sex, the simple absorption of liquor and the animal act which is never anything else but simple even if you're double-jointed and extremely inventive.

There weren't so many evenings like that at Shalott House. Because of their nature they were unplanned; but it's odd that of all the hours I spent there I remember with the most pleasure those which hadn't the least tincture of sin.

Adam, in fact, commented upon this as we emptied the ashtrays and put the glasses and coffee cups away at two in the morning.

'Not one regret,' he said, 'not one cause of Confession. You won't wake up with a hangover or wondering if you hit someone with your car or wondering if the silly bitch has remembered to take her pill. We ought to do this more often.'

'Yes, we ought to,' I said, my brain still happily digesting new ideas and nourishing dreams which, to do me justice, had nothing to do with my own material advancement. 'But we won't.'

We would go on playing the Crying Game, there would be other scenes as ugly in their way as the scene with Carlos, different in kind but no different in degree. I didn't make any dramatic resolutions, I fully intended to keep on living in exactly the same way as before; but somehow or other, watching Adam's face as he'd hit Carlos, disillusionment had crept in.

twelve

It was one Saturday morning in April that Angela asked me to marry her. We were having breakfast at her flat; as if to live up to the bright spring day outside I was wearing a new light grey suit from Simpson's and she a crisp white blouse and scarlet skirt.

We were eating a full English breakfast – cornflakes, orange juice, coffee, bacon and eggs, toast, Cooper's Oxford marmalade – and we were eating it not in the kitchen but the dining-room, facing each other at opposite ends of the big mahogany table. This was her latest whim, not to be relaxed or casual, but to be thoroughly middle-class and formal and although our tongues were to some extent in our cheeks, we discovered that the time we spent with each other was becoming infused with a sense of ceremony, that we were even able for hours at a stretch to forget the world we lived in, to put ourselves back, as it were, on the Gold Standard. We would even dress for the theatre though now we would eat afterwards not at Prunier's or the Caprice as once we had done, but at the flat on something simple but good – Harrods' special pork sausage, Fortnum's game pie, a meat fondue with a bottle of red wine; and as often as not we didn't go out but watched TV or listened to gramophone records and sometimes concerts on the radio. I wouldn't say that the edge had gone off our passion for each other; but it had become quieter, gentler, less frantic, we didn't tear at each other, her bites didn't draw blood.

There was still a part of her life I didn't share. I hadn't yet seen her studio in Notting Hill. And her paintings were becoming more and more obsessed with violence as she herself became more domesticated; I sometimes wonder now if that wasn't the key to the change in her behaviour, if she wasn't narrowing the channel and building up its banks in order that the floodwater might run deeper and faster. But I was content to have two or three nights a week and occasionally a weekend of the new Angela: I didn't ask her any questions about her activities when she wasn't with me any more than she asked me.

When that morning she said in a matter-of-fact tone over the marmalade, 'I think it's time we got married,' it came as no shock.

'Yes,' I said. 'It *is* time we got married.'

'Don't overwhelm me with your enthusiasm,' she said sharply. 'There's no reason why you can't marry, is there? You haven't a wife tucked away somewhere, have you?'

I went over to her chair and kissed her on the cheek. 'I love you, darling. Who else would I marry? I only wish you'd given me the chance of asking you first.'

'I might have waited a long time then, mightn't I?' I saw tears in her eyes. 'Didn't you think I was the same as other women, then? Didn't you know I was twenty-five and I've done everything and I've seen it all and now I want a home and children? We're playing at it now, honey. A good old game of Mummies and Daddies in this smashing Wendy house of a flat – oh, that's what it is really because no-one lives properly here. Even I don't. I'm the care-taker, you know. I keep the place aired. If my dear brother ever does need the place, out I'll go.'

'I sometimes wonder if he exists,' I said. 'Or your father and mother. Am I being kept a secret from them or what?'

'They all exist, don't you worry. But Perry's off to Japan, and Daddy and Mummy have buggered off to the Canaries. They used to go to different places separately, but I suppose they're slowing down a bit now.'

'It's not important, but I'm curious as to their reception of me as a son-in-law.'

'They'll be damned glad it's not someone worse.' Then she added with unusual thoughtfulness. 'No, darling, I don't mean that. They'll be jolly pleased, actually. You see, you're strong and healthy and not decadent. My parents are very hot upon the subject. The father of my children needs to be terribly prole: we're an old and thin-blooded lot. Mummy and Daddy are cousins, you see. They had to have a special dispensation.'

'Oh, I think I'm common enough for them,' I said, not particularly liking the concept of myself as a stock animal, 'but it's keeping you I'm really worried about.'

'I've got some money. And I get rather a lot when I marry. Under my grandfather's will. But it must be a Catholic. There'd been the hell of a row about a cousin of mine marrying a Jew, so he wanted to make sure nothing like that could happen again. At least, not if he could help it.'

'I didn't know people could make wills like that.'

'No-one's bothered to contest it. I mean, who else would I marry but a Pape? Or you, come to that?'

'I don't want your money. Or your grandfather's money.' That was a lie in one sense; I had no objection at all to enjoying an unearned income, no matter from what source. What I did object to was the picture of me dancing to Angela's bidding for the rest of my life.

'It's just the same as any other money. Don't be a fool.'

'Settle it on the children then,' I said. The whole conversation was becoming slightly unreal; large inheritances and allowances were completely outside my experience.

'A good idea. Saves tax. Incidentally, what will your parents think about *me*?'

'They're bound to like you.'

'Let's see them now. Today.' Instantly there was nothing else she could think of, nothing else she would rather do and, though I hadn't the least desire to go to Charbury that day, I could see the Angela I'd first known, the Angela who I sometimes missed. My mother's house – and there is a revealing phrase for you – was always ready for a visit from Royalty and never more so than at weekends but I knew that she liked at least twenty-four hours' notice of a visitor, that she liked to put on a special show. And I had already in mind the film I wanted to see that Saturday, I had been planning the whole day.

'It's two hundred miles away, and they're not expecting us,' I said weakly.

'Phone them,' she said, and went into the bedroom to reappear five minutes later with a weekend case.

And so five hours later we were in Charbury. Once on the road I stopped making any objections. It seems a simple enough thing, but that was the high point of our relationship, keeping at a steady sixty down the M1 in an open car, a pretty girl by my side, only wishing that the car had been larger and grander, or at least an MG Midget or a Triumph Spitfire but not really caring with the wind in our faces on a day warm enough to keep the top down but just cold enough to make my sheepskin jacket and string-back gloves and her ponyskin coat a necessity – one remembers now, whatever happened later, and remembers with gratitude. The open car is changed now for a Cortina shooting brake, driving is at any time a chore, the longer the distance the greater the chore. But I've had the time when it was something more, when a box on four wheels was pleasure and poetry, when I had the same little-boy affection for the car as when I bought it on the day of my graduation from Charbury, when I had no burdens and no responsibilities, when I used to lie awake at night, my glittering hopes better than any dreams.

We stopped only once at a lorrydriver's pull-up for tea and bacon sandwiches. And as we approached Charbury Angela grew more and more excited, exclaiming at the moors around the city and even its black Victorian buildings with a childish delight; it was so harsh, so alive, so real, she'd never seen anything like it before, how could I bear to be away from it for long?

'You've been to Yorkshire before,' I said.

'Not this part of it. It's feudal where my cousins live, the peasants still tug their forelocks. And there isn't any industry —'

'Don't worry, there won't be any here much longer the way things are going,' I said as I turned past the Town hall and into Hurley Lane, the road to Kirkingham and my parents' home, long and straight, the dust of demolition always floating over it, the new supermarkets and blocks of flats making it curiously inhuman, robbing it of even the shabby but authentic personality it had when I was a child and it was a road of slums and pubs and little shops.

Kirkingham was a village of about seven thousand inhabitants a thousand feet above sea-level and the adjective most used to describe it by its inhabitants was *bracing*. There was a sanatorium there though now the new drugs like streptomycin had emptied it of TB patients. But in my childhood and adolescence the ambulance taking new patients to Chalmers Castle, a former woolman's mansion on a sort of bumpy plateau on the highest point in Charbury, was a common sight as were the patients walking around the grounds or actually into the village itself. I would always look at these doomed ones with a special interest, but they appeared no different from anyone else except that they were perceptibly healthier.

I've called Kirkingham a village although it was in fact part of Charbury. It was heavily built up around the southern end but to the north it was open country with a surprising amount of lush pasture before the moors and the sheep and curlew country began. The original village – one straggling main street, three pubs, three clubs and three nineteenth century Nonconformist chapels, one eighteenth century Anglican church and a dozen seventeenth century weavers' houses – still had a life of its own and was dominated by two families, the Jurbys and the Luddendens. They were mostly farmers and woolmen; the Jurbys were Methodists and the Luddendens Anglicans, but so Low Church in their leanings that they might as well have been Methodist too.

Adam always said that the chief recreations of the two families were boozing and incest; he put forward this idea when we were about fourteen and had discovered John Buchan's *Witchwood*. 'They're the Elect,' he said. 'Whatever they do, they're going to Heaven, and the rest of us, particularly the Papists, are going to Hell. So behind locked doors they poke away like mad, elderberry wine running through their veins like liquid fire.' And certainly the village had a secretive furtive air about it; there wasn't much social life for anyone unless they were a Jurby or a Luddenden or practised the Jurby or Luddenden brand of religion.

I had never liked Kirkingham myself; yet whenever in London I felt nostalgic for the four walls of my parents' house, for the parochial school and the church, for the city of Charbury; and now as I drove along the main street only the presence of Angela and the knowledge that I'd soon be safely inside my parents' house staved off what Adam and I used to call the Kirkingham *cafard*.

The house in Luddenden Avenue stood in what had once been a select residential development for professional men. It was still respectable, with more than its full complement of cars, with the small front gardens and large back gardens in good order, the paintwork gleaming and the brass door-knockers polished and the curtains crisp and clean, but the professional men had mostly moved away to Ilkley and Burley-in-Wharfedale and Bingley and Warley and Harrogate; in a street of twenty houses only four were not divided into flats. And Adam's former home in Marlcliffe View, an almost identical kind of street some five hundred yards away, had been converted into flats four years ago.

It wasn't beautiful but it was solid. And when we were inside and I automatically made the sign of the Cross under the crucifix in the hall and smelt a cake baking from the kitchen I was surrounded by security, but because of Angela, rid of the ever-growing guilt which I'd normally bring with me. Two of my sisters were married and the youngest, Judith, away at Durham University, had just got engaged. She was clever enough, and fancied following me in journalism: but she was much too pretty for her fiancé to endure a long betrothal. And the two married ones each had a child; still unmarried at twenty-eight I felt that I wasn't, as it were, standing my corner, that I was bringing no new life into the house. I knew too that both my parents considered Adam a bad influence; as, it occurred to me, Theresa had done. My guilt wasn't so great that it would have made me get married just to please them; but I did want to please them. I did want to make them happy. Money wouldn't have done it, since my father had now more than enough; advancement in my career they would have been pleased by only for my sake. What they wanted was to see me settled down, to be given more grandchildren, more objects of love.

But it would be wrong for me to pretend that I didn't also have a sense of truimph as I introduced Angela to my parents. Her hair, her teeth, her hands, her accent, her ponyskin coat that must have cost at least £300 – it was a prize. I was bringing home, a living token of my victory over London and, even more so, over Kirkingham.

At first my mother and father were a little too well-spoken, just as their clothes were too obviously their best, my mother's face too carefully made up, my father's grey hair too well-brushed, his white shirt too obviously not his usual weekend wear. But the roaring fire in the stone fireplace, the comfort of the room, full of ornaments and furniture but large enough to accommodate it all without strain, soon had its effect, as had Angela, perfectly self-possessed but not cool, warm and friendly, charming in a way I hadn't thought she could be.

The room had always been the Best Room, not to be used on weekdays, except for social visitors or special occasions; the dining-room was in effect the living-room where the TV and radiogram and most of the books were. But it had never become a sort of mausoleum, a shrine of respectability, it had never gone unused for long periods. It had a comfort, a rightness of taste about it which now I acknowledged even the drawing-room at Shalott House didn't possess.

For a while the observer took over and I saw my father and mother through Angela's eyes. That too was a triumph. Neither my mother, still pretty with fair hair untinged with either grey or artificial brightness, still only slightly plump, nor my father, tall and flat-bellied with thick dark eyebrows and a straight back, were what she had been half-anticipating. For the stereotype would have been persistently in her mind as it is with even the most intelligent – Mother with

222

a figure like a sack of coals tied in the middle, with fat legs streaked red from sitting too close to the fire, and beery jolly old Dad collarless and his waistcoat unbuttoned, gesticulating with a stubby old pipe in his hand.

'Isn't there a Guilsfield Manor somewhere near Northallerton?' my mother enquired as she gave Angela a cup of tea (from, it didn't escape my attention, the silver teapot which was only used half-a-dozen times a year).

'Yes, but there aren't any Guilsfields there any more. My cousin Alex didn't have any children, and he couldn't really afford to keep the estate going anyway. So he and his wife are in Corfu now, soaking up the sunshine and playing the devil about the Government.'

'They do right,' my father said. 'If I had any capital I wouldn't keep it here to let those fools at Whitehall rob me of it. You paint, don't you, Angela?'

'I do my best.'

This was unexpected; I couldn't recall having told either of my parents this.

'I saw some of your stuff in a Bond Street gallery when I was there last. You're good with the figure, and that's rare these days. Don't be too keen to get rid of all your stuff. Painting and jewellery and land will keep their value, besides being nice things to have.'

My mother intervened.

'Don't talk shop, Luke. Angela doesn't paint for money. She does it because she has to. And it's something of her own that she'll always have, even when she's married. I've often wished that I could do something like that. But do it really well, it's no use otherwise . . .'

'She is good,' I said. 'Really good.'

Angela shook her head.

'It's no use,' my father said. 'She won't ever be satisfied. You really mean it, Frank, and you're well up in these things, but Angela's not the sort ever to be satisfied by that.'

223

Or by me, I thought, or by anyone else. She seemed happy enough now, talking about her family, asking questions about my sisters, relaxed in that relaxed room, outside the sky turning grey as the sun went behind a cloud; she was happy in this room because she knew that the big wooden crucifix above the fireplace, the framed Nuptial Blessing and the First Communion certificates by the Goya Agony in the Garden reproduction weren't there for effect, that my father and mother – and until then I'd never thought about it – had never slept with anyone else and had brought up their children in the fear of God, or rather in His love. There wasn't any fear in that room or in the whole house; there was only love, because they'd kept the rules, even when keeping the rules must have been hard. My father now was next in line for manager and earning over £2000 a year; but there had been a time when he could have cut corners and doubled his income, there had been a hundred lucrative opportunities which he wouldn't touch because they weren't quite straight, because there was always some detail to be kept under his hat; which, he said, sooner or later meant telling a lie. And my mother, who had a taste for beautiful things, to whom anything cheap caused almost physical pain, refused to return to her job as a secretary until all her children had left school. None of us had ever known as children what it was to come back to an empty house; and she would have resigned her present job in a flash had any of her children needed her.

As Angela and my parents talked, I leaned back in my chair, thinking of these things with a sense of discovery but also with a certain foreboding. My sister Clare came for tea, which was the usual Saturday meal – stand pie, pickles, ham, tongue, salad, fruit cake, trifle – with her husband Brian Leavis and their ten-month old son John. Brian was in the Surveyor's Department at Charbury, a large amiable young man who was so transparent in his reactions that he always made me feel rather ashamed of myself for no good reason. The baby was large and amiable too with round blue eyes; he wouldn't come to me but staggered over to Angela and sat on her knee throughout the meal.

Clare, a younger edition of my mother physically but at twenty-four already acquiring a spare tyre, sat drinking tea and smiling. My other sisters, one way or the other, all had intellectual pretensions, but Clare had never wanted anything more – or, come to that, less – than a husband and children. 'He likes you,' she said to Angela. 'Mind he doesn't spoil your lovely blouse. He doesn't like everybody, I can tell you.' There was no trace of jealousy in her voice.

Angela stroked the baby's fair hair delicately, then his small hands with the long fingers and filbert-shaped nails, his mother's and his grandmother's hands rather than his father's and mine, which are square with short thick fingers, workman's hands. I again had a moment of empathy with Angela: she was a woman holding a baby, a basic need was being fulfilled. What disquieted me as I watched her delicately caressing the baby, was that he was also an object, a model, the material of art. She was watching herself with a baby on her knee, she was playing a part.

And as the meal progressed, the conversation never lagging, it occurred to me that everyone except Clare and the baby were playing a part too. My father didn't normally talk so much about painting nor my mother about women's careers nor did Brian talk about houses so much ('if only I could get the mortgage I'd have a house exactly like this – wonderful workmanship, first-rate materials') nor was I quite so relaxed and modest and eager to please.

Adam's name came into the conversation; it was then that I noted the change.

'I've been trying to get hold of the Pevsner *West Riding* at Rowley's,' Brian said. 'I don't think they even know who he is.'

My father sighed. 'It was different when Adam's father was there,' he said. 'He didn't know much about hanging on to his money, but he knew all about books.'

'What was he like?' Angela said.

'Tall and skinny and dreamy. He had a good bookshop of his own at Islington once, but he was too fond of reading books to do his book-keeping properly. Too fond of helping other people, too, particularly writers.'

'I know Adam was very fond of him,' Angela said. 'But he never talks about him much.'

The baby began to cry; Clare unhurriedly took him from Angela and went out of the room.

'Oh, Adam was fond of him. I don't think he ever got over his dying. He used to nearly live here then, poor little devil.'

'We haven't seen much of him since,' my mother said.

'I don't think he wants to be reminded of his parents,' I said.

'You always thought the sun shone out of Adam,' my father said. 'I hope you're never disillusioned. It's my impression, God forgive me, that your cousin Adam never thinks of anyone but himself. His father was worth ten of him. I don't think he ever had a selfish thought.'

My father and Adam's father had been great friends; both with a West Riding Noncomformist background, both had married Catholics of Irish extraction, and both had become converts, in my father's instance before marriage, in Adam's father's instance four years before he died. Their arguments about religion and politics – Adam's father had tended to be mildly progressive, my own father fiercely conservative – had remained as spirited as ever. I see their relationship now as being, like most long-standing friendships, a sort of marriage with my father as the protector, the practical one. I heard now as he talked the sad calmness of love bereft; he'd cried when Adam's father had died but

226

the crying hadn't been the same as when my sister Dorothy had had a stillborn son. There is more than one kind of love.

'He was your friend,' Angela said.

'The best friend I've ever had. I still sometimes say to myself, I'll walk over to Marlcliffe Terrace – it's only four streets away – and see old Jonathan. Of course, he'd married a Flanagan and his wife always used to have the house filled with them. She was a good woman but a bit too keen on her family. They were always telling him they were praying for his conversion. He'd have turned years before he died if it hadn't been for that.'

'The Rossleas never did that to you,' my mother said.

'Too superior, that's why,' my father said. 'All those bloody – excuse me, Angela – schoolteachers. The Flanagans are more straightforward.' The Rossleas, as my father said, tended to be schoolteachers and professional people, lace-curtained Irish; the Flanagans were mostly publicans and bookies and salesmen. That was one of the reasons for Adam's father, a member of an old Charbury mill-owning family, being virtually cut off with a shilling. My grand-father Batcombe being a woolcomber and a rather boozy one, the Rossleas had done much the same thing to my mother.

'My head's spinning,' Angela said. 'How are the Rossleas related to the Flanagans?'

'It's very simple,' my mother said. 'Frank's father always gets mixed up. My great-uncle Tim and Adam's great-uncle Aloysius were first cousins. The Rossleas have never really got over it.'

At this point, my sister Dorothy, heavily pregnant, came in with her husband Stephen Bandon, her mink coat over her arm. Dorothy had been a teacher of elocution before she married and an amateur actress before the children – there were two now, presumably being looked after by her

227

mother-in-law at their house in Beckfield, north-east of Kirkingham. I knew Dorothy's curiosity wouldn't allow her to stay away; I also knew that within the first ten minutes of our seeing each other she'd find occasion to refer to her husband's Mark Ten Jaguar, her own Mini and her disgraceful old rag of a mink coat, as if none of us could see it for ourselves.

'We just *dashed* in to meet Frank's girl-friend,' she said breathlessly. 'We're off to Charbury to do a show whilst we still *can* –' Her sharp blue eyes were scrutinizing Angela, pricing each item of clothing and her accent was now even more relentlessly impeccable than it had been the last time I saw her.

'I hope you don't give birth in the stalls, that's all,' Stephen said. On the whole I liked him the best of my two brothers-in-law; he had a sardonically realistic approach to life and I often wondered just what had attracted him to my sister.

*　　*　　*

At nine o'clock my father looked at his watch – I noticed that he was wearing the gold Omega that my mother had given him for their last anniversary and not his everyday one – and said with an air of great surprise – 'Just for once I think we might have a little drink.'

He'd been saying this every Saturday night ever since I could remember.

'I believe I'll join you,' I said happily.

'Perhaps Angela would like a drink,' my mother said.

'I'm rather tired,' Angela said. 'I'd much prefer a cup of tea in any case.'

'You're sure you don't mind?'

'Of course not, or else we'd both go with you,' my mother said. I had a feeling of being indulgently sent out to play

228

like a child. I felt a strange drowsy peacefulness settle over me; nothing in this house would ever change.

I stopped outside at the car.

'It's only five minutes to the club,' my father said. 'Haven't you done enough driving for today?' He strode off up the steep hill to the Conservative Club; I kept up with him without effort, relishing the cold air on my cheeks and cold in my lungs after the heat of the Best Room.

The road was a parody of Heath Street in cobblestones with blackened terrace houses each side and even on the left steeply rising steps with handrails leading to a narrow passage between two blocks of houses. The shops were small and dingy, and at the top of the hill there was the Conservative Club and Kirkingham Moors in place of, as it were, Jack Straw's Castle and the Heath.

The Conservative Club was finished just before the war, a large red-brick one-storey building in every room of which, because of some trick of acoustics, could be heard the click of billiard balls, a sound which has always seemed to me lost and melancholy, dissipated in the most spiritless kind of way.

My father and I settled down in the part of the main bar, two tables to left of the centre, which we knew from experience would be the warmest and the most draught-free. (The ventilation at the Club wasn't all that it should be either.)

'She's something like, is Angela,' he said to me after the usual grumble at the beer and the general ineptitude of the architect ('They gave him his qualifications for good attendance. Ten years the bugger must have took to get through.') of the club. 'You can see she comes from a good family. No airs and graces, she doesn't have to tell you she's something better, she just is . . . Has she any money of her own?'

'When she gets married. I don't know exactly how much.'

'Don't you?' He gave me a shrewd look. 'You're not the chap I took you for then. You mean that you don't really care, is that it?'

'I'd marry her if she hadn't a penny.'

'You'd still be doing well for yourself. Stephen's eyes were out like organ stops.'

'I get fed up hearing about that sodding Jag and the mink coat.'

'We all do, Frank, we all do. And the more she went on, the less she impressed Angela. Not but what Stephen didn't take it all in. I hope we don't have trouble there. Why do you think Dorothy tries so hard?'

'She always did.'

'So did you. Perhaps a bit too hard. I only hope you don't get out of your depth. Angela has a will of her own.'

'So have I.'

'Yes, but marriage is different. It won't work just because you're both Catholics, not that it doesn't help. Your mother and I have had hard times, but there's always been that to hold us together. How did you meet her?'

'At Adam's.' He'd never been so inquisitive; these were more the sort of questions I'd have expected my mother to have put to me. But I loved him so much – because of his goodness not simply because he was my father – that I had no option but to answer him truthfully. It wasn't very often, after all, that someone cared and asked for nothing in return.

'Did he know her first then?'

'She was a friend of his fiancée's.'

'He never deigned to tell us he had a fiancée.'

'It was four years ago. It didn't last long. Another woman.' To my amazement I was embarrassed. 'It wasn't Angela.'

'You don't surprise me. He's not the marrying kind, is Adam.'

'I met the ex-fiancée. She committed suicide. Quite recently.'

'Poor silly girl. She wasn't a Catholic?'

'Not that I know of.'

'They live without God,' he said. 'They live as if they were never going to die, and then they realize there's something missing . . .'

Wee, wee, wee, I can't find my way home; night at the crossroads and the owl on the signpost and the dark woods. It had nothing to do with me; give me the bowl of water and a clean towel. I changed the subject.

'Adam's going into business on his own account. He wants me to be his partner.'

'Does he now? I'll tell you why; he wants a general mugabout, someone who'll never try to take over behind his back. You please yourself, son, but you don't know much about business. Or about Master Adam. Don't go in with a friend, particularly when that friend's your cousin.'

He was putting into words what I'd intermittently been thinking ever since Adam made me the offer; but now, perversely, I was angry with him for expressing my own mistrust.

'I don't see why not. You'd think he was a bloody con man, the way you go on.'

'He is.' My father's eyes were fixed somewhere above the portrait of the Queen and Prince Philip on the wall opposite. 'But not for money. He likes to arrange people's lives. His mother was a good woman but she was just the same.'

'You're not trying to arrange mine by any chance?'

'I'm your father,' he said mildly. 'By the way, do you ever see anything of Theresa Carndonagh these days?'

Now – and I don't care to remember this – I was angry. 'Someone's been gossiping. Someone's been nosing around my private life. I won't bloody well stand for it —'

'Shush.' He had never hit any of us but he could still

silence me at will. 'She's related to the Monsignor and the Monsignor has relations too. You think that we shouldn't listen when people talk about our son?'

'It depends upon what they say.'

'She's keen on you but you're in with a bad crowd. Naturally, the Carndonagh version was that she loathed you, but I know damned well that if she wasn't keen on you, she wouldn't even remember your name. Didn't you know the Monsignor had relations? Not here, but in Harrogate and Bingley.' He wagged his finger in mock reproof. I could see that he wasn't entirely displeased to have a son who was considered by the Carndonaghs to be a devil for the women.

'Theresa mentioned it once. I didn't pay much attention.' I ordered another two pints of the Club's special bitter, which was one thing at least they did better in the North, clear and with a good head on it, with a slightly aromatic after-taste.

'What's she like?'

'She's a good girl. But bossy. Looks a bit like Angela.'

'You seem to like bossy women. Your mother now has a will of iron. And it's come out in all her daughters. Even Clare. Clare seems easy-going enough, but she'll not budge an inch from her way.' He smiled. He was full and over-flowing with happiness now, greeting people from time to time, aware that everyone recognized his clever son from London who at twenty-eight earned nearly twice as much as his father (I'd never really explained my expenses to him but I knew that he didn't mind my earning more) and who was as good as engaged to one of the Guilsfields of Guilsfield Manor, a genuine old English recusant family which hadn't sold out to Henry the Eighth and whose name was in itself better than any title.

He asked me about my job which he was always hungry for the least detail of, and as he listened to a suitably edited account of the Glenthorn-Aviemore campaign ('A dirty lot, these bloody socialists, and cunning with it, not like poor old Profumo') I underwent a painful attack of understanding, painful because I loved him; I saw for the first time, that he did no more than endure his job, that its arid details, its undercurrent of pettifogging legalism ('strong stuff, this insurance, if you read the clauses in small print on the other side of the appendix to Page One Hundred' he used to say) had never really suited him. He would have preferred a job like mine, he would have preferred to be in the centre of things, he would even have fancied himself as a writer. But he wasn't as cold as me, he met a good Catholic girl and he fell in love with her and he married her and gave her five children. I resolved that I'd give him a holiday in London – it was easily enough arranged now that he was a senior in his firm, and show him round the paper, take him on jobs with me, get tickets for all the shows and invitations to all the Press receptions. I knew that I wouldn't even as the idea was formulated; I didn't love him enough, I was far too absorbed with my job, the Shalott House circle, and Angela; I could, to be vulgar, see no further than my own prick end. Now that I have enough love, now that I want to give him all that I can, it's too late.

And whilst I thought about this – pluming myself upon my own insight and generosity of spirit – I was occupied with another thought, panic-stricken by it, feeling myself as not an individual at all, but caught in the same old trap – *You seem to like bossy women* . . . And the queer thing was that it wasn't Angela who suddenly seemed ageless and tremendous, but Theresa. It was Theresa's womb that was drawing me in, drawing me in future and freedom and all, Theresa whom I hadn't seen since last winter, Theresa whom I had vowed never to see again.

thirteen

The Editor might have been Jerry Knaphill's brother: the same round face, not effeminate but somehow feminine in cast, the same rather protuberant pale blue eyes, the same fat slouching body, and even the same gold-rimmed spectacles. I think sometimes that there must be only about a dozen English physical types, and one day they'll all be properly and scientifically categorized and one will be able to describe by number.

Jerry, however, always gave the impression of not being quite up to par, of keeping himself going only by alcohol and sex; the Editor, despite his surplus weight, was so abounding in energy, so clean and scrubbed and freshly laundered that, on this wet Monday morning after my visit to Charbury, he made me feel tired, down-at-heel and despite my shower at Angela's flat and my fresh shirt and underwear, somehow unclean, just as the wall-to-wall red carpet and enormous walnut desk and the big picture windows made me feel, thinking of my own steel desk in the Reporters Room, just one stage above office boy.

'It's a *new* murder series,' the Editor said. 'The Victims. Those who get murdered and those who they leave behind. You know Backmuir's not expected to live?'

Backmuir was a child murderer serving a life sentence, who had that weekend been attacked by his fellow-prisoners.

'Good,' I said, feeling cheerful for the first time that morning.

'Doubly good, because all hell is let loose at the Home Office. Backmuir wanted solitary confinement – he's not crazy despite what those effing head-shrinkers said – but the Home Office decided he must mix with the other inmates. To keep him psychologically stable.' He grinned, showing two rows of small white teeth. 'Christ, I thought there could be no-one worse than Soskice until we got Jenkins. Then I thought we could get no-one worse than Jenkins until we got Callaghan. But this new bloke beats them all. And he's done the one thing that won't be forgiven; he's let something bad happen to a murderer. So the time has come to clobber the bastards. And with this series we will clobber them good and proper. I've arranged for you to interview the Alderholts this morning. A change from Judy Aviemore and David Glenthorn, but it'll do you good. We're paying them fifty quid by the way, so you needn't beat about the bush too much. Ask them any questions you like.'

I felt sick. 'I'm not sure it's in my line of country.'

'Why do you think I asked you?' He pulled out a folder of letters from a drawer and began to look through them. 'I'll see you after lunch, Frank.'

When the Editor had asked to see me that morning I had been, as they say in the West Riding, chuffed. To be singled out by Barbury was better than not to be singled out at all; but however important he might be, he wasn't the Editor, nor was he ever likely to be. He was being used, as we well knew, to keep the Editor on his toes; and people who are used in that way rarely are rewarded according to what they consider their lights to be. An hour later in a Council estate south of the river, I was not chuffed. If only I'd been working-class, I suppose that the estate – a thousand or what appeared to be a thousand uniform pebble dash houses under a grey rainy sky – would have been what I was used to, that the people who inhabited these houses would not have been of a different species from me. And if I'd been a public schoolboy, I might at least during the holidays have mixed with boys of my own age at an East End youth club, might even have considered them to be the salt of the earth.

I had gone to St Chad's parochial school, I had gone to St Theo's Grammar School; at the former I was sorted out early, at the latter I was stamped once and for all not so much as middle-class but non-working class. The most frequently used term of disapproval at our home was *Council House*; it was even more withering than *common* or *vulgar* or *crude*. The council house tenants lived off our backs, asking for garages whilst we walked to work to pay the mortgage; it was their children who had nits in their hair, filled the Juvenile Courts, threw stones at trains and later on, took drugs, contracted syphilis, murdered and were murdered, were led into futile strikes by Communists – to me even now a Council estate was not only depressing but sinister. I won't even attempt to justify this attitude; I'm content to record it.

The actual interview was even more harrowing than I'd expected. Even then, before I was married and had children of my own I didn't like to think of children suffering; I had a way of reading the papers and blacking out all the items which dealt with deaths in accidents or by murder and, almost as bad, their ill-treatment. I suppose that this was the result of my having four younger sisters and helping to take care of them; I knew, vividly, what children were like, how helpless and how fragile they were.

Backmuir's victim had been a girl of seven; there was a photo of her on the mantelpiece, amidst all the usual litter one sees on working-class mantelpieces. She had round horn-rimmed NHS glasses with wire sides, which made her death even more unbearable; I could imagine them lying cracked beside her with her Dorothy bag, and the thin white legs obscenely parted.

The mother, a thin rabbity-faced woman, was holding her six-month-old baby to her. His name was Gary; his face was small and pinched and his nose was running. His matinée jacket had been white once but was now predominantly yellow. There was a raw ammoniacal smell from the nappies over the fireguard; my guess was that she didn't wash them properly but simply dried them when they were wet. The four-year old daughter, Sandra, clung to her mother's skirts, peeping at me now and again through her fingers. Two of her front teeth were black with decay. The other child, Roy, was six and was back at school after a series of heavy colds which she'd been frightened were something worse because TB ran in the family; I was glad that the child was better, because to look at Gary and Sandra was almost physically painful. Pity hurts, and the more objects of pity, the more it hurts.

The husband, as thin and rabbity-faced as his wife, sat by the fire smoking a cigarette. I gave him a Mannikin, and the prosperous clubroom smell helped to fumigate the atmosphere a little. I was glad that at least I had fifty pounds in cash to give them – it wouldn't last them longer than a few days, since that kind of person is always feckless, but there'd be a little colour in their lives, they'd be able to buy a few illusions.

'He hasn't worked much since it happened,' the mother said. 'Nerves. She was his pet, you see.'

'Always used to come running out to kiss me when I came home from work,' the husband said. His nerves apparently prevented him from shaving or combing his hair; but even as I thought this I started to cry. I wasn't only crying because of the dead child, I was crying because I had so much and they had so little, because though she was a slattern and he was a layabout, they were kind to their children, Gary's little bony hands clutched his mother's dress knowing they'd never be brushed off, Sandra, when I started crying went over to her father and sat on his knee. They were a family, and a family which had been cruelly attacked; when they saw my tears they comforted me in a surprisingly articulate and tender way and the mother gave Gary to her husband to hold and went into the kitchen to make tea. I accepted the comfort and drank the tea, which was the cheapest kind with leaves floating on the top and tainted by the metallic taste of sterilised milk, and went on with the interview, bearing in mind always what the ultimate purpose of the Victims series was, already editing the words, cutting out the swear words and repetitions – *All I know is, my Miriam's dead and the man who did it is still alive. It won't seem right to me if he doesn't die,* and, most telling of all, from Sandra, *Miriam did go to Heaven, she did, but I want to see Miriam again, I do.* But when her mother mentioned the child's Dorothy bag again, speaking quite calmly as if standing at some distance from the event – *I knew it was hers, because her father had stencilled her initials on it, ever so proud of it she was* – my tears started to flow again.

I gave them the fifty pounds when I'd got as much as needed from them – to have given them it at the beginning would have meant no interview – and went out into the rain, glad to be out in the fresh air, glad even of the physical discomfort of rapidly becoming soaking wet.

When I gave my piece to the Editor that afternoon he read it through quickly, making alterations from time to time, in between answering the telephone. As he answered the telephone his eyes were still on the typescript: I waited apprehensively for his verdict, feeling smaller and younger, just as I used to do in my early days on the Charbury Gazette.

'A cracker,' he said finally. 'A real cracker, Frank.' He

went over to the large bureau beside the desk, opening it to reveal an array of bottles and a large refrigerator. 'You deserve a drink. What'll it be?'

'Scotch, please.'

He poured me a large drink and himself a small one.

'I like to know my colleagues, Frank, particularly the young ones. Because if I don't spot the bright boys and girls some other editor will.' He tapped the typescript with his gold pencil. 'There's feeling here, Frank, real feeling. That piece took something out of you. Perhaps you feel too much but, by God, it's a fault on the right side.' He gave me the typescript. 'Tell them I want this big.' The phone rang again and I left his office feeling better than when I'd gone in, the whisky and the praise chasing away my feeling of emptiness.

There was a note from Barbury on my desk; I considered disregarding it for a moment, feeling that I'd done enough for one day, but remembered that he was still Assistant Editor and I was still likely to see more of him than I was of the Editor.

'Where the bloody hell have you been?' he asked me when I went into his office.

I told him.

'Plenty of others could have done that,' he grumbled.

I shrugged my shoulders.

'It's not for me to argue with him, is it?'

'He might have told me first. Well, don't let us waste our time over it. Aviemore's now definitely left his wife.' He rubbed his hands. 'The balloon is about to go up. I want you to get a statement from him. Don't worry about libel. I'll sort it out this end.'

'And his wife?'

'You'll be lucky. It only broke an hour ago and I've had someone try her. She won't play at all. Not even the old *I have no statement to make at present.* Just – I quote – *If you print*

239

anything about me, be careful to get your lawyers to go through it with a fine toothcomb ... Clever bitch. She's protecting Glenthorn, of course. As long as she can ...'

'Where is Aviemore?'

'You have me there. I've tried everywhere but no soap. Not that it prevents you from trying again.'

'I'm bloody tired,' I said. I was sick of the whole affair; indeed at that moment sick of my whole job. That morning I had bought my way into a family's private grief for fifty pounds; now I was to help break up a marriage and to ruin a man who'd never done me any harm.

'If we don't get the story someone else will,' Barbury said, as if reading my thoughts.

'I'll try,' I said, and spent the next hour phoning every place where Aviemore might possibly be. Then, as I was at the point of admitting defeat, I remembered the name of the drinking club where he'd been on the night of my first party at Shalott House.

When you've been doing any job long enough you develop special instincts. There was no rational explanation for my absolute certainty that Aviemore would be found at the Gearbox; and at that stage in my career I relied upon my instincts sufficiently not to question them.

The Gearbox had had several changes of owner since it was first founded – if that's not too grand a word – sometime in the fifties. It had begun as a rally drivers' club; but the drivers had drifted away as parking in Central London became more and more impossible and as Soho more and more wide open. The name hadn't changed, most probably with the dim idea of attracting the Carnaby Street set. But they preferred soft drinks and coffee and the Beatles and the Rolling Stones belting it out on discs, and the Gearbox was for serious drinking. The surroundings were dingy but respectable, in a narrow street off Tottenham Court Road; there seemed to be a great many mysterious little manufacturing businesses there, and even a few flats. It was an odd corner of Soho, well out of the strip club and dirty book-shop and restaurant mainstream; at half-past five when I got out of the taxi, the Gearbox's pink neon sign was the only evidence of life there.

I ran up the narrow wooden steps and showed my Press card to the manager, a standard Mark I type club manager with a Zapata moustache and black suède shoes.

'No trouble, I hope, old boy?' he asked.

'I'm looking for someone,' I said. 'But there won't be any trouble, I promise you. He might even be glad to see me.' I glanced around the long narrow room. The blue plastic covered benches round the sides, the red carpet, the purple walls with large pink stars, looked garish enough now but later on when the blinds were drawn and the pink-shaded lights switched on it would come into its own, a quiet little drinking club where nobody cared about the last train home and no-one, male or female, would pester you unless you wanted to be pestered. The Burrow would have been a better name for it than the Gearbox, because it was a burrow, a hiding-hole; which was the rationalization for my being there if I needed one.

Two girls, one in a leather jerkin and tight jeans with a fly front and the other in a rather fussy pink dress talked in low voices at the far end of the room. The one in the dress was wearing a wedding ring. At the bar two fat men with Yorkshire accents drank Guinness and discussed cricket with the barman, also a Mark I type with dark greased-down hair and a pale night-time face. A fat little man with a gold bracelet watch and worried eyes sat alone with a large whisky pretending to read the paper, glancing over it from time to time at a young-old woman who sat at the other end of the room, yawning and crossing her black-stockinged legs from time to time to show a glimpse of white flesh.

Aviemore wasn't there; but I knew that he would arrive

sooner or later. I bought the manager a large whisky, keeping to Worthington myself, and interviewed him without him knowing it to pass the time until Aviemore came in.

He was there at a quarter past six, dapper and bouncing in a sober dark grey suit.

'Excuse me,' I said to the manager, having learned by now that no-one likes it being too obvious that one has simply been made use of.

I held out my hand to Aviemore; he seemed the hand-shaking type. 'We met at Adam Keelby's party,' I said. 'Frank Batcombe's my name.' He laughed. I hadn't expected him to be unduly downcast but hadn't expected such ebullient high spirits. 'God I was pissed that night,' he said. 'As pissed as I expect to be tonight. I've left my car behind. In fact, Frank, I've left everything behind. You've no idea what a relief it is.' I saw that he had been drinking; not to excess, but enough to loosen his tongue.

'Add to the relief then,' I said. 'Have a drink.'

He nodded to the barman. 'Bert knows what I like. They have ice here, did you know that? Distributed with a lavish hand.'

He sat down with a sigh of relief and Bert mixed a Martini. The rain drummed against the bleary window and I had a moment of revulsion. What was I doing here, plying a man with drinks to prise the secrets of his marriage bed from him?

'You know I work for the Argus,' I said when I'd brought over the drinks. 'You can tell me to go if you like and I'll go.'

'The palest Martinis in London,' he said. 'The gin says hello to the vermouth ...' He stared at the young-old woman; probably she looked younger to him than she did to me.

'Would you like to say anything about it?' I asked him.

'I summon up your face,' he said, 'from the mists of the

242

past. You work for the papers. I read the papers a lot. My wife's always in the paper these days. Also a certain prick of a politician. You interviewed my dear wife once.' He giggled. 'Don't imagine that one doesn't see what you're trying to do to a certain someone ... Clever Judy couldn't see until I told her.'

'That's interesting.'

'Yes, it is. I'll tell you something, my dear boy. Don't ever marry a woman writer. Don't ever marry a clever woman. I'll tell you who I am: I'm Judy Aviemore's husband. Funny thing is this: she never began to write until she married me. I gave her the time, don't you see. I paid for the nanny and the au pair and the daily help – I wonder if she'll go on using my name? Not my name any more, of course. You meet them at parties and they know your name. Bloody marvellous, you think. I mean, my firm's not the biggest in the world, but I built it up. Then it comes home to you – they don't know who you are, not they. *How wonderful it must be to be married to a great talent like hers, Mr Aviemore. What a privilege!*' He drained off his Martini and nodded at Bert again. 'Privilege my arse. She's not there half the time. In *bed* she's not there. She was grateful enough to be married to the boring old businessman after she'd had a basinful of la bloody vie Bohème with her first husband, the great painter, the great star-crossed genius who started the day with brandy and pep pills ...'

'Would you say that you and Mrs Aviemore have separated, then?'

'Yes. We have separated and I shall be consulting my solicitors. There is no hope of a reconcil – reconciliation. It's a question of my honour.' He looked around the room frantically as if he expected to find his honour there. 'A rotten sneaking bastard has robbed me of my honour ...'

'You wouldn't care, between us, to name the man?'

'He's very well known. Much better known than me. Oh

yes. Believe me, his image is going to get a real old bashing. Yes, I'm going to ruin the bastard, the North-East's darling will be their darling no longer. Very moral they are in the North. It's my honour, you see.'

'You think he's damaged your honour?'

'I've got a right to my honour, haven't I? It's my wife he's slept with, isn't it? I've left home, you see —'

'Mrs Aviemore is staying on at your house?'

'Yes, and welcome to it. I never wanted to live in bloody London.' He closed his eyes and screwed up his face. 'Jesus, the creeps she brings into the house! Long hair like great big tarts, neighing away about bloody Vietnam and bloody Hiroshima and bloody South Africa and how we ought to be kind to the bloody niggers because they're just as good as us . . .' He sipped his second Martini, then his glance took in the two girls in the corner, now dreamily holding hands.

'They're Lesbians,' he said.

'I know.' I began to like him; there was something pathetic about his simplicity.

'Have you heard what they do?' He told me, his eyes wide. 'They don't want men after that.'

'Is that a fact?'

He nodded gravely. 'I don't mind. I mean, I don't like ballet, but some people rave about it. It's all a matter of taste.'

I left him after the third Martini, which appeared to be a neat quadruple gin, and phoned my story, such as it was, to Barbury from the club call-box.

I found myself ravenously hungry, had an omelette and two cups of coffee at the nearby Golden Egg without seeming to taste them, refuelling rather than eating and drinking, and arrived at Shalott House dead-tired but more than physically exhausted. It was one thing to weep for a murdered child, to give sympathy to the poor; it was another to be sorry for a prosperous middle-aged City man drunk in the Gearbox Club. Where did it stop? What was I being paid for? My time? My skill? Or all of me? And if I was selling all of me, was I being paid enough?

I went into the drawing-room ready only for a quiet slow non-professional drink and possibly something to eat when I felt less used-up, when I'd had the chance to feel that once again I belonged to myself and to myself only. I wanted to see no-one else; particularly not Simon Cothill, who was sitting by the fire talking to Adam in the low voice of a conspirator. When I entered the room they both seemed startled; Simon was the first to recover himself.

'We've been discussing our dear friend Barry,' Simon said. Barry was a young actor with whom Simon had had a brief and tempestuous affair some three years ago when Barry, on the strength of a few good notices, had left the comparative security of a long-established repertory company to try his luck in London. It hadn't taken Barry very long to exhaust Simon's usefulness to him; he had moved on rapidly with his tall gangling but expressive body and his sad bony face with the little boy smile, via Sunday night club performances and TV to several successful films and a fiancée from an old and extremely rich County family.

'Adam couldn't make out why Barry wanted to marry her,' Simon said. 'After all, as far as his tastes run to *women*, they run to the petite, not great shambling creatures like Audrey, and rightly is she named. But I said,' Simon paused, holding up one hand, 'I said, My dear, she's the only girl whose clothes will fit him!'

'We were actually discussing Simon's image,' Adam said. 'We are trying to put hair on its chest, to make it dead common. It's an uphill struggle.'

'I think you're absolutely *misguided*,' Simon said. 'Camp I was before anyone but Christopher Isherwood used the word, camp I am, and camp, my love, I shall always be.'

'Then you'll camp yourself into effing Carey Street,' Adam said. He examined Simon's scarlet wild silk jacket and lace shirt with distaste. 'You won't be bloody well told, will you? That outfit you've got on is all wrong for a start. I told you to try to look like a bookie, not a male whore.'

Simon's smooth face corrugated into sulkiness. 'You're lamentably ignorant, Adam. Some raving swordsmen dress *just* like this.'

'That's all right if you *are* a swordsman, Simon. But not for you.' He turned to me. 'Aren't I right, Frank?'

'Oh, Christ, keep me out of it. But if I were paying for someone's advice, Simon, I'd take it.'

'There you are.' Adam poured me a glass of wine as if in reward. 'Frank, if I may say so, you look shagged out. Hard day at the office?'

'Saw the parents of a murdered child in the morning. They live in a council estate south of the river. Wrote my piece, was ready to go home, and that pig Barbury told me to find Aviemore.'

'Judy Aviemore's husband?'

'That seems to be part of his problem. I found him all right – just followed a hunch – but it was bloody depressing. Evidently he's going to cite Glenthorn at last. It'll be the end of him. It's the one thing the PM won't stand for.'

It was a relief to talk about it; what didn't seem strange then, though it did later, was that I never thought about discussing the matter with the woman I was going to marry. When I mentioned Glenthorn's name, both Adam and Simon looked startled; more startled, I realized – without, in my fatigue, seeing any significance in it – than one would have expected them to be.

'Glenthorn?' Adam said. 'Are you sure?'

'He was rather elliptical about it, and also pissed as a newt, but he couldn't have meant anyone else.'

'She didn't mention it to me,' Simon said. 'Still, these

246

things blow up all of a sudden. I didn't think he was that sort of chap, that's all.' He looked at his watch, a platinum bracelet which he always wore fastened loosely so it hung like a bangle. 'An early night for me, dears,' he said. He slipped out so quickly that I scarcely noticed he'd gone.

'It's his honour,' I said. 'That was the expression he used.'

'His honour!' Adam laughed. 'These people have the morals of the farmyard and they talk about honour. It was the booze talking, not Aviemore. You could buy his sodding honour —' he broke off and looked at me with something like solicitude. 'Have you eaten, Frank?'

'I've eaten. I'm feeling a bit better now, actually. The funny thing is —' I was now talking to myself rather than to anyone else — 'what an unpleasant shock it gives you when a plan works. Of course, Barbury knows his job. But six months ago I wouldn't have believed it could be done.'

'I thought it could,' he said. 'I also thought, when you told me, that you weren't all that happy about it. Because, when all's said and done, what's in it for you?'

The big wing-sided chair had never seemed so comfortable, the room so large or so warm, so absolutely representative of the way I always wanted to live.

'Promotion perhaps,' I said.

'A couple of hundred a year more before tax. And you'll still have to have your expenses scrutinised by a bunch of mean-spirited accountants who hate your guts because they never have any expenses themselves, and the only way for them to get on is to question every penny to demonstrate their keenness and their integrity. It isn't good enough, is it, Frank?'

'Not now particularly.'

'Why not now particularly?'

'Angela and I are engaged.'

He shook my hand. 'I'm not surprised but I'm delighted.

You're exactly what each other needs. We'll have a bloody good dinner on this. Do your people know?'

'I took her home at the weekend.'

'That'd please your mother if I know her. I tell you what, Frank, you're always hearing about the silver cord and the Oedipus complex and all that psychological cock, but all the mums I've ever known were absolutely overjoyed to see their sons married. Especially Papist mums, when it's a good Catholic girl. Let's have some brandy.' He poured me a generous measure of Hennessy VSOP. 'Here's to you and Angela.'

It was all so simple. Behind me lay the smell of that Council house, the note of genuine humiliation in Aviemore's voice, the life of the employee. Ahead of me lay marriage to Angela, travel, independence, declaring dividends instead of receiving salary cheques, a life in which all the conniving was on a civilized level in civilized surroundings, the life of the employer, the life in which one no longer took orders. Why had I hesitated so long?

I lifted my glass. 'And to Keelby and Batcombe,' I said.

fourteen

My first quarrel with Angela took place at breakfast one
month to the day and almost to the hour after our engagement. The spring that year had been cold and wet, and now
the summer was beginning badly with gales and hailstones
lashing the trees in the long narrow garden of Montagu
Square.

'This is the first time we've been together for a week,'
Angela said.

'I had to go,' I said. 'It's my job.' I had been to Truro
and to Dublin interviewing authors partly because the
Literary Editor was taking an early holiday and partly
because the Editor, who seemed to be taking a great interest
in me these days, had decided that I needed to diversify
my experience. I had enjoyed myself and had brought back
a monumental expense account; the two authors I'd interviewed and, indeed, practically lived with, had not only
professed themselves admirers of Scott Fitzgerald but had
also seemed to be emulating his drinking habits. I had
enjoyed it all the more since I could now, since my acceptance of Adam's offer, see the date of my release approaching.

'Your job's with Adam now,' Angela said. 'I had lunch
with him on Wednesday and we fixed it all up.'

I came back to the table and sat down. In a severe navy blue dressing-gown, her face innocent of make-up, she looked every inch the Head Girl she once had been, except that on her left hand there was an engagement ring.

'That's nice,' I said, helping myself to coffee. 'You and Adam fixed it all up. At lunch. Have you decided what my salary's to be?'

'You won't get any, just a share of the profits.'

'And when do they begin?'

'Nominally, about four months from now. In actual fact, it'll be more like nine.' She buttered herself a slice of toast. 'You see, Frank, I'm putting up seven thousand. I'm a pretty big shareholder.'

'There isn't any need. In fact, I don't want you to.'

She spread marmalade over the butter. 'That's beside the point. Adam's a good risk.'

'What does your lawyer think about all this?'

'Once I'm married, he can think what he likes. Good God, Frank. I've known Adam for years. Ever since Wendy —' she put the toast down. 'You didn't really know her,' she said. 'You never saw her at her best. She just reached out —' she opened her arms – 'and everything was poured in. She and Adam were a marvellous couple.'

'If they were so marvellous, why didn't he marry her?'

She was silent for a moment. 'He must have told you. Another woman. And his damned male obtuseness —'

'The other woman wouldn't have been you?'

'I've never slept with Adam. Why should I tell you a lie? Oh hell, darling, never mind Wendy. Let's arrange our own lives. We'll have a holiday, a nice long holiday, and then you can go to work —'

'What'll I use for money?'

'I'll pay for it. Be my kept man, honey. What's money for, if you can't do what you want?'

'But I *won't* be your kept man. I'll keep on at the paper

250

until Adam's ready to start, then I'll give up my job.' I was behaving out of character; all my life – it was, no doubt, the inheritance from the Irish side of the family – I had been mainly actuated by the desire to please. I had no gentlemanly scruples about living on Angela's money, because I wasn't a gentleman; but once I took her money I wouldn't belong to myself any longer.

'I'm going to Tangier next week,' she said. 'Come with me. It won't cost you anything, we'll stay with my Uncle Leo.'

'Uncle Leo mightn't like me.'

'Oh, he would. That's why he went to Tangier in the first place, if you catch my drift. But I'll protect you.'

'You're restless, aren't you, Angela? You can't bear to be in this country for too long, can you?'

'I'll settle down, I promise.' She came over and sat on my knee. The material of the dressing-gown was thinner than it appeared; I knew she was naked underneath. 'But now I want some sunshine, I want to get to know you. Give in the proper notice if you want, and then we'll go. Chuck up the damned job now – what's the difference?'

'No.'

She stood up. 'You don't love me at all, you bastard.'

'I do, but you're not going to bloody well dominate me. If you do now, it'll be worse when we're married. If it comes to that, we have quite a few axes to grind. When the hell are your parents coming home? When do I see them? Or am I to be kept secret? Like your bloody studio? Like your lunching with Adam? Like your great friendship with Adam and Wendy?'

'That wasn't a secret,' she said in a low voice.

'Everything's secret. Like your brother. This bloody flat's like something in a fairy story and I mean a fairy story. I don't believe you have a brother, I don't believe you have parents, I don't believe you have a studio —'

'You're jealous, aren't you? You want me to have no freedom at all, you want to smother me, you want me all the time, you want me to wait here twiddling my thumbs whilst you go off God knows where for your lousy scandal-sheet of a paper. You'll meet my parents, I promise you, and you'll even meet my brother, not that he won't forget about you five minutes after he's been introduced. He doesn't give a curse about anyone unless he can make some money out of them . . .' Her face wrinkled up as if she were going to cry and I pulled her towards me, but she broke away.

'You can choose now, Frank. Your job or me. Or are you still going about with that pious little female journalist? Are you seeing her on the quiet?'

'Theresa? I haven't seen her since I met you.'

'Do what you like. God, sometimes I *hate* you. You're so bloody smug, you're so sure you're always right, you're always sitting in judgement on someone or other, and now you don't trust me, you're scared to give up your piddling job, you're scared I might change my mind, you're scared of what my people will say –' She burst into a flood of noisy tears, stamping her foot like a child in a tizzy, the Head Girl losing control.

I kissed her; she wriggled away but I kissed her again, biting her lip hard. The naked body which emerged from the dressing-gown was not the Head Girl's body, nor were her words the Head Girl's words as she straddled me moaning in the chair, shifting, writhing, turning, the living illustration in that high-ceilinged room with the gleaming table to a book of eighteenth century pornography, elegant even in her abandon. The fine lady's body, it occurred to me even as I began to moan too, being pleasured by her footman.

She went to Tangier a fortnight later; we had patched up a kind of truce, had begun, I then believed, to have an

252

uneasy respect for each other. For the first week of her absence I even relished the ambivalence of being free and not being free, of being engaged and of not being engaged, of not having to consider anyone's convenience but my own. I used sometimes to think of how different it would have been if I'd been engaged to Theresa – I'd seen the pattern of the ordinary engagement with my friends in Charbury. One met one's fiancée virtually every night and sometimes at lunch-time too, one spent every weekend with them flat-hunting and bottom-drawer shopping and, occasionally, if the fiancée needed to wash her hair or catch up with her sewing or mending, the fiancée would be allowed leave of absence, which he wasn't really supposed to enjoy. But I was getting the best of both worlds, I had fiancée and freedom and a new job that was much more than just a job, all tied up in a neat and festive package.

*   *   *

But one evening after Angela had been away for nearly three weeks I ran across Theresa and Harry O'Toole at El Vino's. It had been a hot day for once, the dark narrow room was bright with summer clothes. O'Toole was wearing a very pale lightweight suit with a lavender blue button-down collar and dark blue kipper tie which didn't really do anything for him; he was too respectably bulky, already too settled in that respectable bulkiness for the rest of his life. But Theresa looked cool and – for once I was forced to use the word – swinging in a white crochet minidress and orange sunglasses and shoes and bag to match.

They made room for me beside them on the bench; I sat beside Theresa and was unreasonably disturbed to discover that her flank was both hard and taut and soft and yielding, and that already I was wanting her. I'm not an expert upon sex but I have painfully acquired one working rule; our bodies are wiser than we are. To be explicit, they don't get stirred up if there's nothing doing; we want only what we can have.

Sitting beside Theresa I didn't work this out consciously. I was quite simply jealous, and delighted to see that there was no engagement ring upon her finger. With all her faults, she was too good for him. She was too good for me too, I thought atavistically; my father had told me once that the best man born wasn't good enough for a good woman, and he was dead right, he wasn't merely being sentimental, conditioned by an essentially female church and a wife with, as he said to me often, a will of her own.

'Congratulations,' Theresa said, and O'Toole muttered something to the same effect; he was the sort of person given to spasms of embarrassment in the simplest social situations, which was yet another reason for Theresa being too good for him.

'It comes to us all,' I said. 'Are you still with 'Vagina'?'

O'Toole perceptibly winced; not so much, I think, because of the word itself, but because it was being used in front of Theresa.

'I'm sorry,' I said. 'I get so used to calling it that.'

'It's accurate enough,' Theresa said. 'That's about the only part of the female body they haven't shown yet.'

'Give them time,' I said. 'They're still cock-a-hoop about making abortion socially acceptable.'

'It's murder,' O'Toole said. 'Nothing else.'

There he was right at least, there we could find some kinship if we wanted to find it.

'I liked your piece in *The Victims*,' Theresa said. 'I wish you'd do more pieces like that. You know, Frank –' her voice took on a didactic tone – 'that's your real strength. Your *feelings* are right. You're rather strained when you try to be bright and waspish.'

'You mean there's a lot of good in me?' I was pleased that she should have remembered my article, but not so pleased that she should have implied that my range was limited.

'No, there isn't,' she snapped. 'I was thinking about you professionally, that's all.'

O'Toole seemed embarrassed again. I think that he was perceptive enough to see her interest, but not experienced enough to be able to turn her hostility towards me to any advantage.

'Your fiancée paints, doesn't she?' he asked. 'I saw some of her paintings in a colour supplement once. They're rather ... strong ...'

He meant that Angela always put in the pubic hair and the cleft of the vulva itself, and he found the thought rather shocking.

'My editor loves them,' Theresa said.

'I'm sure we could arrange a meeting,' I said.

'Why isn't your fiancée with you tonight? Is she painting in her Notting Hill hideout?'

'She's in Tangier actually. She'll be back soon.'

'Poor Frank, all alone. Still, I dare say you'll find lots of company at Shalott House.' She picked up her handbag. 'We'd better be moving, Harry, if we're going to see this film tonight.' She pecked my cheek briefly. 'I'll see you around, Frank.'

'Perhaps before you think,' I said, but they were already on their way out. She took his hand – he had ugly thick-fingered hands with bitten nails – and I stared at their re-treating backs with a feeling of vague regret which, as I sat there drinking Chablis, became more and more sharply defined.

At closing time I walked along the Strand to Leicester Square and took the Tube to Sloane Square. Every man I saw – including some whom, had I been a woman, I wouldn't

255

have touched with a disinfected barge-pole – seemed to have a woman with him, and only I was alone and free and wishing to be neither.

It had grown no cooler, and the King's Road was positively stuffy; I imagined all the heat of the day, all the carbon monoxide fumes collected in the chalk bowl that was London, somehow concentrating themselves in this one road, mixing with the smell of garlic and hot milk and, above all, the smell of young women. I walked along the road slowly from the Sloane Square end, trying to look both as if I had somewhere to go, and I was in no hurry; I tried to visualize Angela, but kept on seeing Theresa's hand in O'Toole's, the thin white hand in the big red one. And I tried to pretend that I wasn't looking for a woman, wasn't looking for one of the swinging Chelsea birds, fully paid-up members of the Permissive Society. Like every man of my generation I'd often said that sex was no problem; one had only to stroll along the King's Road and bob's-your-uncle. But either I'd been misinformed or all the swinging birds had already been picked up. I was staring at the window of Granny Takes a Trip, on the point of having a drink and going home to an early bed, when I felt a nudge in my back.

'Give me a light, will you?' The voice was rough and Cockney but female.

I gave her a light. She was small with black stockings and long brown hair. Her face was nearly ugly except for the white teeth and large dark eyes.

I smiled at her. 'Would you like a drink?'

She nodded. 'There's no point in your looking there,' she said. 'That sort of gear wouldn't suit you. You're dead wholesome, see?'

In the pub nearby I bought her a drink. She insisted upon a pint of beer.

'You know what they say about girls who drink pints,' I said. 'Wouldn't you rather have a short?'

'Bugger that,' she said. 'I'm thirsty.' She punched me in the ribs again.

'I'm not a pro,' she said. 'I want you to know that. In fact, I'm getting married next month.'

'That's nice,' I said.

'Get you,' she said. '*That's naice.* You don't think it's *naice* at all, do you?' I noticed she had no ring on her left hand. 'In fact,' she said, 'you don't give a fuck, do you?'

I laughed. 'Not really.'

'My name's Janice. Bloody silly name. What's yours?'

'Frank.'

'I'm at a loose end, Frank. The same as you.' Her dress was of the shift kind; when she leaned forward I saw the shape of her pointed little breasts, then it was as if she were flat-chested again.

'How loose?' I asked her.

'My young man's a poet. He's somewhere in Scotland now. Christ knows why. Goes off for weeks at a time, the bugger. What do you do?'

'I'm a journalist.'

'I didn't think you were a lorry-driver somehow. Have you got a girl?'

'She goes off for weeks at a time, like your fiancé.'

My eyes were beginning to smart with the smoke but I felt at home in this pub, as I did in the Salisbury. Basically, whenever it was built, it was Victorian, and there had been no attempt to tart it up for the on the whole well-heeled clientele who filled it these days.

Janice's hand squeezed my knee. 'You're big, aren't you? My Roddy's awfully weedy, though he's very good in bed. He doesn't take dope, you see, though he drinks a lot.'

'Should I know his stuff?'

'No, you shouldn't. He doesn't publish much. Someone asked him to write an article for a magazine the other day, but he wouldn't. He doesn't like writing prose.'

'Who does?'

'Don't be nasty about my Roddy. Get me another pint.'

'Have a short, for God's sake. I told you about pints.'

'What if it's true. Women are much nicer than men, straight they are. You know, just down the street there's a Lizzie club, honest. I went there for a giggle once . . .' Her voice changed, became almost prim. 'No, I didn't. I hate that sort of thing.'

I tickled her palm. 'Do you hate it? Do you really?' We were jammed in a corner by the entrance; I felt light-headed and weightless, and yet my whole body felt as if it were denser than usual, the flesh heavier, the blood thicker. I longed briefly but sharply for a world where girls didn't pick up strangers, didn't discuss their most intimate concerns with them within minutes of their being picked up, didn't hint at being perverted in order to sharpen their appetites. For she was watching my face for signs of excitement, her dark eyes bright, and I felt as I sometimes felt with Angela, that I was about to enter the arena, that the beast with two backs was a simple beast no longer, that it was savage and sophisticated, seeking domination rather than satisfaction. And it passed, it was as if I were deliberately being kept inside the pub by the girls in their mini-skirts and the men with Zapata moustaches and shoulder-length hair – priestesses of Astarte, priests of Cybele? – and I stopped caring and was finally released into a taxi with her, kissing her frantically, almost despairingly, my hand under her skirt and then briefly aware of stumbling up narrow creaking stairs smelling of mice and gas and mouldering plaster; and of pity, a heart-rending pity as I saw her tinselly scarlet pants and her black stockings, one laddered, on the floor beside the bed and then nothing but my sweat stinging my eyes and her voice screaming in the distance; I had the impression of wind against my face, a black wind, a scouring wind from a great tundra I had to travel across alone; the smell of gas grew stronger and then the sunlight prised my eyes open and she was standing beside the bed with a cup of tea in her hand.

'You're good,' she said. 'Nearly as good as Roddy. 'Course you were pissed blind.'

'You were good too, honey,' I said. I found that I couldn't remember her name. My head began to ache, and I said a quick Act of Contrition; I knew I wasn't going to die there and then, but there was time for me to be knocked down by a car between wherever I was and Hampstead.

The smell of gas was explained by the gas ring on the scarred table by the door, which together with a large whitewood wardrobe painted in red and blue zigzags, two red fireside chairs blackened with dirt, two rickety kitchen chairs, a large bookcase with sagging shelves, a large whitewood cupboard no-one had bothered to paint, and the double bed I was lying in, comprised the sum total of furniture in the room.

She pulled her grubby dressing-gown more tightly round her. 'It's effing cold after yesterday,' she said. 'Not that it's ever warm here. Damp. There's a West Indian family in the basement. God knows how they get on in the winter.'

I finished the tea and felt almost instantly better despite the lipstick marks on the rim of the cup.

'Can I get a bath?'

She laughed. 'You must be joking. I have to go home to Tottenham for a bath.'

I swung myself out of bed in one movement and put my trousers on. 'Can I have a wash then?'

She went to the wardrobe and flung me a towel and a bar of soap.

'Next floor down to your right.'

The bathroom was tiny, about the size of two coffins laid side by side. The matchboard partition door was permanently stuck halfway, and the bath and washbasin were splotched with green. The hot water taps had been sawn off both bath and washbasin. The soap was pink and violently scented; I imagined that its cleansing action would be through removal of skin; but the towel was clean and dry and after a vigorous sluicing in cold water my headache began to disappear.

The W.C. – there was a twee little porcelain notice outside saying *The Smallest Room* – was next to the bathroom. This was the size of two coffins laid end to end with an old-fashioned W.C. on a dais; there was even toilet paper on a holder here, and a reproduction of *The Fighting Téméraire*, and the walls had recently been distempered bright yellow. I washed my hands again and ran up the stairs; Janice – her name came back to me now – looked at me sourly from the kitchen table. 'Christ, you do look healthy,' she said. 'Poor bloody Roddy can't even walk up those stairs without wheezing. Want some more tea? I've only got Marie biscuits to eat.'

I ate a couple of Marie biscuits and drank a second cup of tea; after I had had a shave with Roddy's electric razor – a brand new Remington Selectramatic which he'd probably stolen – the process of physical recovery was complete. So complete, in fact, that when her dressing-gown fell open as she leaned across the table to accept a cheroot from me, I was tempted to take her back to bed, to enjoy her and fully enjoy remembering her afterwards. But that would have been a waste of the Act of Contrition. And there could be no certainty that Roddy wouldn't reappear, which she had told me the night before he had a disconcerting habit of doing. She had also told me then – my memory was almost in full working order now – that she and Roddy had agreed that each must be completely free. But I was old enough to know that men in particular consider such agreements to apply only to themselves; and weedy though Roddy might be, a kick in the testicles or a razor slash across

260

the face would hurt just as much from him as from a fitter man.

'I have to go,' I said.

'Do you?' She wriggled, and the division between her breasts appeared. The dark eyes watched me intently.

'I have an appointment.'

'So have I. With a sodding nignog. Just an excuse to have a white woman strip for him. But it's a living.'

'My fiancée's an artist.'

'You told me last night when I told you I was a model.' She began to giggle.

'What's so funny?'

'I'm not laughing at you, straight I aren't.'

'It's been wonderful,' I said. 'I'll phone you.'

She stopped giggling. 'No,' she said, 'you won't.'

'All right, love. I won't, if that pleases you.' I kissed her on the cheek and ran down the steps. I thought that I heard her giggling again, but I couldn't be certain.

The road was off Chepstow Road; the terrace houses had once been the homes of the Edwardian middle classes, had gone rapidly downhill after the 1914 war, and now were being redeveloped into homes for the middle classes again. The exteriors of the redeveloped ones were glistening with paint and polished brass; there were only two shabby ones left. Soon Janice would be without a home and soon, without benefit of official planning, the district would be respectable again.

It was another chapter for the book on London: was it a good thing that the city should be cleaned up in this way, that there should be no areas of disorder and riot left, no places where the defeated and feckless could retreat to, no sanctuaries from respectability and prosperity? These thoughts and the morning paper occupied me happily enough during the Tube journey to Hampstead; as I walked up Heath Street in the sunlight I wished that I had the courage to sing and dance, to visibly and audibly express my happiness.

When I let myself into the flat there was no sign of anybody being awake; it was only half-past eight, and neither Adam nor Basil had to be at their offices until ten o'clock. I showered quickly and, my clothes over my arm, walked naked into my room, intending to change completely from head to foot. There was a woman in my bed, her naked body only half-concealed by the bedclothes. One arm was over her eyes as if to ward off a blow, pulling up one heavy, dark-nippled breast. There was a clump of dark hair in the armpit, darker than the hair on her head, which was fanned all over the pillow. She smelt of sleep and sweat and stale tobacco and alcohol; but it wasn't a bad smell, because she herself had a good personal smell.

As I stood dumbfounded she opened her eyes and yawned. It was Judy Aviemore.

'I'm sorry,' I said. 'I didn't know —'

'It's me who should be sorry,' she said. She made no attempt to cover herself, but smiled at me, perfectly self-assured.

I took a dressing-gown from my wardrobe. 'I'll see you later,' I said, and went out of the room without looking back.

I knocked at Adam's door and went straight in.

'What the hell are you playing at, Adam? Why couldn't you put her in your own bed?'

'I can't imagine anything nicer,' he said calmly. 'But she didn't want to sleep with me or anyone else last night. In addition to being absolutely kettled, she has that bastard of a politician on her mind. Half-past four it was before she quietened down —'

He reached for his dressing-gown at the bottom of the bed. 'I must have a bath before Basil awakes, the sod always makes a meal of it.'

I followed him into the bathroom. 'There's something fishy going on,' I said.

He turned on the taps and took out his bottle of bath oil. 'Simple pleasures,' he said. 'It foams when you put it under the taps. And the bathroom smells delightful – sexy but medicinal, like a Swedish brothel. There's nothing fishy going on, Frank. Judy was working late on the book with Simon and finally they had a few drinks and one drink led to another, and I expect they exchanged sorrows and wept tear for tear. Then Simon passed out, and when he came to, there was no Judy to be seen, only a neat little pile of female clothes. He must have thought he'd had a brainstorm and done her in; I expect all these boys are hostile sub-consciously to women. But needless to say he hadn't.' She knocked at our door at two a.m., stark naked and absolutely plastered, and babbling Glenthorn's name and how she was going to ruin this good and Christlike man whom she loved so dearly ...' He lowered himself into the bath. 'Your campaign seems to be working, my dear Frank.'

'I'd be obliged if you didn't come all moral over me. It's not my campaign, it's the Assistant Editor's. If I didn't do what he asked me to, I'd simply lose my job, and someone else would take over.'

He sponged his back.

'It's quite pleasant,' he said, 'but I must say I don't experience the almost orgiastic sensations promised in the advertisements ... I'm not coming all moral over you, Frank, merely pointing out a fact. J. Aviemore and D. Glenthorn are now indissolubly linked in the public mind. That was the intention, wasn't it?'

'Nothing's happened yet.'

'Well, Aviemore blows hot and he blows cold. And he likes a bit on the side himself. But sooner or later, and now, I think, sooner, he'll actually see his solicitors, and the wheels of the Law will begin to grind. And Glenthorn will

263

apply for the Chiltern Hundreds. I don't think he has any other source of income but his salary; ipso facto, being Labour, he's a sod, but he's an honest sod.' He sluiced his head with the sponge then rinsed it with the shower attachment.

'Judy will get him something.'

'If he'll take it. She told us all this last night in between bouts of weeping and offers to take on any man in the room.' He got out of the bath and began to dry himself. 'The strange thing is how profoundly anaphrodisiac a woman is in that state. In short, one didn't fancy her.'

'I know what anaphrodisiac means,' I said. 'You needn't add a bloody footnote for my benefit.' Everything he had told me sounded feasible: but it was too feasible, the package was too neat. But then, I recollected, he had always loved secrets; he would tell me the rest in his own good time. I went to answer the doorbell.

It was Simon, looking his real age for once, in a pink silk dressing-gown and purple scarf and scarlet Moroccan slippers.

'I expect you've heard it *all* now,' he said. 'Do not, please, look at me, I know I'm an absolute *hag*. I didn't sleep one *wink* last night, I give you my word, what with the vodka and worry worry worry.... Do you think I look *ill?*'

'You look dreadful, Simon,' I said. 'It wouldn't surprise me if you were to drop dead here and now. It often happens like that. And when it does you'll go straight to hell.'

He tittered uneasily, not knowing whether I was serious or not.

'Sometimes I'm *frightened*,' he said. 'In the middle of the night. But I don't believe in all that stuff about hell, so it doesn't apply —'

'Hell is full of people who don't believe in it,' I said. 'They have all eternity to find out how wrong they were.'

'You're a beast, Frank.' Judy Aviemore's amused voice said at my shoulder. She kissed Simon lightly on both cheeks. 'I'm sorry, honey, for being such a drunken nuisance. You can have your room back now, Frank. I'm sorry I gave you a shock.'

'It was a very pleasant shock,' I said. 'I only hope I may have many more like it.'

'That's very gallant of you, but I know I look like hell. I must go upstairs and pick up my clothes. Simon will let you have your dressing-gown back.' She had tidied her hair and in the heavy blue woollen dressing-gown which was a little too big even for me, she looked extremely feminine and, even at this moment, knew it and enjoyed being feminine for all she was worth. As she left the flat with Simon, again I felt that there was something odd in the air, something I couldn't quite put my finger on. And I found myself envying Glenthorn, wishing that like him, I had the guts to ruin myself for a woman.

I went into my room and put on fresh underwear and socks, clean shirt and a new light blue mohair suit which I'd had made from a roll of cloth my father had got cheap for me. Now the underwear and shirt and socks I'd worn yesterday could go to the laundry, the suit to the cleaners; I dabbed my face and forehead with Ambassador cologne and Notting Hill Gate was washed away. I'd been looking forward to this ever since I'd awakened; but somehow it was all spoilt.

At breakfast Adam was the only cheerful one. 'I've changed our brand of orange juice,' he said. 'From now on it must be South African. Not only does it have the full complement of vitamins, but in drinking it we are striking a blow for RASP. And a blow against Canon Collins, Trevor Huddleston, Bleeding Heart Cameron, the Archbishop of Canterbury, and all that dreadful crew . . .' He babbled on merrily; normally we should have added fresh items to the store of fantasy which was accumulating round RASP, have vied with each other to produce the most reactionary opinions. But that morning Basil and I spoke mainly in monosyllables, except that towards the end of the meal, when Adam said casually, 'Where were you last night, by the way, Frank?' Basil said gloomily, 'He was well out of it.'

'Tush,' Adam said. 'If exhausting at the time, it was extremely interesting to a student of human nature.'

'One only hopes,' Basil said, 'that one won't become involved in anything squalid.'

'Judy isn't like Wendy,' Adam said. 'She'll not do away with herself.'

'Wendy seems to be on your mind lately,' I said, remembering all the times her name had entered the conversation since her death.

Basil stood up. 'I repeat, one only hopes that one won't become involved in anything squalid.' He seemed about to say something to me then went out of the room.

There was an uneasy silence. 'What's up with him?' I asked.

'Oh, he's being very professional. Loathes the thought of scandal being anywhere in his vicinity. But where were you last night, anyway?'

'Picked up a bird in the King's Road. Ended up in Notting Hill.'

He appeared honestly shocked. 'You might have picked something else up as well.' I could see that he disapproved of my going outside the Shalott House circle for sex. 'I hope at least you took precautions.'

'Birth control's a grave sin. No use making matters worse. Besides, it's like washing your feet with your socks on.'

'Well, you'll know when your nose drops off . . . Notting Hill . . . isn't that where Angela has a studio?'

'I suppose so. I've never visited it.' To be reminded of the fact that there was a whole area of her existence which I was forbidden to enter profoundly angered me. He changed the subject quickly; but I couldn't get it out of my mind all day; and the more I thought about it, the more clearly I seemed to hear Janice giggling to herself as I left her.

fifteen

I met Angela at London Airport a week after; she was so
deeply suntanned that I didn't at first recognize her, and
wearing a bright red silk dress some six inches above the
knee. I had been buying a lot of new clothes lately, spurred
into it by Adam, who pointed out that what was good enough
for a journalist wasn't good enough for a partner in a
PR firm; I was wearing for the first time a bronze and
black mohair suit from Aquascutum, a fawn silk shirt, a red
Princess Mara tie and red silk handkerchief to match, and
brown sealskin shoes. And I was wearing the gold bracelet
Longines that Angela had given me for my birthday
and the gold cufflinks she had given me on our engagement; against the background of silver aeroplanes and
bright sunlight, and the loudspeakers calling out the names
of foreign places – Rome, Athens, Majorca, Madrid,
Moscow, New York, Teneriffe – and the bottles of whisky
and the jewellery and the expensive clothes in the gift shop
giving the impression that they were free, that they were
about to say *Wear me, Drink me,* like the roast chickens and
lemonade fountain in the song, it seemed to me that we
were the stars in a film with a happy ending, that the quality
of my life would continue to grow richer, and richer, that

what I'd been conditioned to think from childhood simply wasn't true, and that the world of the senses was abundant enough, that the pattern arranged for me was supremely right.

For Adam now was busy arranging the details of the new firm. When I came home at night I would always find him poring over sheafs of figures and manufacturers' catalogues; and when he went out it was always with potential clients. 'I wish you'd let me give you a hand,' I said to him in the small hours returning from a *Son et Lumière* performance with Angela, my mind still reverberating from great events. 'I *am* your partner, aren't I?'

He rubbed his eyes.

'There'll be plenty for you to do once we start. Leave it to old Adam, he'll make your fortune.'

'You'll make nothing if you fall ill,' I said. 'Give yourself a break. Get yourself a bird and come and make up a foursome with Angela and me tomorrow.'

'My father was always giving himself breaks,' he said. 'He had his books, and he had his hobbies, and the days were never full enough. He never pushed himself, he always trusted everyone, and all his capital ran through his fingers like sand. I could do with some of it now.'

But he went with Angela and me to see *Camelot* the next night; he didn't bring a girl along, explaining that he'd been let down at the last moment and hoping that we wouldn't mind him playing gooseberry, but I think myself that he'd taken a vow of celibacy – ridiculous though it may seem – until the firm was finally under way.

There were times when it seemed to me that Angela had taken a vow of celibacy too. It wasn't that she never made love; but nine times out of ten she sent me home with no more than a kiss, and on the odd occasion that I slept with her it wasn't as it had been before. She awoke me with her crying one night, in fact; when I tried to take her in my arms, she moved away.

'What's the matter, darling?'

'Nothing that you'd understand.' She sat upright and lit a Burma cheroot.

'Is it me?'

'No it isn't you. Don't be so bloody conceited.'

'What is it then?'

'I dreamed about – oh, what's the use?'

'Aren't you having a nice time?'

'A nice time? Frank, all my life I've done exactly what I wanted, and now I'm changing and *I don't want to change.*'

She gave me a cheroot. 'I know you don't like them, but smoke it for company ... Listen, I won't ask you again, I promise. But trust me and give up your job now and come away with me. Never mind the job with Adam.'

'The partnership?'

'Oh, Christ, you're so innocent! I love you for it, but you're not fit to be let out alone. The job with Adam. I promise you I'll get you a better one. My brother —'

'I can get my own jobs,' I said.

'If my brother gives you a job, it'll be on your own merits. If we broke up the day after, he wouldn't care.'

'No, love,' I said. 'I couldn't let Adam down, for one thing.'

She kissed me. 'You couldn't, could you? It's my own fault for asking. You've got to take people as they are, not as you'd like them to be ... I still think of that weekend at your home. So warm, so secure ...'

'I was afraid it would be dull for you.'

'You needn't have been. I only wish my own would stay put ... I wish I could myself ...'

I was lost for a moment. What was I doing with this woman? What was all the mystery about? How much better did I know her than the time we first met? Why wasn't anything ever simple and straightforward with her? Then I found myself – or at least my instincts found my body – as she put out her cheroot and pulled down the bedclothes, the tears still glistening in her eyes but her face gloating.

sixteen

'You rotten bastard!' Barbury shouted. 'I'll have your hide for this, see if I don't.'

He was white with rage, the broken veins on his cheeks standing out as if painted.

'Watch your language,' I said, 'or I'll knock your teeth down your throat.'

It had been a scorching hot day; the road was up on the side behind his office and the whole building smelt of boiling tar and stone-dust. I was fighting the desire to sleep after an expense account lunch with a visiting American pop star, a skinny young man who was virtually inarticulate, and I also had it in my mind that I was to meet Angela's parents and brother for the first time the next day. The article wouldn't come right, the sound of the pneumatic drill, the stuffiness of the office, my apprehension of the next day, all combined to drive from my head even the few distinguishable words the pop star had uttered.

Barbury took a deep breath. 'All right, you're not a bastard. You're merely deaf, dumb, and blind. Do you know who's run off with Judy Aviemore? Bloody Simon Cothill! Her bloody housekeeper's just let it out of the bag. No-one knows where they've gone. Cothill,' he said, and spat on the floor. He looked as if it were only by a great effort of will that he didn't spit in my face. 'Raving queer, you said. Jesus, he *lives* just above you. You knew he was seeing her regularly. Who are you bloody working for, eh? Who are you working for?' His voice rose to a scream.

I was too stunned to speak for a moment. Then I remembered Judy Aviemore's visit to our flat in the small hours. Why hadn't I told him? Because all my instincts had confirmed her story. Simon wasn't even double-doored, wasn't even one of those queers who likes a woman occasionally. To sleep with a woman was as unthinkable for him as to sleep with a man would have been for me.

'It can't be true,' I said. 'I know Cothill, I tell you. Someone's having you on.'

'Are they? Do you know why we were so quick with the story? Because we've been having Aviemore tailed, that's why. Should have done it long since. Because what we found out from the same bloody housekeeper is that not so long ago Judy Aviemore spent the night at Shalott House. It wasn't with you or your effing PR mate, was it?'

'There's something peculiar about the whole thing,' I said. 'I can't put my finger on it, but there's something wrong somewhere.'

'It's you that's bloody wrong,' he said. 'Cothill a queer? You tell the British public that now. Glenthorn must be laughing himself sick. The whole of bloody Fleet Street must be laughing itself sick —'

Mislingford entered the office, panting slightly. 'Excuse me for butting in like this, Barbury, but I had to catch Frank here.' He clapped me on the back. Although he was panting with exertion and wearing an old-fashioned heavy blue serge suit with a waistcoat and stiff white collar there was no sweat on his face. 'Frank, you're on my conscience. I never made that luncheon appointment. Wednesday, at the Savoy Grill, one o'clock? Fine. Do forgive me, Barbury.

But I've been so rushed lately that I've got to do these things whilst they're fresh in my mind. We've got to cherish bright young men like Frank, haven't we, Barbury? Not but what it isn't old reliables like you who do the bulk of the work . . .'

He waved his hand as if in benediction and half-ran out of the room.

'He's only one of the stockholders,' I said.

Barbury shuffled some papers on his desk, looking tired and old.

'Only about one of the biggest,' he muttered. 'Maybe I should throw parties too . . . Or maybe I should be twenty years younger . . . Oh, bugger off, Frank, bugger off. Do what you like, I've finished with it.'

He took his hat off the peg. 'If anyone wants me I'm going out to get drunk,' he said to his secretary. 'Blind drunk.'

He brushed past me, his face twitching. I went back to my desk and drank a cup of tea and swallowed two aspirins.

My father grew up in the Western Desert, just as his father grew up at the Somme; and had I been a few years older I might have grown up in Korea or Malaya. I wouldn't care to argue about whether this sort of introduction to manhood is desirable or not; but often I'd envied those who'd experienced it. Now on this hot afternoon, drugged with food and alcohol and tobacco, I had come to maturity. I was in no condition to assume its burdens but perhaps one never is.

My first act in my new estate of life was to phone Shalott House. The answers were all to be found there: I didn't want to find them, but that was irrelevant. The time had come for me to go into action. I knew that Adam was home that day with what he described as a touch of the old leprosy but which was actually nervous dyspepsia, the only illness I ever knew him to suffer from, and which he treated himself with a diet of arrowroot biscuits and soda-water. I got no reply, depressed the receiver and re-dialled, and heard the engaged note. He had taken the phone off the hook and left it there, not wanting to be disturbed. I smiled. Soon he was about to be disturbed to some purpose.

I remembered the piece I'd been working on and finished it more quickly than I'd finished any piece before. The Editor had expressed an interest in it, and I knew now who had the power. There wasn't even any need for me to exert myself unduly in finding out where Judy Aviemore and Simon had gone; they would be discovered soon enough. Barbury had been slapped down; it would be his face that was red, not the paper's. What was necessary now, for my own sake and no-one else's, was to understand how and why I'd been betrayed. I gave my copy to an office-boy and went into Jim Summerhill's office.

Jim was a tall rather scholarly-looking man, who was in his limited spare time a collector of old books. He was, properly speaking, the person through whom Barbury and I should have communicated; I reminded myself to have a browse around the junk shops of Charbury on his account the next time I was there. London, he always said, wasn't much of a field for the impecunious collector, the ground having been thoroughly gone over, particularly by the Yanks.

Jim looked up from *The Clique*, his standard executive pattern heavy hornrims slipping down on his nose and contriving to look like pince-nez.

'Down with Oxfam!' I said.

'Down with Oxfam it is. In what manner may I assist you, Frank? It's a rare but none the less welcome pleasure to be of service to you . . .'

He could go on like this for ten minutes by the clock; it seemed harmless badinage, but I was well aware what it implied.

'I've an inkling where to find Judy Aviemore and Simon Cothill,' I said.

He returned to his magazine. 'I suggest that you see Mr Barbury.'

'In his own words, he's gone out to get drunk, blind drunk. He said I could do what I liked about the story.'

'I should translate that as *carte blanche*, wouldn't you?'

'I would indeed, but the point is whether the Editor would.'

'Excuse me,' Jim said. He picked up the phone. 'Put me through to the Editor, please. This is Summerhill speaking. About the Aviemore story. Do we kill it? Yes. No, he's gone out.' He laughed. 'How shrewd of you to guess . . . Beside me now, in fact. Bright-eyed and bushy-tailed as they say in America. Yes, I'll tell him. Goodbye.'

'Your query was anticipated, Frank. Yes, you do have *carte blanche*.'

'I'll phone you back,' I said.

'I shall be here,' he said. 'Until eight at least. And if I am not here – even I require refreshment from time to time – you may be sure some tried and trusty colleague will be manning this telephone, ready to translate your hasty message into clear sparkling prose. Down with Oxfam!'

'Down with Oxfam!' I said, and went out into Fleet Street, feeling more relaxed than I had done for some time. There'd always been something devious about the way in which I'd been asked to approach this story and, indeed, I had eventually begun to violently disapprove of the purpose behind the campaign. Now the campaign was blown sky-high, those who mattered at the paper knew and didn't care, and I was in the clear and doing a simple straight-forward job.

I leaned back in the taxi and lit a cheroot. I would need this interval of relaxation, the first that day: what lay ahead of me wouldn't be pleasant. I was accustomed to trusting

Adam, to loving him like a brother, I had been prepared to give up my job and enter into partnership with him, a relationship as exacting and intimate in its way as marriage. We'd been friends for eighteen years; or rather he'd permitted me to be his friend. The hero-worship had all been on my side; it had been good and I wasn't ashamed of it, I'd admired him without reservation, copied his way of speaking, his way of dressing, his politics. In a sense he'd be with me all my life. But now I had to face him with the accusation of betrayal, now for once I was going to use him.

Shalott House had never looked so resplendently at its best. It had not long been repainted, the lawn was newly trimmed and sweet-smelling under the sun, the roses and dahlias, red and white and pink and yellow, were out in the borders. For a moment, paying off the cabman, I thought I was going to cry. I should never again be able to pretend it was all mine, I should never dream about it again; it was an Edwardian mansion where I had a share in a flat, and where I was betrayed.

When I let myself in there was no sign of anyone about. Then I heard a woman's voice in the direction of the bathroom. I smiled to myself; Adam had apparently made a miraculous recovery. I went over to the drink cabinet and poured myself a glass of red wine. That cabinet, so massive and heavy, so meticulously finished with its gilt dragons on the red and black foreground, would be one of the things I was going to miss; inanimate objects insinuate themselves into your life like dogs and other people's children, they leave a gap when you don't see them any more . . .

Angela walked into the room in her slip. It was a white one through which I could see the shape of her legs, and her dark hair was tousled. She smelled of sex, that strange marine smell, so intoxicating when one's had the sex oneself, so pungent and nasty – an animal's voiding – when some one else has had the sex.

I dropped my glass; it rolled over the floor and shattered on the brass fender.

'You'd better get dressed,' I said. I didn't feel any surprise; my capacity for surprises had been exhausted earlier in the afternoon.

She stared at me. 'What are you doing here?'

'Working, strangely enough. I wish you'd get dressed.'

Adam came into the room in shirt and trousers, barefoot.

'You'd better watch your feet,' I said. 'I've broken a glass.'

'You're very calm.'

'If she prefers you, there's nothing I can do about it. I didn't come here to catch you out, in any case. It was the last thing in my mind —' I felt the tears coming irresistibly.

'Oh Christ,' he said, 'what a rotten sod I am, Frank. I'd rather you hit me. I won't stop you. I haven't one excuse to offer, not one.'

'You will have,' I said. 'A great many, all plausible.' I wiped my eyes with the back of my hand. 'But I won't listen to any of them.'

'Don't mind me,' Angela said. 'Just pretend I'm bloody well not here. I wish to God you would hit him. Or me. Or both of us. What sort of a man are you, anyway?'

'You should know,' I said.

'Oh, yes, you can put your thing into me. Or into that bloody little whore, Janice —'

'Adam you *are* a bastard.' I walked up to him and slapped his face hard. He didn't return the blow.

'You'll feel better now,' he said gently. 'But I didn't tell her. I'm a rotten swine, but I'm not that rotten.'

Angela laughed. 'I only found out yesterday. You see, Frank, London's a village. Notting Hill's a village. Janice is one of my models. She lives a stone's throw from my studio. I go away, and what do you do? Pick up a dirty scruffy little alley-cat —'

'Because you went away. And how the hell do I know what you were up to when *you* were away?'

She turned and went out of the room without a word. I felt nothing but an overwhelming relief.

'We might as well have a drink,' Adam said. 'I suppose it's no good me saying I'm sorry?'

I shook my head. I wasn't certain whether or not to hit him again.

'I felt a lot better about noon, so I thought I'd ask her over to have a talk about business. Believe it or not, she has a very good business head. Nothing was further from my mind than sex, believe me. We were looking over some figures and – well, that day we read no more.'

'How long has it been going on?'

'This was the first time. I swear to God it was.'

I put down my glass. 'It's not so much your doing it I mind, as you assuming I'm an idiot. I have been an idiot. I've trusted you absolutely, but it's different now —'

Angela returned to the room fully dressed, her hair no longer tousled.

'This *is* cosy,' she said. 'I hate to interrupt your chat, Frank, but just what are your intentions? About *me*, Frank.'

'It's supposed to be up to you.'

'Well then, it's easy.' She took off her engagement ring. 'Will you put the notice in the Telegraph?' She frowned. 'It wouldn't really have worked, you know. You're a bit too bloody normal for me. I need someone who understands what it is to need to be free . . .'

'I'm surprised you don't marry Adam.' My bitterness broke out. 'You've been sleeping with him for years on and off now, haven't you?'

She smiled. I realized that she was happy now, the centre of attention at last.

'So you *do* have some reactions? I'll never marry Adam. It

was the first time today and, honestly, he's not very good.'
I heard Adam gasp as if hit in the belly.

'The first time?' I shouted. 'The first time, you bloody
liar? Do you think I don't know that you broke up his
engagement?'

'Yes, I did.' Her smile was fixed now. 'But you don't
know much about sex, do you? Never mind, you'll learn. I
didn't take Adam away from Wendy. I took Wendy away
from Adam.'

'He's got his own back now, hasn't he?' I asked. I was
drowning now, floundering in a mixture of emotions – pity,
hate, revulsion, bewilderment. I stood up and shook her
hard. 'And where's Wendy? Did it start again when you met
her again? What happened to her when you'd finished with
her? Why don't you follow her, then?'

She pulled herself away from me. 'It didn't start again.
If it had —' Her pupils were dilated, the black nearly
swallowed up the blue. 'You'd like me to kill myself,' she said
in a whisper. 'You'd really like me to.' Her face was the
white of scraped bone. And I saw that she was enjoying
herself, that she could get no more stimulation out of
ordinary emotions than a meths drinker could from luke-
warm lager, that if I weren't careful I should, even now, be
drawn in again, drawn in all the more helplessly for knowing
what I now knew, to be left in the end like poor Wendy,
alone at the crossroads at night, the dark woods beckoning
me. 'I'll tell you something else,' I said. 'You're a lousy
painter. Cheap, sentimental, derivative, pornographic. Not
sexy. Just pornographic. That's why people buy your bloody
paintings. Do you know what Saul Dykenhead said? If they
made special chocolates for brothels, he'd choose you to
paint the boxes. You see, there's a unique soggy heaviness
about your lines —'

'You filthy lying shit!' she screamed, and ran blindly out
of the room. I heard her struggling with the knob of the

outer door and then it banged to, and I slumped down in the nearest armchair, feeling almost sexually exhausted.

'You know damned well that Saul never said that,' Adam said.

'She'll never be sure,' I said. 'Even if she asks him she'll never be sure.'

'You're really vicious, aren't you?' His tone was admiring.

I was already beginning to be ashamed of myself. I had told a lie, I had told the one lie against which an artist has no defence, and I would not have cared, when I told it, if it had driven her to suicide.

'Yes,' I said. 'When my back's against the wall.' I looked at him without emotion; Angela had used it all.

'I can guess what you came for,' he said. Now somehow or other it was as if the old friendship had been re-established; the fact that I'd caught him sleeping with my fiancée seemed not to matter. There were only a few trifling details to be cleared up, his attitude said, and all would be as it was before.

'I'd like you to explain about Simon and Judy Aviemore,' I said. 'As quickly as possible. Because I'm not certain that I shouldn't try to break your bloody neck.'

'You know my problem with Simon. How in short to de-camp him. Well, I reached a dead end. Then another problem came up. Mislingford wanted me to get your paper off Glenthorn's back.'

'I thought Mislingford was well to the left of Glenthorn.'

'Don't interrupt if you want the facts quickly. Mislingford wants to be on the winning side. I mean, I hope he's wrong, but as I've often told you, I keep my own politics out of it. Mislingford is backing Glenthorn, because Glenthorn is a coming man. Your paper's campaign was succeeding rather too well —'

'Mislingford's a big shareholder in the Argus. Couldn't he just have stopped it?'

'By that time I'd had my marvellous idea. It suited us better to have it continue. Suited your editor better too.'

'So Simon running off with Judy Aviemore was a put-up job?' The desire to hit him had vanished; as had my need for revenge upon Angela.

'Of course. Simon is established as one hundred per cent he-man, the heat's off Glenthorn, and J. Aviemore receives some useful publicity. Of course, it wouldn't be the right kind for a politician, but it's just what the doctor ordered for a lady novelist. And Mr Aviemore was paid twenty thousand lovely quids tax free. By Mislingford, of course. Mind you, it wasn't as easy as all that. Judy didn't think much of the idea at first, and Simon was frightened he'd actually have to go to bed with her. And at one stage Mr Aviemore went all honourable on us. That was when his name was a by-word in the City. However, Mislingford doubled his payment, and he took the cash, et cetera . . . That's all, Father. For a penance, I'll give myself another glass of this wine because I'm beginning to be fed up with it.'

'Very clever,' I said. 'Very complicated and very nauseating. I see now what made Judy Aviemore drunk that night. You never thought that you might lose me my job.'

'You're not being fair, Frank. I didn't want you to be sacked. I asked Mislingford to see to that side of it. Didn't he?'

'Yes, he did,' I said rather bitterly. 'I actually thought it was because he remembered me personally.'

'Some people are hard to please,' Adam said. He was perfectly at his ease now, unaware of having offended in any way. 'Christ, Frank, you must see I couldn't have told you about any of this. I've got a duty to my clients —'

'Not to your friends?'

'Frank, Frank, am I not telling you that you'd never anything to worry about? The Editor's on your side anyway. He only cares about taking Barbury down a peg. Even Barbury – not that I know or care about the chap – won't suffer. And believe me, old Mislingford will be a great help to you . . . That is, if you want to stay in journalism.'

'Adam, I've no intention of leaving journalism.'

'I still would like you with me,' he said. 'After all, what's Angela? Hell, there's no shortage of women.'

'There's just one thing,' I said. 'You let me become engaged to her knowing damned well she was a part-time Lizzie. Do you think I could work with you after that?'

He appeared genuinely puzzled. 'It's not the same for women,' he said. 'I honestly thought you'd have guessed yourself sooner or later. Besides, it was just a phase with her . . .' His voice trailed off. Communication had broken down between us at last. I still cannot fathom the reason for his silence; did he think it unimportant or did he want to see someone else, despite it being his best friend, in the same predicament? Or did he think of Angela as being a sort of Commando Course to prepare me for the jungle warfare of public relations?

There's always a question left unanswered, there's always the one instance when someone steps out of character. I could understand, almost forgive, everything else, because I couldn't be sure that in his shoes I'd not have behaved in exactly the same way. But even his sleeping with Angela was less important than his withholding the one piece of information about her which would have put me off her from the start. I took this problem to Theresa eventually and she said that Angela's capital was the obvious answer. But eventually he got the capital he needed from Mislingford; it was never really important to him. I can see it all in perspective now, it's long ago ceased to hurt. Only the memory of this small betrayal – small in comparison with the larger betrayal – still has power to disturb me in the small hours.

'Never mind,' I said. 'What I want now is to know where Simon and Judy are. Can you help me?'

'Nothing easier,' he said, looking relieved. He dialled a

Suffolk number. 'Simon? Have you got it in yet, you naughty boy?' He winked at me. 'Listen, this is important. We've been rather mean to poor old Frank. Just to please me, will you give him an exclusive? Him and no-one else. Another week of unbridled passion —' he winked at me again – 'and then you can come home, you and your new image, you dirty old co-respondent you. O.K. My dearest love to Judy. Bye now.'

I took the address and phone number from him and phoned Jim Summerhill. 'I've got it,' I said. 'I'm off to Suffolk. Can you arrange a photographer?'

Adam smiled benignly. 'There you are. Old Uncle Adam will always look after you.'

I held out my hand. 'I'm off now, Adam. I'll collect my stuff later.'

'Don't be ridiculous, Frank.' He looked as if he were about to cry and stamp his foot. 'Where'll you stay?'

'I'll pack an overnight bag – I'll probably have to stay the night in Suffolk anyway. Then I'll find somewhere, don't worry.'

'God, I feel awful about this. You don't mean that you want to clear out now? At least stay here till you find somewhere to live.' I saw that he was genuinely near tears. He needed me more than I needed him; I had become part of his life, like the furniture and fittings of Shalott House, like Shalott House itself, like his circle of friends. But I was the most important friend, because I was a link with his past being his cousin, a link with his parents' past. I was there to be used, and he would use me but, as much as he could love anyone he loved me. I was the reliable one, part of his past and part of his possessions, the possessions which meant so much to the bachelor.

'I'll give you a months' rent in lieu of notice,' I said.

'To hell with that, he said. 'What sort of peasant do you take me for? I don't count pennies with my friends.'

'I'm sorry,' I said. 'I know you wouldn't. But I can't stay here one moment longer.'

It was a lie; already the room had returned to normal, the stretcher-bearers had carried away the dead and the wounded, the blood and guts had been mopped up. If I stayed out the month, I should continue, as it were, to dine in Mess, and the gaps at the table would close themselves up, I would remain part of his possessions like the grandfather clock or the chandelier or the Chinese lacquer cabinet, loved but owned, I would eventually find myself working with him, scarcely knowing how it had happened.

'These things pass,' he said in a low voice. 'I thought I'd never get over Wendy leaving me for Angela but when I saw Angela again I was glad to see her ...' He yawned. 'Christ, I'm tired ...'

'I've a phone call to make,' I said abruptly, and went to the extension in my room.

'Theresa,' I said eventually, after two wrong numbers and two wrong persons, 'this is Frank. I'm leaving Shalott House.'

'Why should I care?' Her voice was cold. 'Is that all you have to tell me?'

'Wait.' She would nag, she would grumble, she would be jealous, she would expect me home at the same time every night, she'd be hell to live with when she was pregnant, and she wouldn't be happy unless she had at least four children; and there was nothing in her past that wouldn't bear the light of day, there was no hint of corruption about her, she would love me fiercely and honour every clause in her marriage vows if it broke her heart. 'I love you,' I said. 'Will you marry me?'

She gasped. 'What about Angela? Not that I give a damn.'

'That's my girl,' I said. 'It's all off with Angela. All off with Adam too. I was going to go into PR with him.'

'You realize that you've now told everyone on the magazine?' She laughed. 'You'll never get out of it.'

'I'm off to Suffolk on a job, but I'll phone you again from there.'

'Just you wait where you are. I'm coming with you.' She was crying now. When finally she hung up, I sat smiling at the telephone for five minutes. I would never be alone again.

I went back into the drawing-room where Adam had fallen asleep in his armchair, his head slumped forward. I settled down to wait for Theresa. The room was quiet except for the slow tick of the grandfather clock. After a while Adam's mouth fell open and he began to snore, as he would in this same room ten, twenty, thirty years from now.

More top fiction from Magnum Books

Patrick Anderson
417 0227   The President's Mistress   90p
417 0299   The Senator   £1.25

Franklin Bandy
417 0387   Deceit and Deadly Lies   £1.25

Tasman Beattie
417 0212   The Zambesi Break   80p
417 0195   Panic Button   90p

David Beaty
417 0261   Cone of Silence   95p
417 0262   Excellency   95p

Eugene P. Benson
417 0152   The Bulls of Ronda   70p

Thomas Berger
417 0253   Little Big Man   £1.25
417 0298   Who is Teddy Villanova?   95p
417 0433   Arthur Rex   £1.50
417 0440   Sneaky People   £1.25

Rita Samson Bernhard
417 0358   The Girls in 5J   £1.10

John Braine
417 0483   Life at the Top   £1.25
417 0484   The Jealous God   £1.25
417 0210   Waiting for Sheila   75p
417 0199   Stay With Me Till Morning   90p
413 3664   The Pious Agent   85p
417 0175   Finger of Fire   85p
417 0455   The Vodi   £1.25

Matthew Braun
417 0309   The Second Coming of Lucas Brokaw   90p

Pearl S. Buck
413 3670   The Good Earth   95p
413 3669   Dragon Seed   80p
417 0223   Letter from Peking   70p
417 0243   The Rainbow   75p
417 0256   The Mother   75p
417 0255   The New Year   85p
417 0254   The Three Daughters of Madame Liang   95p

Robert Carroll
417 0151   The Budapest Tradeoff   80p

Ron de Christoforo
417 0376   Grease   95p

£1.80

	Parley J. Cooper	
417 0311	The Studio	90p
417 0248	Wreck!	90p
	Simon Cooper	
413 3745	Exhibition	80p
	David Creed	
417 0430	The Watcher of Chimor	£1.25
	Anne David	
417 0310	Kids	£1.10
	Robert DeMaria	
417 0356	Empress of Rome	95p
	Philip K. Dick	
417 0429	Confessions of a Crap Artist	£1.25
	Colin Free	
413 3474	Ironbark	70p
417 0209	Vinegar Hill	£1.25
	Monica Furlong	
417 0170	The Cat's Eye	70p
	Bernard Glemser	
417 0179	Grand Opening	80p
	Ben Healey	
417 0154	Captain Havoc	90p
417 0264	Havoc in the Indies	95p